Love at the

Darcie Boleyn has a huge heart and is a real softy. She never fails to cry at books and movies, whether the ending is happy or not. Darcie is in possession of an overactive imagination that often keeps her awake at night. Her childhood dream was to become a Jedi but she hasn't yet found suitable transport to take her to a galaxy far, far away. She also has reservations about how she'd look in a gold bikini, as she rather enjoys red wine, cheese and loves anything with ginger or cherries in it – especially chocolate. Darcie fell in love in New York, got married in the snow, rescues uncoordinated greyhounds and can usually be found reading or typing away on her laptop.

Also by Darcie Boleyn

A Very Merry Manhattan Christmas
Love at the Italian Lake
Love at the Northern Lights

Conwenna Cove

Summer at Conwenna Cove
Christmas at Conwenna Cove
Forever at Conwenna Cove

Cornish Hearts

The House at Greenacres
The Cottage at Plum Tree Bay
The Christmas Tea Shop

Cariad Cove Village

Coming Home to Cariad Cove
Starting Over in Cariad Cove

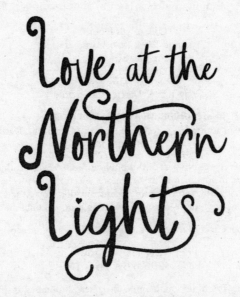

Love at the Northern Lights

DARCIE BOLEYN

CANELO

First published in the United Kingdom in 2018 by Canelo

This edition published in the United Kingdom in 2022 by

Canelo
Unit 9, 5th Floor
Cargo Works, 1–2 Hatfields
London, SE1 9PG
United Kingdom

A CIP catalogue record for this book is available from the British Library.

Print ISBN 978 1 80436 104 7
Ebook ISBN 978 1 78863 118 1

This book is a work of fiction. Names, characters, businesses, organizations, places and events are either the product of the author's imagination or are used fictitiously. Any resemblance to actual persons, living or dead, events or locales is entirely coincidental.

Look for more great books at www.canelo.co

Printed and bound in Great Britain by Clays Ltd, Elcograf S.p.A.

1

For Jimbo, you brought light to my world and love to my heart. We planned on seeing the northern lights together, but you were taken too soon. One day, I will see them for us. Miss you always. XXX

Chapter 1

'Oh my God, Frankie, we're being arrested!'

'What?' Frances Ashford looked up from the flute of champagne she'd been nursing for the past hour, and peered through the dimly lit VIP section of the exclusive London club.

'Get up! It's the police.'

Jennifer Prescott, Frankie's best friend, grabbed her hand and pulled her to her feet, causing her to spill the remains of the champagne down the front of her pink silk dress.

And sure enough, six burly police officers were heading their way.

'But why would they arrest us?' she asked Jen, looking first at the men in their black shirts and trousers with black baseball caps on their heads, then at the rest of her hen party.

'Because we've been very naughty.' Lorna Cartwright, another of Frankie's bridesmaids, smoothed her sleek black hair then adjusted the low neckline of her barely there black dress. She giggled then held up her hands. 'I'm here, officers. Please be gentle with me.'

'This is a prank, right?' Frankie nudged Jen as the men closed in on them.

'Oh, Frankie, darling… just go with the flow. This is your hen night and it's time to have some fun.' Jen cocked a perfectly manicured blonde brow at her, then held up her hands in the same way as Lorna and the other three bridesmaids.

Frankie scanned the club, wondering if she had time to make a run for it, but suddenly handcuffs were locked around her wrists. One of the officers gruffly informed her of her rights, then she was led down the stairs from the VIP area and across the dance floor, as her friends squealed and giggled around her.

Ten minutes later, Frankie found herself squashed onto a narrow bench, between two of the rather brawny police officers in the back of a transit van. Jen and Lorna were with her, but the others had been stuffed into a different van outside the club. It was clearly hen night high jinks, but even so, her pulse was racing and her mouth bone dry. She hadn't wanted any of this, hadn't even wanted a hen night, but Jen and the others had insisted. Frankie had agreed on the condition that it would be a quiet night of drinks at a club followed by a meal at The Ivy. However, it seemed that her friends had ignored her wishes and come up with something completely different.

The air in the van was stuffy and the heavy aroma of cheap aftershave hung around the hot, bulky bodies either side of her. Didn't these men know that less was more when it came to cologne? How anyone could find this exciting, Frankie had no idea. The urge to stand up, kick open the back doors of the van and jump out was building, and she pressed her long French-manicured nails into her palms to try to stay calm. Surely this torture would soon be over?

She looked over at Jen who was smiling up at the officer at her side. He stared straight ahead, as if he'd been instructed to ignore the prisoners, but his lips twitched as Jen whispered something in his ear.

'Jen?' Frankie couldn't bear it any longer.

'What?'

'How long will this last? It's just…' She glanced either side of her. 'I need the loo.' It was a lie, but if it meant this would end sooner, then she'd put on her best full bladder performance.

Jen rolled her eyes. 'Why didn't you go in the club?'

'I wasn't exactly given a chance, was I? It all happened a bit too quickly.'

'Cross your legs, hun. We won't be long, so try to relax and enjoy yourself.' Jen flashed her a smile.

Each jig of the van as it drove through the London streets, made Frankie realize that her bladder was actually quite full now, and that she'd need a comfort break soon. Perhaps it was the shock – and horror – of being subjected to this. Perhaps it was the water she'd been discreetly drinking to avoid getting a headache from the bubbly.

A squeal of tyres brought the van to a sudden stop and the officers jumped up, but because Frankie had been so tightly squashed between them, she was thrust forwards. She raised her arms instinctively to cushion her fall, but the handcuffs kept her wrists together, so she was winded as she hit the carpeted floor. She lay still for a moment, her forehead resting against the itchy carpet that reeked of the adhesive that held it in place, trying to catch her breath as hell broke out around her.

'What the f—! How is that acceptable?' It was Jen. 'Frankie? Are you OK, darling?'

Frankie nodded as best she could, then strong hands took hold of her arms and lifted her to her feet. She sagged, her stomach aching from her fall, as she tried to suck in breaths.

'You absolute idiots! You're meant to look after your clients, not beat them up. You wait until I post a review about your beastly company.'

'Look, love, no harm meant. We weren't to know she'd lose her balance.' Frankie watched the officer at her side, whose squeaky voice seemed incongruous with his size, as he tried to reason with Jen. 'We'll do you a discount.'

Jen sniffed then flicked her long blonde hair over her shoulders. 'You'd better and a jolly good one at that.'

The van doors swung open and the officers leapt out then helped the women down. Frankie had finally caught her breath but knew that her stomach would be tender for days, the same as when she caught a hockey stick to the gut at boarding school.

To her relief, they had stopped directly outside The Ivy Kensington.

'Come on, Frankie, let's get a drink.'

'Was... that it then?'

'What do you mean?' Jen frowned.

'Being arrested. You haven't arranged for strippers or anything as well, have you?'

Jen sighed then hooked her arm through Frankie's. 'The night is young, darling. The night is soooo young.'

Frankie suppressed the urge to scream...

–

'No! Please put the thong back on...'

Frankie bolted upright in bed and blinked. Memories of her hen night the previous weekend were still disturbing her sleep. Following a very pleasant meal at

The Ivy, there had been another nightclub and a return of the fake police officers, followed by stripping and... She shuddered. It was probably a night that a lot of brides-to-be might have enjoyed, but for Frankie, it had been her worst nightmare. Shaved groins, greased pecs and gyrating strangers, all made her extremely uncomfortable. She'd always been quite shy and reserved and never really felt that she fitted in with the people of her social circle. Perhaps it was due to her early years when her family unit had taken a hit, but perhaps she was just a prude at heart. Nothing wrong with the latter, but sometimes she wished she could do as Jen had suggested and go with the flow. If only she could be happy with the life she'd been given. She just had a feeling that something was missing; it had always been missing.

Her mobile buzzed on the bedside table and she reached across the king-size bed for it. Just her alarm, set to wake her in case she slept on. She'd been so tired recently and was finding it harder and harder to get up in the mornings. Of course, the fact that winter was pushing autumn aside and settling onto England with frosty mornings and dark afternoons probably didn't help. They'd even said there could be snow this year, something that had sent Grandma reaching for a second large gin when she'd heard it on the farmers' forecast.

Frankie flopped back on the fawn satin pillows and sighed. Winter could be such a dreary time and often made everything seem so much worse. That was why Grandma had suggested she and Rolo marry in November, to give them something to look forward to.

'Bugger!' She sat up again. 'Married. Damn and blast it!'

Frankie was getting married... today...

She jumped out of bed and ran to the rear window of the double-aspect chamber, then pulled the heavy curtains apart.

Outside, on the expansive lawn, sat a huge white marquee. She knew exactly what it would look like inside: cream chair covers and tablecloths with their silver and gold place settings and crystal glasses. There would be white roses and mistletoe in the vases and the favours would be pinecone fire starters, encouraging the guests to 'Let love warm your heart'. Twinkling fairy lights and evergreen festoons would be draped across the ceiling and around the entrance. It would be perfect, magical and Frankie should be excited.

But she wasn't.

Not. At. All.

She backed away from the window, as if that could erase the image of the marquee from her mind. Her grandmother had organised the finer details of the wedding, like the favours and decor, and the wedding planner her prospective in-laws had hired had taken care of the rest. It had been remarkably easy for Frankie. In fact, she'd barely had to think about what was happening. Which was part of the problem. She was detached from the process, going into the marriage with blinkers on, as if pretending it wasn't happening would make it all easier to go through with.

She was like a pawn being handed over to the highest bidder at a marriage auction, and that bidder had turned out to be Rolo Bellamy. Rolo was – on paper – the ideal match for Frankie, and although their families weren't quite in the top one hundred of the *Sunday Times* Rich List, they had amassed impressive fortunes over the years through investing in property, land and farming.

It was, apparently, also *the right time* for her to get married. All her friends were doing it, or had done it – like Jen – and some were even on their second or third child, except for Lorna – who was younger, at twenty-five – and had sworn never to have babies because it would ruin her model physique. It wasn't that Frankie didn't like Rolo, because she did (at least, she thought she did) and they'd known each other a long time, but if someone had entered the bedroom at that moment and asked her if she loved the handsome, suave and very successful lawyer, Frankie knew she'd have struggled to reply.

She *should* love him. Wanted to love him. But for some reason, she didn't.

Perhaps she was just incapable of love. She'd tried to speak to her grandmother about it, but Helen Ashford had pursed her thin lips and frowned, then raised a hand to silence her. Helen had spouted something about love being for poor romantics and that it was wise to marry for money – or to marry into more money in this case – then love would find a way.

'I wish love would find a bloody way and pretty sharpish seeing as how I'm getting married in...' she checked her mobile, 'four hours!'

Four hours and her fate would be sealed. She would be Mrs Rolo Bellamy – she'd reluctantly agreed to take his name, as he said it looked better than her keeping her own – and they'd be jetting off to a honeymoon on the private island of Cayo Espanto in the Caribbean. Rolo had booked them a 2,100 square feet villa with a large private plunge pool, personal decks and a private dock. She rubbed at her throat, finding it hard to swallow, as she recalled the images Rolo had shown her of their honeymoon destination. Although he hadn't interfered with the wedding details, like the marquee, bridesmaids' dresses and the rest, he had decided where they would honeymoon and for how long. When Rolo had basically insisted she take his name, she'd wondered if he'd try to get her to quit her job – the job she didn't need to have for financial reasons but she chose to have for her sanity. Admittedly, it wasn't the career she'd have picked, had she been able to follow her heart, but it had been the topic of a challenging negotiation with her grandmother, and management consultancy had been one of the routes deemed suitable for a young woman of her wealth and social status. So far, Rolo hadn't seemed interested in persuading her to relinquish that treasured independence. The tight feeling in her throat increased and she had to cough to try to dislodge it.

Rolo, though outwardly nice and respectable, was rather controlling. And Frankie knew she was a bit of an ass for letting him take charge. But she was used to relinquishing control of her life; it had always been the way.

A knock at the door dragged Frankie from her thoughts and she hurried to answer it, hoping that it would be someone who could put her mind at rest and reassure her that it would all be absolutely fine and that she was just having pre-wedding jitters.

Please let it be nothing more than that…

Chapter 2

'Are you all right, darling?' Jen sashayed into the bedroom. She was wearing a plush white robe and rhinestone-encrusted wedge slippers. Her face was already made up and her hair pulled into an artistic mass of shiny curls and freshwater pearl and diamanté clips. Frankie couldn't help but admire how beautiful her friend looked. Almost as if she was the bride-to-be.

If only she was...

But Jen was already married. She'd tied the knot last year with Henry Prescott, City banker, and they'd honeymooned in Tobago. She'd told Frankie that they intended on starting a family as soon as today was done, but hadn't started trying before as Jen wanted to look good in her maid-of-honour dress.

Frankie envied Jen because she knew exactly what she wanted; she always had done, ever since they were ten years old. Jen liked money, the prestige of having more than one property, and was looking forward to being what she described as a yummy-mummy. She was a born socialite, living happily off her family's wealth and now her husband's, and apart from a brief period a few years ago when she'd claimed to be an interior designer, she had never been interested in working. Her job as an interior designer had focused on shopping for imaginary clients – who happened to like Gucci bags and Louboutin heels – and how anyone was meant to use those as decor, Frankie had no idea. Jen had expressed her surprise on more than one occasion that Frankie chose to work, and didn't seem to understand why Frankie wanted to have a career.

'You need some bubbly, Frankie, to get you into the mood. We don't want you blotto, but we do want you feeling rather marvellous.'

'I don't think I do want alcohol. I haven't had breakfast yet.' Frankie returned to the bed and perched on the edge.

'Of course you do. It will perk you up no end and you need to start getting ready. You probably had a beastly night and didn't sleep a wink, did you? What with all the excitement!'

Jen bustled about the room, speaking into her mobile as she did so, and within minutes there was a knock at the door and a stream of people entered and started fussing around Frankie.

She surrendered to the preening and primping, knowing that she didn't have the energy or the inclination to put up a fight. Her whole life had led her to this moment, a life of submitting to her grandmother and not fighting for what she wanted because it was just too difficult. It seemed that this was her destiny, and she had no say in it whatsoever.

–

When Frankie was finally allowed to look in the mirror, she didn't recognize herself. Gone was her straight brown hair, pale face and clear skin. Someone who could give the Kardashians a run for their money had taken her place. Her dark hair was scraped back from her forehead so tightly that her eyebrows sat at least a centimetre higher than usual and the genuine diamond and pearl tiara – that had been her grandmother's – cut into her now tender scalp. She felt sure that at any moment her hair would snap and she'd be left with a short spiky fringe.

'Don't you look fabulous?' Jen squeezed her shoulder. 'Rolo is going to want to jump your bones as soon as he sees you.'

Frankie tried to suppress the shudder that ran through her but her new bright-pink trout pout contorted of its own accord. Jen met her eyes in the mirror and held her gaze.

'It's going to be OK, Frankie. Married life is pretty darned good. You know… you probably won't even see him most of the time. Much as I love my Henry, he's either at work, playing golf or off doing funny handshakes. My life is my own and yours can be too.'

Frankie's heart sank. That sounded like an awful way to view being a newly-wed like Jen. She was also surprised; Jen hadn't admitted anything like this to her before and it made her wonder again at how close they actually were. There had always been something between them, a sense of understanding and compassion, but they weren't exactly bosom buddies in a *Sex and the City* or *Friends* kind of way. Was Jen really happy with her lot, as Frankie had previously believed, or had she missed what was right in front of her because she was dealing with her own issues?

'Come on, Frankie, have some more champagne.'

They clinked glasses and Frankie downed hers in one go. She wasn't a big drinker, unlike Grandma, who called four in the afternoon gin o'clock, and her father, who kept the wine cellar very well stocked, and the warmth from the alcohol soon flooded her system, loosening her inhibitions. She let Jennifer refill her glass several times, then she was led to the dressing room just off the main bedroom. As well as the dressing room and bathroom, the bedroom had its own veranda and antechamber, which had, at one time, been used as a prayer room. Rolo's ancestral home was enormous and Frankie knew that it could take an age to walk from one end of the mansion to the other, especially if you got distracted by the antiques and oil paintings of his mother's side of the family. Frankie loved gazing at Rolo's ancestors, mainly because she was fascinated by the changing fashions over the years, intrigued by the fabrics, styles, shoes and hats.

'There.' The fashion designer – who had a name Frankie had been sworn to secrecy about so that no high-society magazine managed to get a sneak peek at the dress – stood back and admired her handiwork. 'Gorgeous!'

'Absolutely marvellously magical... like a fairy-tale princess.' Jen clapped her hands.

'Oh, Frankie, it's super!' Lorna had been standing in the corner of the dressing room, eyes glued to her mobile while Frankie had dressed. Now she looked up and her eyes widened as she scanned Frankie from head to toe. 'I hope I'll be just as beautiful on my wedding day.'

Frankie smiled her thanks, knowing that Lorna always appeared ravishing, whatever she wore, also knowing that Lorna was well aware of that fact.

'Time to see the results!' Jen said. 'Use the mirror in the bedroom as the light is better in there.'

Frankie obediently trotted through to the bedroom and stood in front of the long mirror. The ivory designer dress fitted her slender frame like a second skin. The strapless corset top pushed her small breasts up so they resembled two tennis balls. They glistened under the electric light because of the copious amounts of highlighter that sat on top of the fake tan she'd had yesterday. The satin of the dress seemed to shimmer as she moved, and when she turned to look at the back, the fishtail stretched across the floor making her feel like some sort of mermaid. Whatever her reservations, she had to admit that the dress was breathtaking. She'd just prefer to admire it on someone else. With her mind in such turmoil and her heart squeezing so tight, it was impossible for Frankie to enjoy being so beautifully clothed. Even thinking about how the designer had created the dress, about the textures of the material and the painstaking stitching that held the magnificent handmade creation together couldn't lift Frankie's mood. She was lost indeed.

As she gazed at the unfamiliar woman in the mirror, she was conscious of the designer, hairdresser and beauticians leaving the room, until it was just her and Jen.

'Frankie, you are truly beautiful. The most beautiful bride I've ever seen.' She smiled. 'You can do this. I'll be with you all the way.'

Frankie turned to her oldest friend and took her hands.

'Thanks, Jen. You've been really good to me today... and over the years.'

Jen nodded. 'I know we haven't been as close as we could have been. I always felt you were holding something back. At times, I wondered if you actually liked me... because, you know, I can be a bit of a drama queen, a bit self-involved and a bit OTT, I guess. And we didn't exactly become friends in an organic way, did we? What with our grandmothers pushing us together from an early age then being at boarding school together. But I do care about you. I always have.'

'I know. Me too.' Frankie tried to smile but her face was pulled so tight that she suspected it came out as more of a grimace.

'I'm going to give you a moment now to compose yourself, to find your inner calm, as my personal yogi says. Oh… and if I forget to mention it later, I packed a few things in your honeymoon case.'

'Like what?' Panic seared through Frankie.

'You'll find out when you reach your destination.' Jen winked at her. 'No peeking beforehand!'

When her friend had gone, Frankie shuffled over to the bed and sank onto the soft coverlet. This was it then. She was trussed up like a prize turkey, about to make promises of love and fidelity when her heart wanted to do neither.

A knock at the door made her stomach lurch. Was it time already?

She tried to stand but the dress was too restrictive and she was worried about popping the delicate seams if she got up too quickly.

'Hello?' she called. 'Who is it?'

The door swung open and relief washed over her when she saw her father, Hugo Ashford.

'You look so handsome in that suit,' she squeaked as he approached the bed. 'I would get up but I can't.'

He smiled then took her hands and helped her to her feet.

'Frances, you are beautiful.'

'I don't look like me at all.'

He shook his head. 'You do, sweetheart. In fact, you look so much like your m—' He pressed his lips together and dropped his gaze to his shiny black shoes.

They stood there for a while, holding hands. There was so much Frankie wanted to ask and so much she sensed her father wanted to say, but, as always, they stayed quiet, understanding that some things were too hard to discuss; some things were best left unsaid.

Finally, he released a shaky sigh. 'She'd be very proud of you today.'

'She would?'

He nodded.

Frankie thought about the wedding invitations she'd written for her mother. Five in total. When it had come to posting them, she'd torn each one into tiny pieces like confetti then dropped them into the bin. She'd wanted to invite her mother, yearned to invite her, but shame and sadness prevented her. After all, her mother had walked away all those years ago and never looked back. Why would she want to know Frankie now? Why would she care that her daughter was getting married? She hadn't been there for all the other things Frankie had gone through, like getting her first spot or her first period, nor for her exam results' days or her university graduation when she'd gained a first-class honours degree in business management and accounting. She hadn't been there when Frankie had cried into her pillow over disappointments and a deep sense of loneliness, when those charity adverts about children in Africa – who had no clean water to drink – broke her heart, or even when she got engaged.

Her mother had never been there for her.

Never. Ever…

'Frankie.' Her father licked his lips nervously then met her gaze. 'I need to tell you something.'

'You do? Oh, Dad… you're not ill, are you?'

'No. No, angel, nothing like that. It's about your mother.'

'I'm listening.'

'If she was here today… she would tell you to be sure that this is what you want.'

'Oh…'

Frankie scanned her father's face, wondering what had prompted this confession.

'Uh… of course it is, Dad.'

'Are you sure? Because I'm not. I've watched you since the engagement and something just seems… rather off.'

'Rolo is a good match. He's one of Buckinghamshire's most eligible bachelors and he's on that society list of most desirable successful young men. Grandma showed it to me. Many times. I'm a lucky woman.' She gave a strangled laugh.

'Are those your words or my mother's?'

She swallowed hard.

'I would never interfere, Frankie, because I don't feel I have the right. If you can tell me hand on heart that this is exactly what you want, then I'll forever hold my peace. However… if you have an inkling of doubt in your mind, then don't go through with it. Marriage is a huge commitment. It's not just rings, flowers and swimming in tropical waters while you sip fancy cocktails. Sorry, darling, I sound patronizing now but… There's so much more to it. It's hard… even when you love someone very much.'

Frankie took a slow deep breath then released it.

What did her father want from her? She couldn't run away from this today, could she? It would be wrong and so many people had gone to so much trouble and expense. Grandma would be spitting-teeth mad and Rolo would be furious that he'd been humiliated in front of all his friends. His parents would be irate, the wedding planner would be shocked, the wedding dress designer would curse her name and…

Her vision blurred. All the reasons for going through with it and none of them were the right one.

'I don't love him, Dad.'

He nodded. 'Then don't do it.'

'But I—'

He held up a hand. 'Don't make any more excuses. You know in your heart what's right. I'm going to go now and I'll be waiting downstairs. You decide what you want to do and if I don't see you for the ceremony, I'll know why. Just remember that it's better to walk away today than in a year's time.'

'Like once I've had a baby.'

His eyes widened. 'Exactly. That would be far, far worse.'

'I love you, Dad.'

'I love you too, princess.'

He shut the door quietly behind him and Frankie was left alone with just her reflection for company. The woman in the mirror was wearing the most beautiful dress she had ever seen and yet her eyes were pools of sadness.

From outside, she could hear the crunch of tyres on gravel and car doors closing, as guests arrived at the front of the property. She was running out of time. It was make or break.

She knew what she had to do…

—

Frankie hurried across the landing, cursing her high heels, with her bag hooked over her shoulder and dragging her Versace baroque-print leather suitcase behind her. By the time she reached the servants' staircase, she was already sweating, and the biscuit-curry aroma of the fake tan was rising from her shiny décolletage.

Step by step, she bumped the case down the carpeted stairs then round the first landing and down the next set of steps. When she reached the bottom, she peered around but the coast was clear. She shuffled along the parquet flooring to the nearest French doors, trying to ignore the judgmental glares from the oil paintings of Rolo's ancestors that hung on every wall, and pushed them open, dragging her suitcase out behind her. She took a step forwards but found that she was pinned in place by her fishtail, so she tried again and a loud ripping sound made her cringe.

'Bloody hell,' she muttered, as she pulled at the fishtail, causing another tear that left the end of the delicate material trapped under the glass door. She paused for a moment and looked back at it, regret that she'd destroyed such a perfect creation filling her, but it really was a case of her or the dress, and today it seemed she was going to be guilty of many things, so committing a crime against fashion was the last thing she should be fretting about.

The November day was bright, the sky clear, promising a fine afternoon, albeit a cold one. She kept close to the house as she made her way around the side, ready to duck behind the large stone planters if she spotted someone, but it seemed that everyone was over near the marquee, preparing for the ceremony. Shame crawled over her skin as she thought of them waiting there, sipping their Pimm's and expecting her to appear within the next half hour, all ready for a grand old knees-up and a uniting of two wealthy families. She was letting them all down, but if she'd thought of going back before, her torn dress made her keep running, because she'd never be able to explain this one to the designer, let alone Grandma.

She dashed towards the maze that spread out to one side of the driveway, and used it as cover as she hurried away from the house. This was the coward's way, she knew it, but she couldn't turn back.

'Oh, hello.'

She froze.

It couldn't be, could it?

'Frankie? Where on earth are you going?'

She turned to the neatly trimmed evergreen hedge at her side where the plummy voice was coming from, and spotted him, peering at her through the leaves.

What the hell was he doing out here?

And how the blazes was she going to explain what she was doing?

Chapter 3

'Frankie?'

'Rolo?'

'What are you doing?'

'Oh… uh… I was just…'

'I'm not supposed to see you before the ceremony, you know, or it's bad luck.'

Bad luck be blowed! Wait until you know why I'm out here.

'Well, you can't really see me, can you? Just a part of me.'

She shivered as a gust of wind whipped at the thin material of her dress. It would've been fine in the heated marquee, but outside, in the chilly November air, the dress was doing little to keep her warm.

'You haven't answered my question.'

'No. Right. I was just…' She sighed. What was the point in lying to him now? He'd soon find out and at least if she told him, he'd be prepared to deal with the aftermath. 'Stay where you are and I'll come to you.'

She tucked her case under the hedge then retraced her steps to the front of the maze and hurried through to where she'd seen Rolo. It took a while to reach him as her heels kept sinking into the soft earth, but as she rounded a sharp corner, she almost ran straight into him and threw up her hands to prevent them cracking skulls.

'Bloody hell, Frankie, look at the state of you! You look absolutely beastly! I hope you're going to sort yourself out before people see you. Mother will completely flip out and if your grandmother spots you like that... Well, rather you than me, what?'

She glanced at her torn muddy hem and the bodice of her dress where fake-tan had streaked the sections under her armpits then bled into the rest of the fabric. She folded her arms over her chest, as much to hide the mess as to try to keep warm.

'Yes... I am in a state. Not exactly what you were expecting, right?'

'Not *exactly*.' He frowned, and she realized that he was holding one arm awkwardly behind him.

'What's behind your back, Rolo?'

His eyes widened a fraction, a sure sign that he was hiding something.

'Nothing.'

'Really?'

'No... not really.' He shrugged then showed her the cigarette packet.

'You were smoking?'

He moved his foot and showed her a cigarette butt that he must have hastily stubbed out.

'I didn't know you smoked.'

'I suspect there's a lot we don't know about each other, Frankie. Like why you're running around the gardens in your,' he eyed her up and down, 'rather soiled wedding dress. Didn't that cost your father around forty thou—'

'Don't! Just... please don't talk about that right now.' Her chest ached with guilt. There had been no need for such an expensive designer dress but it had all been part of the charade that Frankie had gone along with. And perhaps part of her had fallen in love with the bespoke dress that made her think of fairy-tale castles and handsome princes who didn't make their fiancée feel like she was often in the wrong, who didn't secretly smoke in their family maze and… was that another cigarette butt with lipstick on it just behind Rolo's fancy black brogue? He didn't look like he was wearing lipstick.

'Are you going to answer my question now?' He pulled a cigarette from the packet and slid it between his lips then lit it with a rather fancy-looking butane lighter engraved with his initials. People bought lighters like that as gifts, so presumably someone had bought that for Rolo. But who? The only people she knew who smoked were her grandmother and Lorna, and now Rolo, and she couldn't imagine Grandma sneaking out here for a cigarette.

As smoke drifted from his nostrils, Frankie thought back to times when he'd kissed her – not that often, in all honesty – and he'd smelt strongly of peppermint and cologne. She'd wondered if he was trying to hide something from her then and now she knew. Rolo was a smoker… possibly something else judging from the hint of Chanel No 5 that she could smell on him as he moved closer.

'Well, Frankie?'

'Rolo, I'm so sorry but I can't do this.'

'Don't be ridiculous! Go on back in and tidy yourself up post-haste. I don't really want to hang around talking when we're getting married in what…' He pushed up his left shirt cuff and peered at the diamond-studded gold Rolex Frankie had given him to celebrate their engagement. 'Gosh, is that the time? Thirty-two minutes.'

'No, Rolo… what I mean is that I can't marry you. I can't go through with it.'

He shook his head. 'Don't be such an ass, Frankie. Of course you can. You're just in some sort of a state. This is the right thing to do.'

'The "right thing to do"? Bloody hell, Rolo, is that how you see joining ourselves together for the rest of our lives?'

His light-blond eyebrows rose slowly up his clear, square forehead.

'What's wrong with that?'

'It's not exactly romantic, is it?'

'Romantic? Frankie… we've known each other for yonks, dated on and off since we were seventeen and been together properly now for two years. What we have might not be a grand passion but it's… well… it's all right.' He shrugged as if he was talking about wine or a suit, not about the relationship they were preparing to commit themselves to for life.

She stared at him, wondering if he realized what he was saying or if the nicotine had gone to his brain and made him more tactless than usual. He dragged on the cigarette hard then exhaled a long plume of blue-grey smoke that was carried away by the breeze.

'Is that enough for you then? To spend your life with a woman who's all right? Not the love of your life or someone you can't spend a day without thinking about?'

He puffed on the cigarette again then dropped it and ground it out with the sole of his shoe.

'I guess so… It made our grandmothers and our parents happy when we got engaged.'

'But it's not about them, is it?'

'No. We're a good match financially and we've got that prenup, so neither of us loses out if something goes wrong, because we know what we're getting into. I oversaw the finer details myself. Besides, we have to go through with it now.'

'No, we don't.'

'The money, the guests, the vicar, the... the bloody fancy marquee.' He gestured behind Frankie in the direction of the house. 'The honeymoon if nothing else!'

His cheeks and the tip of his nose had reddened, revealing his annoyance as he realized he was losing control of the situation. Frankie normally went along with things because it was easier than putting up a fight with Grandma and with Rolo. She let Rolo choose where they would eat, park, shop, holiday and more.

But not today.

Not any more.

Something inside her had changed.

'Rolo, everyone else will get over this but we won't. Not if we make a mistake. I don't love you the way I should. I care about you but I've been drifting along with all of this, doing the so-called right thing and thinking I could live with it. This morning, when it all became real, I woke up. I'm so sorry for the mess I'm leaving behind but I can't do this. I can't stay.'

He frowned then nodded slowly. 'You're serious about this?'

'I am.'

Am I?

'Are you sure?'

'Yes.'

'Bugger! Nothing I could say to change your mind?'

She shook her head.

'Well... I'll still go on the honeymoon, Frankie. I'm not missing out on that.'

'You do as you like, Rolo. And I really am sorry to leave you in such a bind.'

But as they hugged quickly, their lower bodies arched outwards so they didn't touch as they rapidly patted each other's backs, Frankie knew that Rolo was already far away, working out what to tell people and how to turn the situation to his advantage. He was good at that. Perhaps it was the lawyer in him, used to creating convincing arguments to support his clients and to finding the best in a situation when a case had been lost. Their relationship had been a lost case from the start, the verdict a forgone conclusion, and if it hadn't happened today, then it would have happened somewhere down the road. Possibly with far worse consequences, like hurt or abandoned children. For Frankie, the idea of abandoning or upsetting any future children was a physical pain and one she would avoid at all costs.

'Goodbye, Rolo.'

'Wait! Uh… Before you dash off… What shall I tell people?'

'You'll think of something.'

He nodded, his brow furrowed with concentration.

'Where will you go?'

'I don't know yet, but I do need to get away.'

He huffed. 'Yes, because Helen is going to be baying for your blood. Probably send the hounds after you!' He laughed at his own joke but Frankie knew it had been bandied around, in certain circles, that Helen Ashford had a team of private investigators – nicknamed 'the hounds' – whom she used to look into people she was considering going into business with, or even associating with. In fact, she'd apparently used them to vet all the prospective wedding guests before inviting them.

Frankie winced at the use of her grandmother's name. She'd been trying not to dwell on how furious the older woman would be at losing face, money and control over her granddaughter.

'So I'd better get going.'

'Take care, Frankie.'

'You too.'

She lifted her hem and made her way back out of the maze then dragged her suitcase out from under the hedge. This was the hardest thing she had ever done but she knew it was for the best. Rolo hadn't even seemed upset, not at all. In fact, as his expression had changed to become the one she thought of as his court face, she was sure she'd seen a flicker of relief in there too. He'd made no sweeping declarations of love, no heartbroken pleas and seemed to care more about the idea of losing the honeymoon than about losing her. She straightened her dress, tucked a stray strand of hair behind her ear and took a deep breath. Then paused. Was that a female voice coming from the other side of the hedge? She shrugged. It was probably the wind howling through the leaves, and if it was anything else, like a woman who'd been hiding in there as she'd spoken to Rolo, then what did it matter?

She had definitely done the right thing for both of them.

But Rolo had asked a good question.

Where the hell was she going to go now?

Chapter 4

Just as Frankie was heading down the drive, she heard the crunching of gravel behind her. She turned around and her heart plummeted.

Grandma!

In hot pursuit.

She thought about speeding up but knew that would only delay the inevitable showdown, so she'd just as well grit her teeth and take it on the chin here and now.

She let go of the handle of her suitcase, pushed her shoulders back and watched as Grandma approached, surprisingly fast in her three-inch heels and lavender two piece, her antique pearl and peacock feather fascinator bobbing on the side of her head.

'Frances!' Grandma's chest heaved as she reached her. 'What are you doing?'

'I'm… I'm leaving.'

'Don't be so beastly! You can't leave… this is your wedding day. Oh blazes! What have you done to your beautiful, beautiful dress?' Grandma pressed her veiny hands to her mouth in horror, and Frankie saw that her long nails matched the colour of her suit.

'Grandma, I can't do this. It was a mistake. I thought I could, but marrying Rolo isn't what I want.'

'What you want?' Her grandmother chuckled. 'Jolly good, Frances.'

'Why is that amusing?' Frankie put her hands on her hips.

Her grandmother's slate-grey eyes bored into hers. 'This wedding is a union of two families. It is a demonstration of our wealth and a joining together of two names that mean something in this country! It is not about a spoilt little girl and her foolish dreams. Wake up, Frances, and stop acting like some seedy romantic.'

Frankie's legs were trembling as she stood there trying to be brave in the face of her grandmother's wrath. Throughout her entire life, she'd given in to this woman, allowed the matriarch to bully her into doing whatever she wanted, even allowed her to destroy her own dreams of becoming a fashion designer. Grandma's word had been law and Frankie had rarely questioned it. And where had that got her? She was twenty-nine, in a career that had been a compromise because she'd needed something outside the home and family, and she'd agreed to marry a man she didn't love. She didn't know her own mother and had even allowed Grandma to prevent her from trying to find out more about her.

Frankie was, she had to admit it now, terribly unhappy. 'I'm sorry. I just can't.'

Grandma's face turned red right up to the roots of her white hair – that sat in a style she'd copied from the Queen, and that she'd had for as long as Frankie had known her – and she raised her hand. Frankie instinctively stepped back, fearing a physical blow or that Grandma might grab her arm and drag her back to the house, but instead it was a barrage of words that hit her full force, and a shaking finger that cut through the air between them, the lacquered nail at the end like some sort of blade.

'If you go now, Frances Ashford, you will be leaving everything behind. If you embarrass me by walking down that drive and putting me in the awful position of having to explain where you have gone, then I will never forgive you. I will cut you from my will, throw you out of my house and you will be penniless. Do you hear me?'

Frankie glanced down the driveway to where freedom beckoned, then she glanced up towards the stately home where a lifetime of unhappiness awaited, then, finally, she met her grandmother's cold gaze again.

'You can do what you like with your money. I truly am sorry that you will be embarrassed but I can't see another way of dealing with this situation. If you like, I'll stay and face people. I'll tell them why I can't marry Rolo and let them see me… like this.' She gestured at her stained gown. 'Is that what you want?'

Grandma's lip curled and she bared her teeth.

'Get out of my sight! I should've known you'd end up being as much of a disgrace as your mother!'

Frankie opened her mouth, a thousand recriminations on the tip of her tongue, but she knew that venting them would make nothing better. Grandma had never listened to what she had to say; why would she start now?

So she pulled the handle of her suitcase up again, lifted her chin then set off down the driveway, trying to ignore the insults that Grandma muttered in her wake, and trying to ignore the ache in her heart.

—

At the airport, Frankie made her way to the toilets. The Uber driver she'd called hadn't blinked when she'd got into the back of the car still wearing her wedding dress.

He'd just popped the boot and put her suitcase in there then chatted about the weather and latest headlines as he'd driven her to Heathrow. It made Frankie wonder how often he actually picked up runaway brides from the bottom of the driveway of stately homes. Waiting there had been hell, as it had been busy as guests arrived, so she'd spent the thirty minutes diving behind a nearby hedge every time she heard a car engine, until finally the Uber driver had pulled up and beeped the horn. She'd sprung from her hiding place like a highwayman in wait, and hurried over to the vehicle; another thing that the driver hadn't commented on. After her exchange with Grandma, she hadn't wanted to encounter anyone, knowing that seeing Frankie in her soiled and torn gown would only fuel the gossip when Grandma and Rolo announced that the wedding had been called off.

As she entered the bright white toilets, she looked around. Thankfully, it was quiet, so she didn't have to deal with the curious stares of strangers. She dragged her suitcase into the disabled cubicle and locked the door, then lowered the lid of the toilet and sank onto it.

Exhaustion blurred her edges and she closed her eyes for a moment. It felt as if this morning had happened to someone else. It was all so surreal, like something she'd heard about or watched on TV. Even her conversation with Rolo now had a dreamlike quality to it, especially the smoking. How had she been unaware all this time that he was a smoker? But then, as he'd said, there were probably lots of things they didn't know about each other. Why he'd hidden it from her was something else she was confused about. She didn't smoke herself and never had, except for the few cigarettes she'd tried at boarding school when one of the girls had sneaked a pack in, but she hadn't enjoyed the taste or the dizziness it brought, so she'd left it alone. However, she'd never stressed a vehement opposition to it either, so Rolo's secrecy was odd. Unless… perhaps he'd wanted to have secrets from her. Rolo liked people to see him a certain way, depending upon who they were, and it was highly likely that that applied to Frankie too.

She opened her eyes and stared at her suitcase. She'd packed it for her honeymoon on a tropical island and a quick mental recap informed her that it held tiny bikinis, sarongs, silky slips and her ereader – well, she had suspected that she'd have time to read as the passion between her and Rolo hadn't exactly burned brightly, so she'd known she'd need something to while away the hours. She recalled packing some linen trousers and shorts and T-shirts as well, but hoped she'd included some jeans and a jumper, or at least a hoodie. It was really cold outside and waiting for the Uber had confirmed that for her, as she'd stood there shivering in her strapless wedding dress.

'Just as well open it and find out,' she muttered, as she knelt next to the suitcase then unzipped it. 'Oh, Jen, what have you done?' she screeched as the contents of the case burst out and rolled off onto the cubicle floor. 'I was going on honeymoon, not auditioning for *Fifty Shades of Earl Grey*.'

'Are you all right in there?' A voice from outside the disabled cubicle made her freeze. 'There's a cord you can pull if it's an emergency.'

'I… I'm fine, thank you.'

'Are you sure?'

'Yes, quite sure, thank you. Just reading my texts.'

'While you're on the toilet?'

Who was this person and why wouldn't they go away?

'Uh, yes.'

'That's not very hygienic, you know. Your mobile will be covered in all sorts of germs.'

'Uhhh… thanks for that. It's a habit but I'll conquer it.'

'I should hope so.'

Footsteps informed her that the disembodied voice was heading away, so Frankie sat back on her heels and surveyed the carnage that was her suitcase contents. Jen obviously thought this was funny, or kind, knowing Jen, but it certainly wasn't. What about when the case had gone through the airport scanner? If Frankie had been stopped with it then this would have been incredibly hard to explain. It would be even worse now that she was alone and didn't have the excuse of being part of a honeymoon couple.

She started picking through the offending items. The Earl Grey teabags she put back in the case, but the other items that Jen had packed on top of her clothes she put into a small pile. Frankie had never seen the like of some of them before, from the lacy black teddy to the electric-blue vibrator with a pink tip to the black leather crotchless panties and the edible nipple tassels. Her best friend had obviously had a field day as she'd shopped. There were hold-up stockings in all colours of the rainbow, furry handcuffs and what seemed to be a rubber mask.

'Bloody hell, I was going on honeymoon but this makes it look as though I had every intention of committing a saucy bank robbery.'

When she'd rooted around inside the case and didn't find anything else that appeared to be of the sex toy/fetish kind, she shook her head. If she had actually got these through customs – albeit totally oblivious to their presence – and pulled them out at their destination, what would

Rolo have said? He might have begged for an annulment, as never once in their time together had he asked her to dress up or try anything remotely risqué. She'd wondered about it sometimes, as wasn't that what couples did? Didn't they enjoy adventurous sex lives where they sometimes wore costumes and used titillating toys, especially when they wanted to spice things up a bit? That's what she'd heard her friends laugh about and what she'd seen on TV and in movies, but she'd never wanted to do it and Rolo had never asked. If they had been a bit more exploratory in their love life, would they have been closer? So many questions that would never have answers…

Now, what to do with them? She eyed the sanitary bin. She could throw them in there then leave the cubicle and never come back, but what if someone found them? Some poor unsuspecting person who couldn't open the lid properly, or a cleaner? Frankie would surely be captured on CCTV entering the toilet with her case and they might trace the items to her. Cold sweat prickled her armpits and trickled down her spine. She was in a pickle all right, and wondered if the day could get any worse.

–

Frankie stuffed the erotic paraphernalia into a tote beach bag that she'd packed for sandy flip-flops – thinking that she could decide what to do with it all later – then rifled through her clothes. She settled upon a pair of soft black lounge pants that she remembered packing for the flight home, expecting to be cold after spending two weeks in a tropical climate, and a black T-shirt that she covered with a pretty purple crochet cardigan. It wasn't perfect for the November weather but it was preferable to a wedding dress, then she exchanged her heels for a pair of purple pumps. Thank goodness she'd packed them just in case, even though she'd expected to spend most of her honeymoon barefoot or in her flip-flops.

Once she'd stuffed the wedding dress into the case, she zipped it up then hooked her bag over her shoulder, picked up the tote bag and grabbed the handle of her case. There was no one outside the cubicle now, so she went to the sinks and met her eyes in the mirror.

She looked at her reflection. Her make-up was not as flawless as it had been, so she pulled a pack of wipes from her handbag and wiped off as much of it as she could, then swilled her face with cold water. But as for her hair… there was so much hairspray in it and so many clips that she despaired of managing to get them all out. Even the tiara was welded to her head, so she decided to leave it for now. Besides, in spite of her anxiety about the whole situation, she realized she was hungry. She'd drunk all that champagne on an empty belly and needed to eat something before she zonked out completely.

'You can do this. You can do anything, Frankie. You just need to decide where to go now.'

A thought struck her.

Did she have her passport? She couldn't recall giving it to Rolo, even though he'd asked her about fifty times, but she just kept forgetting. Or did she? Was it a subconscious thing that she'd done because she didn't want to hand him that bit of control too?

She dropped the tote bag and placed her handbag on the sink unit to peer inside. She flicked through the main compartment then the one side pocket and another. She heard people enter the toilets but panic was surging through her so she carried on searching. Finally, inside her year planner, she located it. She pulled it out and pressed it to her lips as tears filled her eyes. If she'd had to return to their London house now, she knew her grandmother would probably be there already, likely having been helicoptered home so she could deal with her wayward granddaughter then force her to return to the stately home and her wedding, even if she had to pick up an off-the-peg wedding gown on the way. Grandma probably would assume that Frankie would go home, and would possibly want to change the locks before she got there just to punish her properly.

At least she wouldn't need to go home; she could go wherever she liked. As far away from Grandma's fury as possible.

'Look, Mama!' A tiny child toddled across the floor, chuckling as she went. 'A wiggle toy.'

Frankie turned to watch them, admiring how the woman crouched down to smile at her child. 'What have you got there, sweetheart?' The mother held out her hand.

Frankie's heart ached then, for all that she had never known, for the mother who had abandoned her when she was younger than the little girl in front of her.

'Oh my God! What *is* that? Where did you get it?' The woman stood upright and held the offending buzzing item aloft. It was the electric-blue vibrator and the woman stared at it in horror as the tip twirled round and round, flashing like the lights on a police car. She scanned the toilets and her eyes landed on Frankie. 'Is this yours?'

Frankie swiftly kicked the tote bag further under the sink unit.

'No.' She squinted in the woman's direction. 'What is it?'

'It's…' the woman lowered her voice, 'it's a vibrator.'

'Oh! No! That's definitely not mine. Never seen it before in my life.'

'I have no idea where she got it from.' The woman's face dropped. 'Oh shit! It could be... dirty!' She flung it into the nearest sink where it continued to buzz and rotate, then grabbed her daughter and doused her hands with liquid soap from the dispenser before scrubbing them thoroughly.

Frankie dashed out of the toilets, taking only her handbag and her suitcase. That was close and she knew that she didn't want a repeat performance, so she left the tote bag and its variety of erotic delights behind. Right where it belonged. She just hoped that whoever found it wasn't too shocked and that it didn't spark a security alert.

Chapter 5

In the airport cafe, Frankie tucked her suitcase under the table then wrapped her hands around the mug of coffee. She could see the entrance to the toilets from here and winced every time someone went in or came out, wondering if she'd see someone emerge carrying the tote bag of treats. The light was fading outside and she realized she had no idea what time it was or how long she'd been sitting there, lost in her thoughts.

Her bones ached and she wished she could curl up under the table and sleep. Instead, she picked up the almond croissant she'd purchased and ate it quickly, washing each mouthful down with coffee, aware that she needed to put something into her empty belly.

Soon, the croissant and coffee raised her blood sugar and the headache she'd blamed the tiara for began to fade. But there was still a question burning inside her: what was she going to do now?

'What time's your flight?' The woman at the next table spoke into her mobile. 'Uh… aha… right. Well, see you when we get there.'

She cut the call then looked at Frankie.

'My brother.' She waved the mobile. 'He's getting married in Cuba next week, so we're heading out there early to take in some of the sights first.'

'Cuba?'

'Yes and I'm so excited. It's my first holiday with my boyfriend too.' Her eyes sparkled and her cheeks were rosy, presumably with the first flush of love.

'That's nice. I'm sure you'll have a wonderful time.'

'Thank you. Where are you going?' The woman's eyes flickered over Frankie's tiara and she touched it self-consciously. It probably did look strange with her casual attire.

Frankie opened her mouth to answer, hoping something would spring to mind, but a tall sandy-haired man arrived at the woman's table and she jumped up and hugged him, so Frankie was spared the embarrassment of admitting she had no idea. The couple gathered their bags then left the cafe arm in arm, leaving Frankie staring at the table they'd vacated. It must be wonderful to truly love someone. Sure, she'd enjoyed spending time with Rolo in the early days and they'd had some fun – in fact, she'd hoped it was love that she felt for him – but she'd never experienced a burning need to see him, to touch him and to be close to him. In reality, they'd been a lot more like polite acquaintances than lovers about to marry. Perhaps that had been because she'd known she didn't really love him and had been holding back. And what had been holding her back? Not just a lack of love and desire but her need for independence. Her need to experience freedom, to know what it was like to be happy with who she was and what she was doing. Had she ever really had that sense of personal satisfaction?

No.

Not in her job. Not in her relationship. And certainly not in her home life, where even though her father had tried hard to fill the gap left by her mother, it had been there... a chasm of emptiness and sadness, a constant awareness that the woman who should have loved her more than anyone else had walked away from her and not cared whether she lived or died. It had also, unsurprisingly, been laced with a bitter anger.

Until she dealt with that, Frankie realized, she would never be able to move on and be happy.

She drained her coffee then opened her bag and pulled out her purse. She had a variety of credit cards and some cash, so she could easily book a flight. At the back of her purse, folded over, was something she carried with her. Always. She pulled it out and unfolded it, then pressed it flat on the table and gazed at the image of a snow-covered landscape. It was dark and the trees cast bushy shadows across the ground. It made Frankie shiver just imagining how cold it must be there. But above the snow, brightening the dark sky with swathes of luminous green, blue and purple, were the northern lights.

Every time Frankie had looked at this postcard over the years since she'd turned eighteen, something had tugged at her heart and made her yearn to see these lights in person. They were beautiful, mystical, magical. Even though she'd read about them and knew their true cause, Frankie still believed that there was magic in nature if it could create such beauty. And, of course, she wondered if her mother had seen these lights… if she had thought of her daughter as she watched the shimmering display.

Her mother had sent cards every year on birthdays and at Christmas when she was growing up. They had been pretty cards featuring beautiful paintings but the messages inside had been brief, almost impersonal, as if her mother had either not cared to write more or had been holding back. However, now that she thought about it and tried to rationalize it, perhaps her mother *had* cared if she was alive and well. She'd noted every changing of the year in her daughter's life, hadn't she? And yet... how much did sending a card really prove? Was her mother actually just assuaging her conscience and nothing more?

Frankie wanted to believe that it was more than just that but what proof did she have other than cards?

She turned the card over and ran her eyes over the familiar words, words she knew without needing to read them, but still, looking at them again helped her confirm that they were real and not a figment of her imagination.

> *Dear Frances,*
>
> *Happy 18th Birthday. I knew this day would come and yet, I cannot believe how the years have flown. Now that you are an adult, I feel able to give you my address. Please know that you are welcome to come and visit me anytime you wish. I would love to see you. However, I understand if you do not want to come. I will not contact you again unless I hear from you, because I don't want to trouble you if you would prefer not to hear from me.*
>
> *Yours truly,*
> *Freya X*

The postcard had arrived in a sealed envelope, presumably to prevent Grandma from reading the message, and Freya's address was printed in the top-right corner, leaving her to make the decision. She had not gone when she was eighteen, nor when she was twenty-one, nor when she turned twenty-nine. It had seemed better to leave things as they were, to build her own life and not rake up the past. She didn't want to hurt her father or upset her grandmother, and knew that visiting her mother could well do both. Her grandmother was a stern, aloof woman, but she had always been around – she had not left Frankie behind – and because of that, Frankie owed her loyalty – although her behaviour earlier today had made Frankie question her grandmother's motives. Her father had been a kind and caring parent, but he had a haunted quality about him, as if he'd never recovered from losing his wife. Frankie had felt protective of him, even though he had been the adult and she the child.

But now, she couldn't deny that the loss of her mother had impacted upon her whole life. Had Freya passed away instead of leaving her, then she would have suffered, but it would have been a different kind of pain enforced upon them both. As it was, Freya had chosen to leave her, and that cut Frankie deeply. It had influenced all her decisions, affected all her relationships and now she could see clearly that the life she had created wasn't fulfilling at all. Her job paid well but it didn't excite her. Her home, where she still lived with her grandmother and father – although she and Rolo had been about to move into a large apartment in Kensington that they had been in the process of renovating – was warm and luxurious, safe and familiar. Her fiancé was… well, he was Rolo, and she already knew how she felt about him. Finding a suitable apartment then renovating it, a process that had taken a considerable amount of time, had given them both some breathing space and – Frankie could see now – an excuse not to move in together until after the wedding. And seeing as how that apartment had been Rolo's choice, Frankie realized she would need to consider where she would live from this point on too.

She turned the card back over and ran a finger over the swirls of colour in the Norwegian sky. Such beauty, such purity, such a perfect escape...

She had some freedom over the next few weeks, as she had told her clients she'd be off for six weeks because of the wedding and honeymoon, then Christmas would soon be upon them, so apart from a few meetings and emails, she hadn't been expecting to do much until the new year rolled in. The admin staff that she and her colleagues employed at the rented offices they shared could deal with any emergencies. It was easier to have a London base for work and for clients, and sharing the costs had seemed like a good plan, and it also meant that whenever she or her colleagues wanted a break, someone else would be available for their clients.

Frankie knew where she was going. She would head to Norway and try to find her mother. She had no idea if Freya would be at the same address, as she'd heard nothing from her after she turned eighteen. Freya had left the snowball well and truly in Frankie's court and she had not picked it up or thrown it; she had left it there to melt. Eleven years had passed and with each changing season it had seemed harder and harder to do something.

Now, however, it was time.

Chapter 6

Frankie spent the early morning flight to Norway wriggling in her seat. She was aching all over from trying to sleep on the hard plastic airport chairs and all she wanted was a hot bubble bath and her own bed. But that wasn't possible and she didn't know if she'd ever be able to go home again.

The man to her right flashed her a few irritated glances and she tried not to look at his laptop screen to see what he was typing. He was likely a businessman heading to an important meeting and trying to use the flight time to prepare. She imagined that he was a successful CEO of a big company or a human rights lawyer on his way to support an international client. Did he have a wife and children at home and two loving parents who'd retired to a cosy cottage in Cornwall or a retirement complex in Florida? Was his life perfect in ways Frankie could only imagine? Peace of mind was such a precious thing to have and she wondered if she'd ever achieve it.

She gazed out of the window but the clouds limited what she could see, so instead she flicked through a magazine that she found in the pocket of the seat in front of her. It featured images of glamorous models advertising perfumes that would make her life successful and happy, if only she spent the three hundred pounds that each one cost. There was an article about an author who'd found overnight fame when she'd written about her backpacking adventures and wedding under a waterfall in Thailand. And there were lots more adverts for all sorts of products and gadgets, and as she scanned them, Frankie felt emptier than ever. She'd tried to fill the space left by her mother with things, and she knew her grandmother and father had done the same. She'd had every material comfort and luxury she could have asked for, and Grandma had certainly kept her busy, filling her time with ballet and piano lessons, tutoring during the school holidays – when she came home from boarding school – and exotic breaks that included yachts, secluded villas and hot lazy days spent in the company of other people with money. But through it all, through every single cocktail party, gala and polo match, Frankie had felt as if she didn't quite belong. In fact, sometimes she'd had to sneak off and spend time alone, trying to fill her lungs with fresh air because they'd constricted so much that it actually felt as if she was suffocating. When she'd gone to see the family GP about these episodes, he'd diagnosed mild depression and anxiety disorder and said it was quite normal in this day and age, so he'd prescribed a course of mild antidepressants to help her through. Frankie had accepted the prescription but never taken the tablets. Leaving the doctor's surgery, she'd been lower than ever, aware that she'd wanted him to tell her why she was unhappy and why she didn't fit in, not to give her something to blur the edges and make her accept her life without question.

Then there was the guilt. She had so much to be grateful for and knew many people would love access to the lifestyle she had. What they didn't know was just how lonely it could be.

When she landed, Gardermoen airport in Oslo was the same as any other, with people bustling about as they prepared for flights as well as those arriving and keen to get home. It was filled with the scents of coffee and pastries from Starbucks, cleaning products and people's colognes. High heels clicked across the floor tiles and new loafers squeaked, as people surged all around her, carrying their bags or dragging their luggage behind them like ants returning to their nest.

In spite of the thoughts she'd had on the flight, Frankie actually felt a flicker of excitement. She was doing something she'd never done before, stepping out of her comfort zone and about to embark upon an adventure. Of course, there was nothing to say that she would find her mother and there were no guarantees if she tracked her down that her mother would want anything to do with her now. But what she did know for sure was that she wanted answers and she wanted them in person, so she would try to get them.

At last.

The single terminal made it easy for Frankie to find her way around. She was, she admitted as she claimed her suitcase then dragged it out of the airport, also curious about the woman who'd carried her in her womb, given birth to her then walked away before she could even crawl. What made a woman leave her husband and child behind? What kind of woman would she find when, or if, she finally located her mother?

–

The Flytoget train was incredibly convenient and Frankie boarded it to get to the centre of Oslo. The train was clean, sleek and silver, and the journey only took twenty minutes. From her seat, she watched as the landscape outside flew past, a mixture of trees, fields and patches of snow. She'd expected to see more snow but when she checked her mobile phone, using the train's wi-fi, she read that it was possible to see some snow in Norway in November but it wasn't guaranteed.

Oslo city centre train station was a light, bright hive of activity. As Frankie wandered through the cavernous building, she heard a variety of accents and languages, and wasn't able to identify them all. It was a cosmopolitan centre and the excitement that had flickered earlier, now fizzed inside her.

She left the station and stepped out into a cold grey afternoon. She'd brought up a map of Oslo on her mobile during the train journey and taken a screenshot, so now she peered at it again to get her bearings. According to the map, it would take her about nine minutes to walk to the First Hotel Grims Grenka, the hotel that had appealed to her when she'd researched places to stay in Oslo, during her wait at Heathrow.

She walked through streets that consisted of a mixture of old and new architecture. There were lots of trees and the pavements were impressively free of chewing gum and litter. When she reached the hotel, the building's red-brick façade and square shiny windows loomed above her and her stomach fluttered. She was really going to do this, to stay in Oslo alone, and possibly meet her birth mother.

She took a deep breath then headed up the stone steps and into the hotel. The lobby was predominantly grey and cream, with square lines and minimal decor. It reminded her a bit of a private hospital where everything was hushed and calm, creating a serene atmosphere for visitors and patients alike.

Frankie booked a room for four nights, with the possibility of extending her stay if need be, then followed the directions – from the incredibly friendly receptionist with impeccable English – to her floor. Her room was light and airy with lots of wood and large square windows with a view of the buildings on the opposite side of the street. The white and green bedspread continued the forest theme. She parked her suitcase next to the bed and kicked off her shoes then wandered through to the bathroom and sighed. Because there, taking pride of place in the bathroom, was a huge bath. Just what she needed to ease her aches and pains!

She turned on the taps, poured some of the hotel-issued bubble bath under the flow, then went to see what she could find in her case to pull on after a long soak in hot soapy water.

Five minutes later, Frankie sat in front of her empty suitcase. She'd gone through the contents and tears stung her eyes. Although back in the Heathrow toilets she'd managed to find the outfit she was wearing, once she'd pulled everything out, she realized how little she had in there that was actually practical for her current circumstances. If she was going to manage at all, she'd need to go shopping for some clothes to tide her over. Luckily, she'd noticed there was a boutique next door to the hotel, so she'd pop in there in the morning and see what she could find.

For now, she'd take a bath, get into the fluffy white hotel robe, then take a nap. The events of the past twenty-four hours, along with the travelling, had taken it out of her and she knew she needed some sleep in order to reboot her brain.

Everything would surely seem more manageable after she'd had some rest.

Chapter 7

Frankie surfaced from sleep like a diver returning from the seabed. She was so comfortable, it was as if she were floating on air and she was tempted to keep her eyes shut and drift off again. But her stomach let out a loud growl and she knew that she needed to eat.

She opened her eyes and reached over to the bedside table for her mobile phone and peered at the screen. It was 7:35 pm, which meant that it was 8:35 pm as Norway was an hour ahead of the UK. If she was quick, she might make dinner!

She flung back the covers then wandered over to the window. She pulled one of the curtains aside and winced. It was light. There was no way it would still be light at this time in the evening in Norway in November. That meant...

Frankie had slept through the previous afternoon and all of the night. She'd lost half a day. And yet, she felt so much better. Evidently the lavender bubbles, and removing the vice-like tiara, had relaxed her and she'd conked out, which she must have needed.

She'd been tempted to switch her mobile off because it had buzzed constantly as her grandmother tried repeatedly to contact her. In the end, Frankie had fired off a quick text to tell her grandmother that she was fine and would ring her soon, but to please allow her some space and time.

The radio silence that had followed had made her think that perhaps Grandma had got the message. Or perhaps she was currently trying to contact one of her private investigator friends to get them to track down Frankie's phone. Why she even wanted to contact Frankie after the showdown on Rolo's driveway baffled her, but then Grandma was a control freak, so now she'd had some time to think about the situation and possibly cool down a bit, it was likely that she wanted Frankie back where she could keep an eye on her.

Her stomach growled again and she pressed a hand to it. Would she make it in time for breakfast? Only one way to find out.

Downstairs, Frankie found a table in the dining room and filled a plate from the breakfast buffet. Once she'd eaten, and drunk three cups of the deliciously bitter coffee, she was wide awake and ready for a day of exploring. Then she looked down at her outfit, the same one she'd worn to fly, and grimaced. She really needed a change of clothes, so she'd have to check out that little boutique next door.

Just as she left the dining room, her mobile buzzed in her bag. She paused, wondering if it was Grandma again, then shrugged. If it was, then it was. She pulled out her mobile and breathed a sigh of relief as she saw Jen's name on the screen.

'Hello.'

'Hey, sweetie, how are you?'

'Oh… hold on.' Frankie pressed the lift button. 'I'm OK, thanks.'

'Where are you? Of course, if I see Helen, she'll likely try to force me to tell her.' She gave a nervous giggle. 'But I swear I won't give you up!'

'I know you won't and I'm sure you can keep it secret from her. I'm in Oslo.'

'Oslo?'

The silver doors opened and Frankie stepped into the empty lift, frowning at her reflection in the floor to ceiling mirrors.

'Yes. But please, as I said, keep it to yourself.'

'Oh, darling, I won't tell anyone. I swear. You know you can trust me. I can keep a secret when I need to.'

'Thanks.'

'How'd you end up there, though?'

'Well, I went to the airport and knew I needed to get away and—'

'Oh! You've gone to find your mother?'

Frankie heard the incredulity in Jen's voice.

'Uh… well, kind of, I guess. No, not really. Well… I went to Heathrow and when I was sitting in a cafe there, I found the postcard from Freya in my bag and it just made sense to see if I could find her. I mean, I've wondered about her for so long, and about why she left and…'

'I understand, Frankie. I really do. But you could… get hurt.'

'I know that. I also know that this could be a really bad idea but I have to try, Jen. It's high time to find out once and for all.'

'What about you and Rolo? Is that all over now?'

The lift doors opened and Frankie walked out onto her floor and headed to her room.

'I don't think it ever really began.'

'Oh. Well… that's good then. I mean, it's really sad but I'm relieved you feel OK about it.' Jen exhaled loudly then clicked her tongue against the roof of her mouth; a sign Frankie knew meant that she was harbouring some doubts.

'It is?'

'Frankie… I don't know if I should say anything.'

'Please do or I'll be worried.'

'Well, are you sure about Rolo?'

'Yes. Sure as I can be.'

'OK. Well, he's gone on your honeymoon.'

'He said he would do. He didn't want to waste the money we spent on it.'

'But, see… he didn't go alone.'

Frankie dropped her keycard and fumbled to pick it up again, her long bridal nails making everything more difficult.

'Did you hear me?'

'I heard you.'

'He went with… with Lorna.'

'Oh.' Frankie's breakfast felt heavy in her belly. 'With our Lorna?'

'Yes. Are you all right? Gah! I shouldn't have said anything, should I?'

Frankie managed to get the card into the slot and her door opened. As it closed behind her with a swoosh, she went to the bed and sat down.

'Frankie? Are you there?'

'I'm here, Jen.' She rubbed her eyes with her free hand and tried to loosen her shoulders by rolling them backwards. Rolo had gone on their honeymoon with Lorna? That, she hadn't been expecting. Lorna was her friend; she was going to be one of her bridesmaids, for goodness' sake. 'It's just… this is all a bit surreal, to be honest.'

'I'm sorry.'

'It's fine, honestly. It's even a good thing.'

'It is?'

'Well, yes. At least this proves that I did the right thing. If he can replace me so quickly, then perhaps he really isn't bothered at all.' She recalled the cigarette stained with lipstick in the maze and the female voice she'd passed off as the wind. Had he been with Lorna then? Had this been going on for some time? How bloody awful!

'I don't know. I do think he cared about you. But Lorna... well, she's a lot of fun and perhaps he just wanted some company.'

Frankie nodded. 'She certainly is a lot of fun.' *And she must have been laughing at me!* 'I actually feel a bit better... knowing that he didn't have to go alone.' She lifted her chin and pushed her hair back from her face.

'You're not hurt or jealous?'

Frankie searched her feelings, wondering how she did feel after hearing the news, but nothing surfaced other than the twinge of disappointment that someone she'd seen as her friend – albeit not a close one – had happily stepped into her shoes. Had possibly already been wearing them.

'Nope.' She gave a small laugh. 'I'm glad I know. It proves that Rolo wasn't just a bad match for me but also a bad catch overall. Rather than taking the time to think, he's hopped into bed with another woman. They're welcome to each other.'

'Thank goodness for that. Mind you, I don't think it's anything serious. Just after you left, Lorna made a point of comforting him and he invited her along. She told me he said he needed to get away and that some company would be nice if she fancied it.'

'Well... good for them. Who knows though, perhaps they were already involved in some... capacity.' She decided not to tell Jen about the cigarette with the lipstick and the voice in the maze. It was all too exhausting to think about, let alone continue to discuss, and she didn't have concrete evidence that Rolo and Lorna had been involved already, even if there were clues that suggested they were seeing each other. 'Uh, Jen?'

'Yes, darling.'

'You... you packed some interesting things in my suitcase, didn't you?'

'It wasn't just me. That was the girls too. They all bought something to put in there. I was only actually responsible for the lacy black teddy. The toys and whatnot, well, they were from the others, including Lorna, funnily enough. I did wonder what would happen if you were stopped at the airport.'

'I wasn't, thank goodness, but I found the items in the airport loos and... well, it's a long story and one I'll tell you when I see you.'

'I'll look forward to it. What're you going to do now?'

'I need to find some clothes, seeing as how I'm in Oslo in late November and I packed for the tropics, then I think I'll have a wander around the city.'

'When will you try to find your mother?'

'When I'm ready. I need to pluck up the courage first.'

'Stay in touch, won't you? Just so I know you're OK.'

'I will.'

They said their goodbyes then Frankie flopped back on the bed. She'd often wondered about her relationship with Jen, about how close they really were, but after speaking to her now, she was convinced that Jen did care. She'd heard the concern in her voice and Jen wanted her to know about Rolo, so she didn't get hurt by hearing it from someone else or seeing it splashed all over Facebook.

Frankie knew she'd have tried to do the same for Jen too, although she hoped that was something she'd never have to deal with.

Right, it was time for a quick shower then some shopping…

–

Frankie peered through the window of the boutique next to her hotel and sighed. How hadn't she noticed yesterday that it was a dance boutique? She could go in and see if they had something, anything, more appropriate than her holiday clothes, something a bit warmer at least, then once she had something to wear, she'd hit the town properly and invest in a new wardrobe.

The shop was cavernous. Glitter balls dangled from the ceiling, sending tiny circles of light across the floor and walls, and music drifted from speakers set high in the corners, lively theme tunes from movies that Frankie recognized from school discos and weddings – some of them probably from before she was even born.

Aromas of peppermint and dried flowers hung in the air and Frankie wondered if it was deliberate, or if it was the perfume of choice of the owner, an elderly woman who stood behind the counter folding tights and occasionally peering over her small round spectacles.

Frankie wandered around, resisting the urge to bob her head in time with the music, looking for something that would pass as daywear and not make her look as if she was auditioning for *Fame*. She picked up some grey and black leggings, three pairs of legwarmers, some tights and dance underwear. Then she spotted what she needed: across the shop was a rail of jogging bottoms and hoodies, baggy tops and other warm-up gear. Having done ballet as a child and into her teens, she'd hoped to find these items here, and it seemed that her luck was in. They weren't exactly high fashion but she'd be warm.

Frankie took the clothes to the counter and waited while the older woman finished folding then came to serve her.

'Hello.' Frankie smiled then got her purse out of her bag. She wanted the shopkeeper to know she was English before she spoke to her in Norwegian.

'Oh, you're English?' The woman smiled warmly. 'Me too.'

'You are?'

'Yes, dear. Came out here thirty years ago and married a Norwegian. Never went back.'

'You're happy in Oslo then?'

The woman nodded. 'Oh yes. It's such a lovely place and my family is here too. I have three sons who live here with their wives and children.'

'That's lovely.'

'Plus, I had reasons for not wanting to go back to London.'

'Don't we all?' Frankie muttered.

Frankie pushed her credit card into the machine then keyed in her pin.

'Are you on some kind of dance trip, dear?'

Frankie frowned.

'The clothes?' The woman nodded at the bag she'd put the clothes into.

'Oh! No...' Frankie shook her head. 'I, uh... was meant to be going somewhere warmer but I... changed my mind.'

'Well, these will keep you warm, that's for sure. But if you need more variety, there are plenty of clothes shops in Oslo.'

'Thank you.'

'If I can be of help in any way, just call in again. Actually…' The woman pressed a finger to her chin. 'I had some stock come in a few days ago that I haven't had a chance to put out yet. One of my son's wives said it might be good to add some more variety to the range we offer. Wait here and let me check for you.'

'Thank you.' Frankie stood by the counter and waited, wondering what the woman might have that she thought would be of interest to her. She hoped it was something suitable because she'd hate to have to decline whatever was offered when the woman was trying to be helpful.

'Dear?' the woman called from near the changing rooms at the rear of the shop.

'Yes?'

'Come have a look.'

Frankie weaved her way through the rails to the woman and watched as she opened two boxes then started pulling out garments in clear plastic wrapping. She gestured at the clothes, so Frankie started to look through them and relief coursed through her.

Twenty minutes later, she had a navy wool tunic with purple flowers embroidered around the neck and sleeves, three beautiful silk scarves in black, purple and pink, a dark grey waterfall cardigan, a grey silk maxi dress with a deep V-neck and a pair of grey sheepskin ankle boots.

She paid for them then waited as the woman put them into bags.

'Thank you so much.'

'It's a pleasure. I had no idea if we'd sell any of these items but it seems my daughter-in-law was right; variety is important. Business has been OK but this might increase the takings, especially if we get more pretty young Brits in who've brought unsuitable clothing for the Norwegian winter.' She smiled, revealing small white teeth. 'I hope you have a wonderful holiday and find whatever it is that you're looking for.'

'Pardon?'

'You have the eyes of someone in search of a dream. Good luck with it.'

Frankie nodded, then picked up her bags and made her way out onto the street. Outside, she gulped down lungfuls of cold air, keen to expunge the emotion that had welled inside her in the shop. Perhaps it was just the woman's kindness, perhaps it was tiredness after the events of the past few days, or perhaps it was because she was closer than ever to meeting her mother, but she couldn't deny that the shopkeeper's kind words had affected her. The woman was a mother of three, married and happy in Norway where she'd restarted her life.

Sometimes life needed a reboot and perhaps Frankie was here to do exactly that.

Chapter 8

Frankie had the address on the postcard for her mother, but it was, presumably, a home address and she might well have moved by now. She pulled out her mobile and typed *Freya Ashford, Oslo* into the search engine.

No results. She flopped back on her hotel bed and closed her eyes.

Think...

She held her phone up and tried again with *Freya Ashford, artist, Oslo*.

Still nothing.

Then it dawned on her that her mother may well have reverted to her maiden name, so she typed in *Freya Jensen, artist, Oslo...*

A series of entries appeared and she scrolled through them. Freya had taken part in a variety of exhibitions over the years, had been active in local events and had been interviewed by local press. One entry caught her eye: it was an address for a gallery. She took a screenshot then brought up Google maps and typed in the address.

Her heart thundered and a cold sweat formed on her brow.

It was an eight-minute walk from her hotel.

Just eight minutes and she could meet the woman she'd always wondered about.

She changed into the navy tunic dress she'd bought at the boutique earlier and paired it with navy leggings and the dark grey waterfall cardigan, then she pulled on thick socks and the grey ankle boots. She looked in the mirror. Something was missing to give her outfit that special touch… She added the purple silk scarf, savouring the way it slid around her neck then fell elegantly to her waist. There was nothing like a scarf to finish an outfit, she just hoped she'd be warm enough in the thick cardigan, but if not, she'd make sure to find a coat once she'd located the rest of the shops.

She left the hotel then followed the directions from the Google map. This was it; she would meet Freya today!

Tucking her cold hands deep into the cardigan's pockets, she walked along unfamiliar streets, past cafes, banks and offices, trying to appreciate the scenery as she went and trying even harder not to overthink what she was doing. It was as if all of her childhood hopes, dreams and worries had been packed away until this moment and she didn't know if she wanted to punch the air, lie down in the gutter and cry, or run to the toilet.

When she reached the point where the map veered right, she turned and found herself in what appeared to be a shopping square with a large Levi's shop, as well as some others with Norwegian names. She noted the Levi's shop as worth returning to in order to add to her Oslo wardrobe. Grandma had not been a big jeans fan, but Frankie loved denim and intended to wear more of it as she enjoyed her new-found freedom.

As she carried on along the route, she realized that she'd returned to the square where the station was located but had come a different way and this gave her a sense of relief because it meant that she could place some familiar landmarks. Another glance at the map told her that she'd gone too far, so she returned the way she'd come, took another left and the map showed that she was where she'd intended going.

She scanned her surroundings, taking in the arches that ran all the way along the building to her right and the large rectangular windows of the buildings across the road to her left, a style that was becoming familiar to her in this city.

Then her heart skipped a beat when she spotted the sign on a shop front: *Freya's Gallery*.

Now that she'd found it, she had no idea what to do next. Should she go in, or walk past and try to see if her mother was inside? Should she peer through the window and get a look at her mother first or just charge in and confront her?

What to do...

As she was pondering, the door to the gallery opened and a large man stepped out into the street. Frankie watched as he locked the door then checked his watch before glancing around. She turned quickly and feigned interest in the shop window, appearing to gaze at the clothing inside but actually watching the man's reflection. He had the keys to her mother's gallery so perhaps he worked there. He had to be about six foot four with a mane of thick blond hair that fell to his shoulders. A gust of wind lifted it from his face and in profile she saw a thick beard and strong nose. She willed him to turn so she could see his face properly but instead he dropped to one knee to tie a shoelace, then threw a rucksack over his shoulder and marched off along the street.

Then he was gone and Frankie was left staring at the dark window of the gallery opposite.

It was possible that the man had gone for lunch but it didn't look as if there was anyone else inside. She could wait but the idea of hanging around didn't appeal, so she crossed the road. A sign in the corner of the window informed her that the gallery was 'Closed for the afternoon', so there was no point in waiting here. She decided to go for a walk, grab a coffee and some more clothes and decide what to do next.

But as she wandered along the pavement, she couldn't help wondering who the man was. Did he work with her mother? Was he a son she'd had after arriving here? Or – the thought that made her chew her lip – was he some sort of boyfriend? What if her mother had taken a younger lover who resembled a Viking? It was perfectly possible; it could happen. Couldn't it?

And with that thought in her head, she returned to find the Levi's shop, keen to get some comfy jeans to keep her warm as winter blew through the streets of Oslo, and doubt and insecurity settled once more in her heart like ice.

–

After she'd purchased more clothes, and a warm black padded jacket, Frankie took them back to the hotel and laid them out on the bed. Combined with her initial purchases from the dance boutique, she had sufficient outfits to get her through a week or two.

She'd grabbed a sandwich and a takeaway coffee for lunch and now had the afternoon stretching out in front of her. A walk around Oslo seemed like a plan; it would be good for her and allow her some time to see the city where her mother had started a new life all those years ago.

She retraced her footsteps to the square by the train station then looked around. There were several options, including organized tours, but she wanted the freedom to wander as she pleased, so she set off in the direction of the Aker Brygge Wharf. Her new jacket kept the worst of the chill out and she was glad of the goose down quilting inside it. The jacket might not be that fashionable but it was warm and practical. She knew that a few small changes could make it more interesting, like some embroidery on the cuffs and the pockets, and she smiled as she thought about the type of winter range she would design if she had the chance.

Even though the breeze was chilly, the afternoon sun broke through the clouds and warmed her face, and she pulled her sunglasses from her bag. It might be the start of winter but sunglasses were a must. It was also hard to feel anything but optimistic with the sun on her face and the wind tousling her hair and she hoped it was a good omen.

The inner harbour area was busy and evidently popular because of its restaurants, shops, apartments and office buildings. There were plenty of places to eat and drink, and Frankie wondered about the location's history, so she stopped in a quiet spot and pulled out her mobile to find out more. According to the information she found, Aker Brygge was the site of an old shipyard, Akers Mekaniske Verksted, which explained the combination of old and modern architecture. It was no wonder the area was popular, with its wonderful views of the marina and the Oslo Fjord.

Frankie put her mobile away and wandered around, admiring the scenery and the wharf itself. Everything seemed so clean and fresh and the light bounced off the windows and the water, creating a sense of brightness that lifted Frankie's spirits and increased her sense of optimism. If Freya had come here all those years ago and felt this same positivity, even though at that time the city might not have been as developed as it now was, then no wonder she had stayed. Frankie loved England and her home but also enjoyed visiting new places and had travelled to many different countries during her lifetime. But there was something different about Oslo. Perhaps it was because she knew that Freya was here and perhaps it was because she'd just walked away from making a huge mistake by marrying Rolo, but she felt lighter than she had done in an age. Whatever happened with Freya, Frankie knew that she'd be glad she came and that she wouldn't regret not marrying Rolo. Her only regret was not calling things off between them sooner, but then she might not have decided to come to Norway, so in that respect it was surely a good thing.

She stopped in front of a cafe with tables outside. It seemed like a perfect spot to while away an hour or two, drinking coffee and watching the world go by, so she took a seat and perused the menu.

Half an hour later, she was enjoying a generous slice of *verdens beste*, what the menu described as Norway's National Cake or World's Best Cake. It was a delicious combination of two thin slices of fluffy sponge sandwiched together with vanilla cream then topped with baked meringue and almonds. Every bite was like a mouthful of heaven and Frankie wondered how she'd managed her whole life without it. She washed it down with a cup of strong black coffee, appreciating being able to enjoy both al fresco with such a beautiful view.

–

Frankie was suddenly conscious of a loud snuffling. It seemed to be muffled at first, as if someone was shouting to her from inside a car, but then it became louder and it dragged her awake.

She opened her eyes and gasped. A huge wolf was staring at her, its furry coat thick and grey and its mouth oozing drool. What had happened? Had she somehow wandered into the wilderness where she'd be eaten by wolves?

Wait… what wilderness? She was in the city of Oslo and… still sitting outside the harbour front cafe.

'Are you all right?' The noise, now distinguishable as a voice speaking English laced with Norwegian inflection, attracted her attention and she raised her gaze to find the most piercing blue eyes she had ever seen burning into hers.

She opened her mouth to answer but couldn't find any words.

'Are you ill?'

She watched as the full pink lips set between a golden beard and moustache moved again.

'Miss? Can I get you help?'

She shook her head.

'No. I'm fine, thank you. Except for the wolf.'

The huge man nodded then stepped backwards, taking the wolf – who Frankie could now see was on a lead – with him.

'You were sleeping at the table.'

'Was I?'

'People… I… was worried that you were ill.'

'How did you know I was English?'

'I didn't but I tried several different languages and that was the one that woke you up.'

'Oh.'

'Do you need to see a doctor?'

'No. I'm all right. I'm just… tired, I guess.'

Had she been so tired that she'd dozed off in a public place? She remembered drinking a coffee and eating that amazing cake while people-watching, then checking Facebook on her mobile and seeing… some photographs on Lorna's page of her and Rolo snorkelling in crystal-clear waters, but she'd been feeling fine. A bit peeved that one of her friends and her ex-fiancé were evidently having such a great time, but still relieved that she wasn't there with Rolo herself.

Perhaps she was still suffering the effects of months of stress and worry. It had all built up and now her body and mind were trying to recover by resting. She just hoped that it wasn't stress-induced narcolepsy that would seize her randomly, rendering her unconscious, as that would be rather difficult to manage. A girl at boarding school had suffered from it when they'd been studying for their A levels and the poor sixth former had often snored through lessons and library time.

'Go to bed earlier, perhaps?' the man suggested, a hint of a smile playing on his lips.

'Ha! Yes, good idea. I will do. Thanks.'

'And it's not a wolf. Luna is a husky.'

Frankie looked down at the beast sitting in front of her, its head tilted as it observed her, its blue eyes so light they were almost transparent. The unblinking and intelligent stare unnerved her, as if it could see right into her heart. And when she looked up again, it wasn't much better looking into the stranger's eyes, because his were just as… knowing… and familiar?

'Do I know you?' she asked, realizing that she recognized him with his shoulder-length blond hair and impressively broad frame.

He shook his head. 'You're mistaking me for someone off TV. Some people do. It's a bit... embarrassing.'

'I don't think so. I mean... what could I have watched that you might be in?'

'*Thor*?' he suggested.

Frankie stared at him. He could be mistaken for Chris Hemsworth; he was about the right height and build.

'Or that actor who plays Ragnar Lothbrok.'

'Who?'

'In *Vikings*.' Above his beard his cheeks flushed. 'See what I mean? It's embarrassing.'

'I can't say I've watched that series but why is it embarrassing?'

'I get stopped, and people ask for selfies and signatures.'

'Signatures?' She frowned. 'Oh, autographs!'

'Yes. I'd prefer not to, if you don't mind.'

'I can understand that.' She realized what he'd said. 'Oh, no, I don't want your autograph.'

'Good. I am relieved. And even more embarrassed now. Are you here for long?' he asked. 'With your... family, husband or boyfriend?'

'No. None of those. But I'm not sure how long I'm staying.'

'You are here on business then?'

'Yes. Kind of.'

'And... you're sure you are OK?'

'I am and thanks again.' She stood up and held out her hand.

'Good.' He shook her hand and she suddenly felt tiny, her fingers lost in his grip. He towered over her, creating the strangest feeling inside her… it was unusual in a way that she had never experienced before. It wasn't unpleasant at all, in fact, it made her skin tingle and when she looked up, she found him gazing at her curiously.

Then she realized where she'd seen him before and she released his hand as if it had burnt her and stepped backwards. He was the man from Freya's gallery, the one she'd seen locking the door. No wonder he'd made her feel a bit funny; he must know her mother. He frowned for a moment then shrugged.

'Take care now and enjoy Oslo!'

'I will. Goodbye.'

She lowered herself into the chair, aware that her legs were shaking, and watched as the man disappeared into the crowds, his dog jogging along beside him. She realized that although she'd shaken his hand, she'd been too distracted by his touch to tell him her name or to get his.

As she raised her hand to request another coffee from the waitress, she found herself hoping that he wasn't actually Freya's son or younger lover, but she dismissed the thought because she wasn't here to admire the locals or to interfere in her mother's love life. She was here to find out the truth.

Chapter 9

Jonas walked briskly along the promenade. It was a beautiful afternoon and he was out with Luna, his two-year-old husky. He'd been to the gallery in the morning and closed up at lunchtime for Freya, as she'd had a lunch appointment with a buyer and had left early. He slowed his pace and led Luna towards a bench where he sat down. Luna sat on the ground in front of him gazing out at the birds swooping into the water, her ears pricked and her tail curled around her legs. Her high prey drive kept her constantly alert when they were out and about, and Jonas kept a tight hold on her leash, not wanting to see her launch herself into the water.

This was a typical afternoon for him when he was in Oslo – he'd walk Luna to burn off some of her excess energy and they'd often enjoy a stroll along the front – but today something was different. He breathed deeply and tried to enjoy the sensation of fresh air and sunshine on his skin but something had unsettled him. Well, not exactly something, but that English woman he'd found sleeping in front of the cafe.

Of course, it wasn't every day that he found someone sleeping on the harbour front, but something about that woman had troubled him. She'd seemed exhausted, sad and vulnerable. Jonas hated to see anything suffering, whether human or animal, and he knew he had a soft spot for wounded creatures. His mother had teased him enough about it growing up and told him it was because he was so intuitive and in tune with nature.

But it was more than that. He filled his lungs with air, counting each exhalation out slowly as he allowed his mind a few moments to mull it over.

What had it been about that woman?

She was strikingly beautiful. He'd noticed that immediately, it had been obvious even when she was slouching at the table, her head turned towards the sun. Her silky brown hair had fallen over her shoulder, strands of it deep red and golden brown as they caught the sunlight. Her skin was clear and free from make-up and her dark lashes had fluttered on her cheeks as she slept. And then… when he'd finally managed to wake her, he'd seen her eyes, as green as the northern lights and just as rousing.

He shook his head and smiled. Sometimes he sounded almost poetic but he knew it was the artist in him. When he saw something beautiful, whether scenery, animal or person, he wanted to capture that beauty in a photograph, to preserve it for ever, and that was what he had felt when the woman had sat up and met his gaze. He'd almost asked if he could take her photo, but she'd likely have become suspicious about his motives and he hadn't wanted to do that to her. She was probably in Oslo on some kind of business trip and he didn't want to ruin that for her by making her wary of the locals.

But she was beautiful…

And strangely, she also seemed familiar. There was something about the shape of her eyes and the tilt of her chin, a sense of pride and independence he felt sure he'd seen before. Perhaps it was just an English thing and she reminded him of an actress or celebrity. After all, he had accused her of mistaking him for Thor or that *Vikings* actor, so it could be the same for her.

What did it matter?

Jonas came across many beautiful women in his line of work and many interesting tourists, but that was all they would ever be. He loved his life, his freedom and his job, and no woman was ever going to change that for him.

His mother had warned him that one day a woman would come along and steal his heart but he was thirty-two and it hadn't happened yet. He couldn't see that changing.

And that was just fine with him.

–

'Dad?' Frankie answered her phone.

'Frankie, darling?'

Emotion welled in Frankie's throat and she swallowed hard.

'Are you all right?'

'Yes… I'm fine, Dad, thanks.'

'Jolly good. I'm so glad.'

'I'm in—'

'No, it's OK, Frances, don't tell me.'

'Why, will Grandma torture you to get the information?'

Her father gave a small laugh at the other end of the line.

'Well… perhaps not torture but she does have the ability to make my life hell.'

'Oh, Dad.' Frankie wiped her eyes with the back of her hand.

'I know. I should have moved out years ago but I hated the thought of leaving her alone.'

'She's tougher than you think.'

He didn't reply and Frankie knew better than to push him on this. Her father was so gentle and kind-hearted and he'd always put her feelings and Grandma's before his own. Whenever Frankie had tried to get him to stand up to his mother, he'd always explained that Grandma was getting older and that she wasn't as tough as she seemed. She'd been devastated when her husband had died when Hugo was just fifteen, and it seemed to Frankie that, ever since then, she'd relied on her son more than was healthy for either of them. It wasn't that she thought her father was a wimp – because he was a strong and successful businessman – more that he was too considerate of his mother's feelings and never wanted to upset her by standing up to her. But it was something Frankie had tried and failed to get her father to change, so she knew better than to push the subject now.

'How are you anyway, Dad?'

'Missing you madly, but glad you did the right thing for you.'

'But not for Grandma? Did she tell you that I saw her as I was leaving the Bellamy estate?'

'She did say that you'd had words.'

'She had words. I bit my tongue... as usual.'

'She'll survive, darling. It's given her a bit of a mission actually... which is why I want you to be careful who you tell about where you are.'

'She is looking for me then?'

'Uh...'

'I had visions of her employing fifty of her private investigators to track me down.'

'I've asked her to leave you alone so you can have some time out, and I explained that you felt you and Rolo rushed the whole wedding thing.'

'How'd she take that?'

'Not well but what can you do? She'll be fine.'

'I wish you'd had more children then it wouldn't have all fallen on me... Oh... I'm so sorry. I didn't mean that. It just came out.'

Frankie winced, as she knew it wasn't her father's fault that she had no brothers or sisters. He'd never fallen in love after Freya had gone. Besides, he'd told her he couldn't bear for her to feel replaced or overshadowed by any other children he might have had from a subsequent marriage, so he'd preferred not to get involved again.

'I understand. I know that some siblings would have taken the pressure off you a tad.'

'As it would have done for you.'

'Indeed.'

'Anyway, Grandma will get over it in time. I'll come back in about ten years, shall I?'

'To be honest, I think she's more shocked at what Rolo's done. Dammit! You don't know about that, do you?'

'That he went on our honeymoon with Lorna?'

'Jen told you?'

'She didn't want me to hear it from someone less tactful or to find out via the photos on social media.'

'I'm sorry, darling.'

'Don't be, Dad. I'm fine about it, honestly.'

'As long as you are.'

'Well, look, I'll keep in touch by text and phone call. I don't know exactly how long I'll be away but it probably won't be long. I just—'

'You need some time. I know and I understand. Love you, princess.'

'Love you too.'

Frankie ended the call then stretched out on her hotel bed. She could just imagine how furious and frantic Grandma would be right now, and it was all the more reason to stay away for a while. If she went back this week, then Grandma wouldn't have had time to calm down and that would mean Frankie would be subjected to all manner of difficult conversations. Sometimes, it was as if she was still a little girl, not a 29-year-old woman with a job and a life of her own.

She knew Grandma worried about her – or her reputation, rather – and that she'd taken over the role of mother figure in Frankie's life after Freya had left, but sometimes, life with Helen Ashford could become… claustrophobic. That was why boarding school had been a surprising blessing for Frankie; she'd been able to escape Grandma's shadow for weeks at a time, and to have a chance to assert some independence. She wondered if her father had always been so overshadowed by Grandma, or if it had happened after Freya had left. She couldn't imagine a woman marrying a man so henpecked by his mother and wondered if Freya had stood up to Helen. It would take a strong woman indeed to say no to Grandma. Frankie had experienced the disapproval of her grandmother many times, something that was often followed by a rolling of eyes and mutterings that suggested that she reminded Grandma of Freya, so perhaps her mother had been strong. It could even explain why she had felt the need to walk away…

But without her baby?

The hurt pierced Frankie's chest and she pulled her knees up and hugged them. She didn't know if the hurt of abandonment was something she'd ever be able to forgive and forget, whatever Freya's reasons were. Although she couldn't deny that she'd like to try — if the simmering anger that hid in the shadows behind the hurt would allow her to.

Chapter 10

Jonas finished his coffee then returned the mug to the kitchenette at the rear of the gallery. He'd opened up at ten, the gallery's usual time, as Freya was having the morning off. She usually ran the gallery herself but when Jonas was in town, he liked to help. Freya had initially put up resistance when he'd offered, but she soon came round to the idea, especially when he reminded her that she was helping him out by displaying his photographs for free.

He swilled his mug then walked back through to the gallery. It was a bright airy space with art and photographs displayed on the light grey walls and on boards that were set at right angles along the centre of the gallery. It was a haven of calm and tranquillity, where people spoke softly as they wandered around gazing at the art, and a place that could transport visitors to many other places and times – some of them real as in the photographs, and some straight out of artists' imaginations. Jonas loved being outdoors, but if he had to be inside, then the gallery was a good place to be.

Jonas was very fond of Freya. She was a strong and independent woman, quite a lot like his mother, and she was also generous and compassionate. She'd give anyone who walked in off the street the time of day, and Jonas sometimes worried that someone would take advantage of her. He'd even tried to speak to her about it on a few occasions but she wouldn't hear of it, explaining that everyone deserved a chance and who was she to judge anyone?

He'd met Freya around five years ago, when a mutual acquaintance had introduced them. He was back from a year of travelling and photography. He'd been to Iceland, Switzerland and Italy, using the money he'd saved and some of the savings his mother had put away for him after his father had died. He had a whole load of photographs to sell and Freya had been interested in seeing his portfolio. She'd been so taken with his work that she'd invited him to display it at her gallery, insisting that she didn't want any commission from sales, and it had been too good an offer to refuse. Jonas had been struggling a bit financially, and though he hadn't told her as much, it was as if she sensed that he needed help.

He walked to the window and looked out at the street, seeing the same grey stone buildings opposite and the same people going about their daily routines. There was something comforting about familiarity but also something that made Jonas long for the wide-open spaces of the countryside, and he knew it wouldn't be long before he'd pack his rucksack and camera, hop on a plane and head off again. Then something caught his eye... A young woman wearing dark leggings, boots and a black padded jacket with her shiny brown hair falling around her face. She was walking slowly along the opposite side of the road and staring at the gallery. As soon as she'd passed, she turned around and walked back the way she'd come. It seemed as if she was pacing up and down, waiting for something.

His pulse quickened.

It was *her*... the sleeping woman from yesterday. The woman he'd woken and who'd been startled by Luna.

What was she doing out there? Why would she walk up and down like someone casing a joint in a movie?

Suddenly, she crossed the road and headed straight for the gallery. Jonas raced to the desk in the corner and sat down just as she opened the door. The little bell, that Freya refused to replace with an electronic device, tinkled and he slowly raised his eyes from the papers he'd grabbed and pretended to be reading. But she wasn't facing him; she was gazing at the far wall where Freya had put Jonas's Northern Lights collection.

She approached the photographs and stood in front of each one in turn, tilting her head at times then stepping back to see them better. He tried not to stare but he found her fascinating. It seemed such a coincidence that she had come to the gallery after he'd spoken to her just yesterday. But then, more rationally, he thought, why wouldn't she come here while in Oslo? Freya's gallery had a fabulous reputation and anyone interested in art and photography, who asked locals for recommendations, would automatically be directed here.

As the woman moved on from his photographs and started looking at some of the paintings, he put the papers he'd been holding – rather tightly – down on the desk and pressed them to try to flatten the scrunched edges. He had to admit that this woman intrigued him but he couldn't pinpoint exactly why. She was attractive, yes, and she had that vulnerable aura to her that he'd seen yesterday, but he met lots of women on a daily basis and they rarely captured his attention for long. It was probably just her English accent and those stunning eyes of hers that had somehow found their way into his dreams last night. But so what? He'd seen a pretty foreign woman and his subconscious had run away with his desires while he slept.

Jonas was no monk. He appreciated beautiful women and had enjoyed spending time with them over the years, but he'd never had any yearning to settle down or to even make any of his relationships into something monogamous, or permanent. He had lots of female friends and sometimes dated, but he always made his position clear and the women he spent time with usually felt the same. There was nothing wrong with spending time with someone as long as you both wanted the same thing. Perhaps… if this woman was in Oslo for a while, she'd like to go out for dinner. There was no harm in that, surely? He hadn't seen a wedding band and when he asked if she was with a man yesterday, she'd told him she wasn't.

He smiled then stood up. He really should ask if she wanted any help.

–

Frankie's heart was pounding as she made her way around the gallery. She'd been outside for about half an hour before she'd finally plucked up the courage to come inside. When she'd entered, she'd kept her gaze lowered, too afraid to look over at the desk in the corner in case she saw her mother. She'd needed to come inside first, to try to slow down her heartbeat and to get some idea of who Freya Jensen was by having a look around her gallery.

The photographs that caught her attention were incredibly beautiful. They featured snow-swept landscapes, the black shapes of craggy rocks rearing up against the night sky, and the ethereal glow of the northern lights. In spite of her nerves, she'd become quite emotional as she'd gazed at them, wondering how someone could so perfectly capture natural beauty with a camera lens.

But someone had, and that someone must have a very good eye and an enormous talent. She'd love to meet the photographer just to ask how he or she had taken these photographs and what it was like to see the lights in person.

As she walked around, she was aware that someone was watching her, and the tiny hairs on her nape rose as if stirred by a gentle breath. She wondered if it was Freya, if the woman who'd given birth to her was looking at her right now and if she recognized her. Would she know her daughter at first sight as people in movies or on those talk shows where families were reunited always did? Would she be happy, sad or shocked to see the daughter she'd abandoned all those years ago?

Suddenly, it was all too much and she needed to get out of the shop. Immediately!

She marched towards the doorway but froze when a large figure blocked her path.

'Hello again.'

She raised her eyes to the face of the man from the wharf. His smile was warm, his blue eyes twinkling. She took in his dark denim jeans, the slightly creased pale blue shirt that clung to his broad shoulders and muscular arms, enhancing the blue of his eyes, and how he'd pulled his hair back from his face into some sort of bun at the back of his head. In his casual clothing, with his beard and long hair, he was everything Frankie had never been attracted to in a man. He was too big and too golden and he exuded a calm, quiet confidence, so unlike the blatant arrogance of the men she'd dated before and yet… she found him incredibly attractive. It was as if he stirred some primal corner of her psyche and she found herself digging her nails into her palms to prevent herself from reaching out and running her hands down his shirt front to see if his stomach was as hard as the outline suggested.

'Oh…' she squeaked. 'Hello.'

'Can I be of assistance?'

His Norwegian accent made the words sound so much sexier than they were intended to be and she took a small step backwards, just to try to free herself from his intoxicating scent. He smelt like she imagined the outdoors would on a snowy day: of sandalwood, fresh air and something else that she could only describe as raw masculinity.

Pheromones!

The term pinged into her mind and she smiled in spite of her situation. Yes, she would blame her attraction to this man on pheromones and the fact that she was in an unfamiliar city and dealing with some complex emotional issues. It was probably natural to want to throw herself at the closest hunky man, some kind of throwback to times when men – apparently – assumed the role of protector. Of course, in reality, Frankie had never relied on a man to protect her. Her father had been there for her but not exactly as an alpha male, and she'd never go for that type anyway. She was a modern woman, strong and independent, and had always gone for the more modern man. Like Rolo. But was Rolo really a modern man? Part of her had always known that he was a tad chauvinistic. He was actually downright controlling, for goodness' sake, so of course he wasn't modern. But she'd wanted to believe that he was, told herself that he'd allow her to pursue a career and to be her own woman. Yet the fact that she'd even thought the word 'allow' had made her hackles rise and she'd had to squash her yearning to run for the hills.

She could see now that it had all been a charade, a hoax, and she was responsible for helping to maintain the whole darned thing. Rolo was not only a fraud but a cheat and the way he had moved on so quickly with Lorna was evidence of that.

She shook her head.

What was she doing? She knew nothing about this man standing in front of her. He might not be at all protective, alpha or any of those other things. He could be a complete sweetheart, gentle, kind, tender and respectful.

And that wasn't helping with her rising desires, either.

Just stop thinking about him and focus on why you came here, Frankie!

'You can. Hopefully.'

She turned away from him, needing to stop breathing the same air as him, and walked over to the photographs of the northern lights.

'Tell me about these.'

'First let me introduce myself, please. I am Jonas Thorsen and I work here… occasionally.'

'Hello, Jonas. I'm Frankie Ashford. Nice to meet you… *properly*.'

'Properly?' He frowned.

'Oh… well, yesterday we didn't exchange names.'

He nodded as they shook hands and smiled politely at each other until Frankie forced herself to look away.

'So… the photographs?'

As Jonas described the locations of the images, Frankie listened carefully. She nodded and made the right noises to indicate that she was listening, and her heartbeat slowed and the tightness in her chest eased. Jonas spoke so enthusiastically and so knowledgeably about the setting of each photograph that Frankie felt she was right there in the wilds of Norway, gazing up at the magical light display. She could imagine the bitter cold making her nose numb and her fingers tingle, the crunch of boots on the snow and the anticipation before the light show began.

When Jonas finished speaking, she was breathless, as if he were a master storyteller and she a captive member of his audience.

'They're just perfect. In fact, I'd like to purchase one.'

His smile lit up his whole face.

'Do you know which one?'

She shook her head. They were all so beautiful.

'Which is your favourite?' she asked him.

He pursed his lips. 'I suspect that might be similar to asking an author which book they wrote is their favourite or even asking a parent which child they prefer. They all have their own… significance and allure.'

Frankie walked up and down the gallery, gazing at the photographs again. She could easily afford to buy them all but doing that would be hasty and somewhat frivolous, especially seeing as how she had no home of her own to hang them in now that she'd split up from Rolo, and if she was really going to make a go of life on her own, she would need to rein in her spending from now on.

'I'll take this one.' She pointed at one of the photographs featuring a small, dark hut surrounded by snow. In the distance the dark shapes of trees reached into the sky, their shadows cast across the snowy ground in front of them. The sky above was black except for streaks of lilac, pink and luminous green. She wished that she could visit that hut, sit outside it and watch the magical display happen right above her head. Then perhaps she would find the answers to her questions, the freedom from being the woman others had expected her to be, when all she had ever wanted was to know herself, to understand who she really was. And she was convinced that finding her mother would play a big part in that.

'If you're sure that's the one you want. Come to the desk and I'll take some details and payment.'

Frankie followed him to the corner and he pulled out a chair for her. When she sat down, he took the chair opposite and typed some details into the computer keyboard.

'I'll just pull up the information then I can get to know more about you…' He winced. 'I mean, get your address for shipping and so on because it's quite big and I suspect you won't want to try to get it on the plane yourself.'

Frankie nodded and watched him as the glow from the monitor lit up his face and reflected in his blue eyes. Perhaps this wasn't the wisest thing to do, buying a photograph from her mother's gallery, but she'd fallen in love with it and with the way that Jonas had spoken about the Norwegian wilderness and about the northern lights. In fact, it was almost as if he'd taken the photographs himself.

'Do you know, Jonas, I forgot to ask who the photographer is. He or she is extremely talented.'

He moved his gaze from the screen to meet her eyes and she saw colour rise in his cheeks.

'It's uh… it's me.'

'Wow! I'm very impressed.'

'Thank you.' He smiled and his colour deepened but he didn't say anything else.

As he took her address and payment details, Frankie had to admit that she was impressed with more than his photographic skills. She was impressed with him, with how he handled himself, with his modesty and with his quiet respectful manner. If she'd praised Rolo for making her a piece of toast, he'd have expected her to keep on about it all day, let alone if he'd done something like take a good photograph. And practically all the men she'd known in her life, except for her father, had been pretty much the same. Realization coursed through her. Had she been going after the same type then? Associating with men who were arrogant and self-assured, who saw women as an extension of themselves and not as real individuals with hearts and minds of their own? Men who married a suitable woman from their own class, a woman with a good fortune to equal their own and a woman who knew how to behave in their social circles.

Why would she have done that to herself? Been a clone for Rolo and his family, a woman who was always conscious of her manners and her behaviour. Would she have sacrificed her own secret desires and yearnings just to satisfy Grandma and Rolo?

She almost had.

And why?

But she suspected that she knew the answer. Rolo and his peers came from a different world to men like Jonas. The majority of them grew up with money and every material item they could wish for. Their parents were often absent, leaving them in the care of nannies and au pairs or sending them to boarding school where they learnt to fend for themselves, and when the children went home for the holidays, they were taken to high-class events and on luxurious holidays. Everything came so easy that a lot of them didn't know what it was like to need to work for something. Their beliefs were often already formed by their families and went back a long way, to those who had lived in their large homes before them. Not that Frankie would say the same of everyone from her class and social circle, because there were exceptions, of course there were, but she was thinking now of Rolo and his friends, as well as some of the women she'd spent her days with, and to a certain extent, herself too.

But she couldn't deny that Jonas and Rolo were worlds apart, and it had to do with more than just the fact that they'd grown up in different countries.

It was refreshing. Jonas was refreshing.

So refreshing, in fact, that when the door opened and the bell tinkled, Frankie didn't even look up until a shadow fell over her. She'd almost forgotten why she was in the gallery in the first place.

Almost…

'Hello. I would ask if you needed any help but I can see that you're in Jonas's careful hands, so in that case, can I offer you some refreshment?'

The voice was strange yet familiar, as if stirring long-buried memories, and the accent was English, just like her own.

Frankie raised her eyes and her mouth fell open.

Chapter 11

Jonas watched Frankie's expression change when Freya entered the gallery. It was as if she'd brought an icy draught in with her because Frankie's face drained of colour and her green eyes widened as she peered up at Freya.

As he stared at them both, Jonas realized why Frankie had seemed so familiar when he'd first seen her: it was because she reminded him of Freya.

How was that even possible?

'I'll get some coffees.' Freya was in her efficient professional business mode. He'd seen it many times before, the slow lifting of her chin and pushing back of her shoulders, the gentle patting of her hair then the determined way she put one foot in front of the other.

Frankie, on the other hand, seemed to have slumped in her chair.

'I think I have all the details I need now.' Jonas tried to get her attention.

She nodded but stared at her hands.

'Frankie?'

'Uh?'

'I said I have everything I need for now but I'll give you my number in case you think of anything else. Or change your mind.' He gave small laugh, trying to thaw the atmosphere that had changed when Freya had walked in, but Frankie seemed oblivious to his attempt at a joke.

'Why would I change my mind?'

'Some people do, especially if it's an impulse buy.'

Frankie shook her head. 'I won't change my mind.'

Jonas nodded then pushed his chair back. 'I'll see if Freya needs a hand. Be right back.'

He left Frankie sitting at the desk, suspecting that for some reason or other she needed a few moments alone, and walked through the gallery to the kitchenette.

Was she running away from something? She certainly had that shell-shocked air of a woman needing some space from something that life had thrown at her. He was also puzzled about her reaction to Freya. He knew Freya had left England almost thirty years ago and that she'd had a troubled time there, but she'd never told him everything. In fact, she'd said it was too painful to speak about in detail but that she'd loved and lost and that she often wished she could turn back time and start over. But that wasn't possible because life didn't have a rewind button.

Freya was practical and philosophical and Jonas looked up to her. He admired her artistic talent, although these days she didn't paint that much, and he found her attitude towards life inspiring. She was a free spirit too; he recognized it in her but she also had a haunted quality that told of harder times, of a broken heart. She'd been out with him a few times on his tours to experience the freedom of the Norwegian wilderness first-hand, but he sensed that she was wishing someone was with her on those tours. Perhaps more than one person...

Whoever it was that she'd been forced to leave behind when she left England.

'Everything all right, Freya?' he asked, as he entered the small kitchenette and found her making coffee.

'Yes, Jonas, thank you, although I do have a bit of a headache today.'

'If you'd like, I could make the coffee and take it through. That customer... Frankie Ashford... has just bought one of my Northern Lights range.' He got three mugs from the cupboard then pulled the milk from the fridge. 'I forgot to ask if she wants milk.' He frowned.

'Did you say Frankie Ashford?'

He turned to look at Freya and her eyes bored into his. He'd never seen her like this before. Her calming presence, her *joie de vivre*, had dispersed and it was like looking at a stranger.

'Freya, what is it? You're worrying me.'

'Oh, Jonas, I knew that one day my past would catch up with me but I didn't know exactly how.'

'Your past?'

'Yes.'

'I don't understand.'

'I know and it's a long story.'

'I'm a good listener.'

'I will tell you, I promise. You've been a good friend to me and you deserve to know. Of course, it could just be a coincidence and perhaps it's a different Frankie Ashford.'

'I don't understand.'

'I know.' She shook her head.

'I don't want to pry, Freya, I just want to know that you're all right.'

She placed a cool hand on his arm. Her silver bangles jangled as they always did and her short purple glitter nails sparkled.

'You're not prying, Jonas, and you have a right to know the truth. You're like a son to me.'

89

He swallowed hard at the compliment. He knew that Freya respected him and his work but to say that he was like a son to her was more than he'd expected. She didn't have anyone else and she led a quiet life, and sometimes he worried about her because of it, but whenever he'd tried to ask if she was OK, she always brushed off his concerns. He hugged her with one arm, almost embarrassed to make contact but sensing that Freya needed it.

She smiled up at him. 'You sweetheart! Thank you. Right, I have an idea. Seeing as how that young woman just made a purchase, I think we should take her out to dinner to celebrate. What do you think?'

He swallowed his response about the fact that she'd only bought one photograph and that would probably pay for one meal, because Freya looked so keen that he didn't want to disappoint her. 'I think that's a great idea. Will you invite her?'

She shook her head.

'You do it but make sure she doesn't refuse. If she can't come tonight, then suggest tomorrow, and reassure her that we do this with most customers. I'll stay out here, so you tell her I've got caught up with an international customer on the phone.'

'Will do. The usual place?'

'Yes. I'll book a table for eight.'

Jonas placed two mugs of coffee on a tray along with a small jug of milk and some sachets of sugar then carried it through to the gallery. Freya was acting strangely but she'd asked him to trust her and told him that she'd explain everything, so he'd try not to worry. He was also glad that he had the excuse to ask to see Frankie again.

She was special in some way and he wasn't quite sure what it was, and she was linked to Freya or the gallery or to some aspect of their lives too, he felt sure of it. So there was no way that he could let Frankie walk out of their lives today without ensuring that they'd see each other at least once more.

—

'Thank you.' Frankie accepted the mug of coffee then shook her head to milk and sugar.

'Freya sends her apologies but she's on the phone to an international customer.'

'Oh… right.'

Frankie sipped her coffee to try to hide her disappointment. She didn't think that Freya had recognized her but she'd wanted her to, and the fact that her mother had just walked away without a second glance was making her chest hurt.

She winced as hot coffee filled her mouth and tried not to spit it back out. Instead, she rolled it around her mouth then swallowed. What was a bit of physical pain compared to the heartache she was suffering? She'd been stupid coming here, stupid hoping for more. Sometimes, answers never came and she should have just accepted that. She'd drink her coffee then get up, walk out and go home. What else could she do?

'Frankie, how would you feel about dinner tonight?'

She met his gaze.

'Dinner?'

'Yes. With Freya and me.' His cheeks coloured in that way she already found endearing and he glanced away as if he was uncomfortable before meeting her eyes again. 'It's a standard thing we do with most customers.' He frowned. 'Especially ones from abroad. I would have liked to ask you out to dinner anyway, even if you hadn't made a purchase, but Freya would like to come too. Not as some kind of gooseberry, you understand. But then it's not a date. Oh stop talking, Jonas.' He tapped his forehead and smiled. 'I will start again. Frankie, would you like to join Freya and me for dinner so we can tell you more about beautiful Norway and convince you to visit Oslo again someday?'

'I'd love to.'

'Tonight?'

'Yes. Why not?'

Her heart skipped. Her mother wanted to have dinner with her, even if it was as a customer, and so did Jonas. Although it seemed that Jonas would've liked to take her out anyway and she wasn't quite sure how to feel about that right now. It made something inside her flutter, but she needed to process what was happening, and if this was the right thing to do. After twenty-nine years, she was going to have dinner with her mother. She wanted to jump up and down and punch the air and scream and cry and run up and down the street. But she'd do none of those things because then they'd wonder what on earth was wrong with her.

So instead she calmly asked, 'Where are we dining?'

'I'll write the details down for you.' He eyed her outfit. 'It's smart dress. Not that you're not smart. I think you look great. Like… really great.' He rolled his eyes. 'Here I go again. What I meant was that they don't allow casual attire in the restaurant.'

'That's fine. No problem at all.'

Frankie took the paper he'd written the restaurant details on then tucked it into her bag. She'd need to hit the shops again to find something to wear this evening.

And that was fine, because if there was one thing Frankie knew how to do, it was to dress for dinner.

She stood up then he walked her to the door and she shook his hand again.

'I'll see you there at about eight then. And by the way, I think you look pretty good too.'

She flashed him a grin then stepped out into the Oslo afternoon, her stomach full of butterflies but her heart lighter than it had felt in years.

Chapter 12

Frankie was ready to go. Well, she was dressed and standing in front of her hotel room door ready to open it and make her way to the restaurant to meet Freya and Jonas, but... she couldn't do it.

She walked back into the room and paced in front of the bed.

Reasons to do this: She'd waited all her life to get to know her mother. She'd waited all her life to ask her mother why she'd abandoned her. The friendly, attractive woman she'd met today intrigued her, and even if Freya wasn't her mother, she'd have wanted to know more about her. Like, how did she end up owning a gallery and what did she like to paint? And... there was Jonas. Frankie wanted to get to know Jonas better too, especially if he was involved with her mother in some way.

Reasons not to do this: Freya didn't know who she was and might not care. Freya had walked away from her and barely tried to make contact all those years ago. Frankie hadn't contacted her after she turned eighteen, so now Freya might not want to know Frankie. This was going to be really difficult and Frankie was downright scared but also a bit angry. Freya had looked absolutely fine, not like a woman who had walked away from her husband and child. She didn't look heartbroken at all, not in the way Frankie realized she had hoped she would. She'd expected to find a remorseful woman, possibly a broken woman, but Freya was successful and, by the looks of it, quite well off financially, so it was highly possible that she harboured no regrets at all about leaving her child behind. After all, she'd never come back and knocked on the door, had she? Never banged on the door until Frankie appeared then told her how sorry she was. So perhaps she wasn't sorry at all.

She stopped walking and took a few slow deep breaths. Right, this was silly. If she didn't go out for dinner this evening, she'd regret it for the rest of her life. She'd always be wondering *what if…* and Frankie was sick of what if?

So she was going to go and meet Freya and Jonas and, hopefully, have a good evening. It would be interesting anyway. Plus, she'd bought a new dress, shoes and bag for the occasion and had her hair done in the salon along the road. Luckily they'd managed to fit her in this afternoon and the stylist had created a smart, chic updo for Frankie that went well with her silk purple dress.

She checked her mobile and saw that it was seven forty-five. It was now or never; this chance wouldn't arise again.

–

Jonas was confused. He was sitting in the restaurant waiting for Freya and Frankie to arrive but he couldn't stop thinking about what had happened earlier that day. The way that Frankie had reacted when she'd seen Freya had definitely suggested there was some sort of spark there. But what could it be? Freya hadn't elaborated yet about her reaction when she'd found out Frankie's name, and Jonas had no intention of pushing her. He knew Freya would tell him what was going on when she was ready.

And if that time never came, then that was fine; it was Freya's prerogative, after all.

He drank some more water to try to settle his stomach. For some reason it was swirling like a concrete mixer and he tried to think about what he'd eaten that might have upset his system but nothing stood out to him. Unless…

He shook his head. This was so uncharacteristic of him. He was nervous about seeing Frankie again. Jonas never got nervous about anything. Over the years, he'd been a bit of a thrill-seeker and had taken some risks to get the perfect shot, whether abseiling off cliffs, jumping out of planes or getting up close to bears and wolves. Nerves didn't affect him any more because he always knew the risks and was ready to deal with them should something go wrong. And here he was, about to have dinner with two lovely women, one of whom he'd known for a while and was good friends with, and yet… his stomach felt as if he'd just snowboarded in the Winter Olympics. Not that he'd ever managed that standard of snowboarding; he boarded recreationally, not professionally. However, he knew how it felt to soar through the air and pull a few 360 spins, and that was enough to send his stomach churning.

'Evening, Jonas.'

'Freya.'

He stood up and pulled out a chair for the older woman then kissed her cheeks.

'You look really nice.'

'Ha! Thank you. I wasn't quite sure what to wear. I mean it's not every day you get to meet your—' She bit her lip. 'A new customer from England, eh?' She gave a wry laugh but her eyes were wide and she seemed stiff and uncomfortable, something Jonas had never seen before. Freya was usually so calm and confident, so relaxed within herself, and he suspected it had something to do with all the yoga and walking she did. But this evening, she was tense and coiled, as if she'd spring from her chair at any moment.

'You always look nice, Freya, but your dress is very pretty.' Freya was wearing a navy knee-length dress with lace sleeves and a cowl neck. She also had heels on, which she only wore when they had a customer dinner or an exhibition. Her bobbed hair was pulled back behind her ears with two silver slides and she was wearing seed pearl earrings. As she reached for a glass of water, her trademark silver bangles jangled.

'Thank you, Jonas. You're very kind.' She smiled at him. 'You know… I will explain why I'm all… aflutter. But after this evening. I want you to enjoy dinner and to make your own mind up about a few things.'

'OK, Freya, you're the boss, but I have to be honest with you… I'm a bit confused.'

She nodded. 'Perhaps I should just go ahead and ex—'

'Hi there.'

Jonas turned to find Frankie standing at his side. Her scent filled his nostrils, vanilla and coconut, sweet and sensual, and made him think of beaches and hazy summer days, of paddling in warm water that lapped gently at his skin. He stood up and smiled at her, aware that the heels she was wearing made her about two inches taller than usual.

She stepped closer and he automatically leant forwards and kissed her cheeks. It was a greeting he reserved for friends but he felt as though he knew her somehow, as if their acquaintance stretched out for longer than just a day.

When they were seated, the waitress arrived and took their wine order, then handed them menus.

'Thanks for inviting me. It's really nice to have some company.' Frankie smiled at them, the low lighting of the restaurant making her green eyes darker, sultry even, or was it the kohl pencil she'd outlined them with? Her hair was wound into a chignon, leaving her neck bare, and Jonas made an effort not to stare at the soft white skin of her throat and the hollows of her collarbones that were framed by her short-sleeved purple dress. He was no fashion expert but the dress looked expensive, as did her shoes. She looked as though she had money, as though facials and manicures and the like were routine rather than rare treats, as they were for his mother and most of the women he knew.

Then he looked from her to Freya and back again, realization dawning now that he could see them so close together. They had to be related in some way, even if it was a distant link.

Once the wine arrived and had been poured, Jonas raised his glass.

'A toast to Frankie for buying one of my photographs. I hope you have somewhere to display it?'

'Oh yes, I'll find somewhere for such a perfect piece.'

He nodded. 'I'm glad it has gone to a good home.'

'How long are you in Oslo, Frankie?' Freya asked, leaning on the table, her arms folded loosely.

'Well, I haven't decided really. A few days was my initial plan but I'm thinking now that I might stay a bit longer.'

'You should. There's a lot to see and do.' Heat rushed into Jonas's cheeks and he cursed inwardly. Nerves and blushing! What was this woman doing to him? But he also wondered how many people could afford to add extra days to a trip. Was money no object for her?

Freya flashed him a knowing smile.

'Jonas is right. I'm sure he could show you around if you wanted a guide.'

Frankie smiled and nodded then sipped her wine. 'Mmmm. This is good!'

'It is. I'm rather fond of good wine.'

'My father has a cellar full.' Frankie's eyes widened. 'I mean… he likes wine, you know, so he buys a lot. Even invests in it.'

'I see.' Freya sat back in her chair. 'And does he have his own place?'

'Sorry?'

'What I meant was… is he single or… married?'

'Oh… no. He was once but he never got over my mother leaving him.'

Jonas felt like a tennis referee, his head was turning from one woman to the other so quickly.

'He's… single then?'

'Yes.'

There was tension in the air and Jonas wasn't sure why but he didn't like it. Freya's face had blanched and Frankie's cheeks now glowed. How had they got on to this subject anyway? It was evidently not a good one for them to discuss.

'How about your job, Frankie? What do you do?' Jonas tried to change the subject.

'It's really not that interesting.' She shrugged.

'Well, try to explain. I'm interested.'

'OK. But try not to fall asleep.'

–

Frankie threw her head back and laughed again. She was having such a good time. The evening had started a bit awkwardly when Freya had asked about her father but then Jonas had stepped in and changed the subject, and Frankie was incredibly glad that he had. He'd listened to her speaking about her own job that she realized she had no enthusiasm for at all, because try as she might, she couldn't make it sound interesting. Then Jonas had taken over and told her all about what he did, a combination of running tours to see the northern lights and selling his photographs. He was so happy with how he made a living, and so relaxed about life, that he made Frankie yearn for a similar existence. Of course, it could have been the wine, she realized, as the waitress delivered the third bottle to their table, but she didn't care. She was having fun and actually felt happy.

She was also learning about Freya, as the older woman added to Jonas's stories and started to reveal small details about herself and her life. It seemed that she'd come to Norway for a break then never left. She'd spent the first few years there painting and selling her art, then she'd saved enough to open her own gallery. From what Frankie could gather, there had been no more children, although there had been a few gentlemen friends, but nothing serious.

When Freya had asked about her father, Frankie felt sure she'd seen something in her eyes, a haunted longing, perhaps. Again, she could blame the wine for letting her fancies run away with her. What would be better than to find out that Freya had never stopped loving her husband and still thought of him often? It would be a just punishment for a woman who'd left her husband and child behind. But Freya had no idea who Frankie was, did she? She'd said nothing and shown no signs of recognizing her.

And that was the way Frankie wanted to keep it for now. She wanted the opportunity to get to know Freya a bit better before dropping the bombshell that she was her daughter. Freya might turn her away right now if she found out, and what would Frankie have achieved if that happened? Not even the chance to ask her questions. If she remained a customer, then Freya would have no reason to be anything other than warm and polite towards her.

She couldn't deny that she felt a bit bad about the deception, but she tried to justify it by telling herself that Freya might seem nice right now, but she had abandoned her life and her family, so there must be a tougher side to her than what Frankie had seen so far.

'What do you think, Frankie?'

'About what?' She sat up straight in her chair, aware that she'd been lost in her thoughts and not heard what Jonas had said.

'About taking a trip and seeing some of this yourself.'

He smiled at her, his blue eyes twinkling and his hair shining like a golden halo around his head. His beard was neatly trimmed, and she could better see the strength of his jaw than earlier that day and wondered how he'd look completely clean-shaven. Either way, he was a good-looking man, if a bit more rugged than Frankie usually found attractive.

She smiled back at him, the wine making her more relaxed and even flirtatious.

'I think that I would definitely like to see some of this myself.'

'Fantastic. How does this weekend sound?'

She swallowed hard. This weekend? Heading off into freezing conditions where wolves and polar bears still roamed. It seemed great as a future prospect but right now?

Her mobile starting buzzing in her bag so she excused herself for a moment to peer at the screen. It was her father's number. He said he wouldn't contact her as long as she stayed in touch so something must be wrong.

'I'm so sorry. I have to take this,' she whispered to Freya and Jonas then swiped the screen before heading to the toilets.

'Hello? Dad?'

'Hello, Frances, I've got hold of you at last.'

Frankie's stomach churned at the familiar voice, so she headed into a cubicle and locked the door behind her. She had a feeling she was going to need the privacy.

Chapter 13

Frankie ended the call then stared at the blank screen of her mobile. She'd known that speaking to Grandma again wouldn't be easy but now that she had, she felt a million times worse than before. Her grandmother had used her father's mobile to contact her, suspecting that she'd answer a call from him.

She put the toilet lid down and sank onto it, turning her mobile over and over in her hands. Grandma was still absolutely furious and she had let Frankie know it in no uncertain terms. She was also still incredibly embarrassed, and berated Frankie for showing her up in front of her friends and acquaintances, repeating some of the things she'd said on Rolo's family driveway and adding a few more insults for good measure. Frankie had stayed quiet, allowing Grandma to speak, knowing from past experience that it was easier to let Helen Ashford get it all off her chest. Interrupting her would only have stoked the furnace and besides, Frankie's growing guilt made her feel that Grandma deserved the opportunity to have her say.

However, when Grandma had insisted that Frankie return home on the next available flight, something inside Frankie had sparked, that stubborn flame that she'd always tried to suppress and that had got her into trouble with her grandmother in the past. Grandma had demanded to know where Frankie was, but she'd stayed quiet; there was no way she was going to make it easy for her grandmother to track her down. In the end, once Grandma had vented and finally exhausted her repertoire of put-downs, Frankie had told her that she'd be home at some point, that she loved her and would stay in touch via text message, but asked her not to phone again as she needed the time and space to think about what she wanted from life and for her future. She'd ended the call then before Grandma could attempt round two.

She held up her hands, the left one still clutching her mobile, and saw that they were trembling, and no wonder.

What could she do? How could she free her mind and decide what she wanted?

She needed to get in touch with nature, to breathe fresh clear air and escape everything that reminded her of her old life. She wiped her eyes and blew her nose, then let herself out of the cubicle, washed her hands and splashed some water over her face.

It was obvious now, what she had to do. She would go on a tour with Jonas and see the Norwegian countryside. If she was going to return to London and possibly to her life there with all its entrapments, customs and acceptable behaviour – although she wasn't yet sure that she could face this course of action – then she would allow herself some time out first in a true wilderness.

Out there, away from everything, perhaps she would find herself.

–

Jonas stood up when Frankie returned to their table and when they sat back down, he had to bite his lip not to ask if she was all right, because she clearly wasn't. Her eyes were red-rimmed and watery, so she'd either been crying or had a massive sneezing fit.

Freya, however, was not going to let it go.

'Frankie, was that bad news?'

Frankie dropped her mobile into her bag hanging on the back of her chair then shook her head. 'Oh, no, just someone from home.'

'But you've been crying.'

Frankie sipped her wine then looked at Freya and Jonas in turn. 'It was my grandmother. She's a bit… annoyed at the moment.'

Jonas felt Freya stiffen beside him. 'Your grandmother? What's her problem?'

Jonas glanced at Freya and was surprised to see that her hands were scrunching up her napkin on the table. She was always so calm and in control that it was a shock to see that she actually seemed angry.

'Oh…' Frankie waved a hand then a tear ran down her cheek. She wiped it away quickly but another soon followed and another until she raised her napkin and covered her face. 'I'm so sorry. This is really embarrassing. I honestly didn't mean to cry in front of you. I barely know you but I'm just feeling a bit… emotional at the moment.'

Freya got up and went to Frankie then wrapped an arm around her shoulders. 'It's all right, Frankie, we all have our off moments. Jonas and I don't mind at all, do we?'

'No… not at all. I'm always making women cry in restaurants.'

Frankie snorted.

'That's right, he's so rude and gruff sometimes, Frankie, that he sends women into floods of tears.'

'Floods.' He coughed. 'Regular brute I am. I blame my Viking ancestry.'

Frankie lowered her napkin and peered at them both then accepted a tissue from Freya.

'I can't quite see you as a brute.' She smiled at Jonas and something inside him loosened, as if he'd been holding himself tight and he'd just relaxed a bit.

'He's not, really, Frankie, he's one of the sweetest men I've ever met.' Freya patted his hand and he smiled.

Frankie dried her eyes then shook her head. 'I really am sorry though. This isn't me at all. I don't cry when I'm out with strangers. I barely cry at all. Stiff upper lip and all that.'

'We don't have to be strangers,' Freya said, and Jonas turned to her. Something in her tone told him that there was more to her words than the kindly reassurance of a customer.

Frankie opened her mouth as if to speak, then glanced at Jonas and sighed. Whatever she was about to say to Freya, she'd decided not to because he was there.

'I'll, um... just pop to the toilet.' He was about to get up but Frankie reached out and held his arm, gazing up at him with watery eyes full of emotion.

'Jonas. I've decided that I'd really like to see the northern lights. Would you take me on one of your tours?'

'Of course. I'd be happy to take you. There's no guarantee that we will see them at any point, I should warn you of that, but we often do.'

'Well, I'd like to go. When's the next one?'

'As I mentioned, I'm actually heading to Tromsø on Friday.'

'This Friday?'

He nodded.

'That's perfect. The sooner the better.'

'Do you have appropriate clothing, Frankie?' Freya asked. 'It's pretty cold up there.'

'You do need proper gear.' Jonas ran his eyes over her face, taking in her red eyes and nose and her pretty mouth. The need to make her smile surged through him and he knew that seeing the lights could lift anyone's spirits. He'd do his best to ensure that she had a good weekend.

'Oh, I don't. I can get some though, if you just tell me what I need.'

'How about if I take you shopping tomorrow?' Freya asked. 'I know what you need to get.'

'That's very kind, thank you.' Frankie smiled. 'I'd really like that.'

Jonas had a feeling that he was witnessing something special happening here between these two women. It was more than just an agreement to go on a shopping trip. He didn't know exactly why but he suspected it would soon become clear.

—

Outside her hotel, Frankie stopped and turned to Jonas.

'Thanks for walking me back. You didn't need to.'

He shrugged. 'It was a pleasure. Besides, after eating so much rich food I needed to walk some of it off.' He patted his flat stomach and she smiled.

'The food was delicious.'

'Are you OK now?' He tilted his head as he gazed at her and she realized again how handsome he was.

'Yes… I'm fine, thank you. My grandmother is just a tricky customer at times.'

'She must have said something very mean to make you cry.'

'No. Well, yes. But it's my fault. I kind of deserved it.'

'I find that hard to believe, Frankie. I know I hardly know you at all but from what I've seen so far you're a good person.'

'You never know though, right? Everyone has a dark side, don't they?'

'What, like a Star Wars character?'

She laughed. 'Exactly.'

'I'm sure your dark side is much brighter than a lot of people's.'

'Perhaps. But I have done things I'm not proud of.'

'So has everyone. Don't beat yourself up about it, though.' He reached out then and gently brushed her cheek. 'You had an eyelash there.'

'Thank you.' Her heart fluttered with the impact of his touch. How could such big hands be so gentle? He had barely touched her skin and yet electricity fizzed through her body, making her light-headed. She put up a hand to steady herself and he took it.

'Frankie?' She met his eyes and saw concern there.

'It's all right. I think it's just the wine.'

'You need to get some rest.'

'I do.' She squeezed his hand then released it. 'I'll see you soon?'

'You will. I can't wait for you to see the beauty of northern Norway. I have a feeling you'll love it.'

'I'm sure I will.'

'Goodnight, Frankie.'

'Goodnight.'

She walked into the hotel and as the door closed behind her, she turned back to wave and found him watching her. He was such a gentleman, kind and caring, and also surprisingly bloody sexy. As she crossed the lobby then stepped into the lift, Frankie was certain that she'd never met a man quite like Jonas Thorsen and she liked the way she felt when she was around him.

Chapter 14

Jonas made his way back to the gallery. He'd left his mobile phone there that afternoon and thought he'd better get it before he went home. As he neared the gallery, he could see light coming from behind the blinds. He frowned. Had they left a light on when they'd closed up? He couldn't remember doing so and he was always careful to check everything before he left for the day. Besides, Freya had been with him, so there had been two of them to make sure that everything was off.

He pulled his set of keys from his pocket and opened the door then locked it behind him. What if they were being burgled? It was possible that someone could have broken in through the back door and that they had come to steal some of the paintings. Art thieves! It could happen, although it hadn't in all the years he'd worked with Freya.

He picked up a vase from the shelf behind the desk then crept through the shop. As he passed his photographs of the northern lights, he smiled at the SOLD sticker next to one of them. If Frankie loved the photographs so much, what would she think of the real thing?

A rustling from the office next to the kitchenette caught his attention and he hurried towards the door then pushed it open, preparing to smash the vase down on the intruder's head, but he froze when he saw Freya slumped at the desk.

'Shit, Freya! I thought we were being robbed.'

She shook her head but didn't look up. 'What're you doing here? I thought you were going home after you'd walked Frankie back to her hotel.'

Her voice sounded different, very unlike the confident, happy tones of the woman he knew.

'Freya?' He took the seat opposite her and noticed the glass of whisky on the table in front of her. 'What is it?'

She met his eyes and he could see that she'd been crying.

'I clearly need to improve my social skills,' he blurted.

'What?'

'Well, first Frankie, and now you. I've been out with both of you tonight and both of you have ended up crying.'

'Jonas, it's not your fault.' She laughed but her cheeks glistened in the electric light. She placed something on the desk in front of him so he picked it up.

It was a photograph taken with a Polaroid camera. It showed a tiny baby dressed in pink lying on a crocheted white shawl.

'Is this you?' he asked.

She shook her head. 'Turn it over.'

He did and saw faded writing on the back of it. 'Frances Hannah Ashford. 1989.'

He looked at the picture again.

'Is this...'

'Yes, it's Frankie.'

'But how? I don't understand. How do you have a photo of her as a baby?'

'Because I'm her mother.'

Jonas felt his mouth drop open as everything fell into place.

'You might need this.' Freya poured him a whisky too.

An hour later, everything was clearer. Freya filled Jonas in about her past in detail and he had been surprised, shocked and even angry as she'd told him about her life in England and about what had made her leave her baby daughter behind. Freya explained that she'd never told him before because it was just too painful to talk about, and she'd also worried about what he'd think if she told him the truth. After all, she had walked out on her family and what kind of a woman did that?

In light of what she'd told him, Jonas said it was completely understandable, but he got the impression that it would take a lot to convince Freya of that now. His main concern was what she intended on doing about what she'd told him. She thought that Frankie knew and that it was why she'd come to Oslo, but she wasn't certain and therefore wanted to handle her daughter carefully; Freya wanted to know more about her daughter and why she had come before having a frank conversation. If Frankie was oblivious to who she was, then she wanted to tell her but it would need to be done gently.

It had made Jonas's head hurt just thinking about how complicated it all was. He cared deeply about Freya; she had been friend and mentor to him and like another mother. Finding out that she'd carried this heartache all this time, that this was in fact the reason why she'd always seemed haunted by something in her past, made him sad. She always came across as strong and independent but she'd been so hurt and so wronged that it made his blood boil. Whatever happened though, he knew that he'd be there to support Freya. It was evident now that he was all she had.

However, if she could form some sort of relationship with Frankie, who seemed like a lovely young woman, then surely that would be a good thing for them both?

'You should come with us.'

'Sorry?'

'You should come away this weekend, Freya. It will give you the chance to find out more about Frankie.'

'But what if she doesn't want me there?'

'I'm sure that she will do. Whether she knows who you are or not, it's clear that she likes you. When you go shopping with her tomorrow, tell her that you're coming too and see how she takes it. Besides, I hate to think of you here alone after what you've told me.'

'Jonas, I'm old enough and tough enough to manage on my own. I've been doing just that all these years.'

'But now it is different.'

'It is?'

He nodded. 'Now I know that you have reasons to be sad and I'm worried about you.'

'Well, that's very kind of you but I'll be fine. Although, perhaps you're right and coming would be a good way to get to know Frankie.'

'Then it's agreed. And, Freya, it is OK to rely on some people. I'm here for you, just as you have been here for me.'

'Thank you. That means a lot.'

'You can trust me. I will not let you down.'

'You're a good man, Jonas.'

He smiled then raised his glass.

'To family.'

'To the family we create for ourselves.'

They clinked glasses then Jonas sipped his drink, savouring the smoky taste and the warmth as he swallowed the twelve-year-old single malt.

He meant every word. Freya was his family and he would be there for her, and hopefully ensure that she didn't get hurt again.

Chapter 15

Freya had sent Frankie a text and asked her to meet at the gallery at eleven the next day. She'd said she had some paperwork to sort before they went shopping.

When Frankie arrived at the gallery, she paused outside, her stomach feeling as though she was on a roller coaster. The dinner she'd had with Freya and Jonas had been an intense experience and she was still trying to work out how she felt about everything. For a start, there was Freya, who seemed nothing like the woman her grandmother had told her about, and then there was Jonas. Frankie had not been expecting to meet a man like him when she came looking for her mother. Jonas was undeniably a welcome addition – her emotions about Freya were so complicated, and so long developed, that he was proving a useful distraction. Even if she had to admit that she was confused by her reactions to him. Jonas was everything she'd never have gone for in a man before but she was starting to question her previous thoughts and behaviour, to wonder at what she'd thought was attractive in a man.

Preconceptions… hers were certainly being blown apart since she'd come to Norway.

'And long may it continue,' she said as she pushed open the door to the gallery.

'Good morning.' Jonas was sitting at the desk going through some papers with a customer opposite him.

'Morning.' She smiled but didn't go over, as he was clearly busy.

'Freya's out the back,' Jonas said. 'She won't be long.'

Frankie nodded then went to look at a new display of photographs that had been set up on one of the central boards. They were beautiful depictions of Norwegian wildlife, from foxes to squirrels to wolves, all going about their daily routines, oblivious to the fact that they were being captured on camera. There was a name next to them that Frankie didn't recognize.

'She's a friend.'

Frankie turned and gazed up at Jonas who had joined her, leaving his customer at the desk looking through a brochure.

'The photographer?'

He nodded. 'Sigfrid Nilson. Aren't they incredible?'

'They are. She has such an eye for detail.'

'She's very talented.'

Frankie was surprised by the pang that pierced her at Jonas's praise of his friend. For one thing, it was irrational on so many levels to feel, what was it... jealous, and it was so unlike her to experience that emotion. She'd never been jealous when Rolo had praised other women; she hadn't even been jealous when Jen had told her that Rolo had gone on their honeymoon with another woman. Well... perhaps a tiny bit peeved that he had moved on with his life so quickly, after Frankie had given him years of hers, but not jealous.

But now it was as if she were waking up from a long sleep in which her emotions had been dulled or not properly formed. She didn't even mind experiencing a flash of the green-eyed monster in this instance, even though it was irrational, because she was just glad to be experiencing more intense emotions. It proved that she could care about other things, that she did have a range of emotions available.

'I'll have to introduce you to her when she's back in town.'

'I'd like that.' *I think…*

'Frankie!' Freya breezed through the gallery, her black waterfall cardigan billowing around her slim frame. She kissed Frankie's cheeks, leaving a wave of floral perfume in her wake. 'Apologies for the delay. Have you been waiting long?'

'No, I've only just arrived.'

'Excuse me,' Jonas said to them both, 'I'd better get back to Mr Hanslow. He's trying to decide upon a suitable gift for his wife for their thirtieth wedding anniversary.'

'Thirty years?' Frankie gasped. 'Wow!'

'Exactly what I said.' Jonas nodded. 'See you later.'

He returned to the client and lowered his large frame into the desk chair. Frankie watched him for a moment, admiring how his black shirt showed off his broad shoulders and strong arms. She could just imagine him working out. But then, he was probably one of those naturally muscular men, who stayed in shape doing traditional manly things like chopping wood and pulling a sled.

Chopping wood? Pulling a sled? Jeez…

She realized that Freya was watching her watching Jonas and heat rushed into her cheeks.

'He's very handsome, isn't he?' Freya smiled knowingly.

'Uh… yes. Yes, he is.'

'And a good man.'

'Yes.'

Frankie willed the heat to leave her cheeks. This situation could have been so different if Freya had been there to raise her. Would they have discussed things like boyfriends and crushes? Would Freya have advised Frankie about all the things mothers traditionally did? Frankie had relied upon Jen and the girls at boarding school, magazines and blogs for advice about things like romance, periods and growing up. It was at times like that that she'd missed having a mother more than ever. She'd longed for a mum to hug her and make her dinner, then cuddle her on the sofa as they'd watched a movie together. There'd been none of that with Grandma; it just wasn't her style. And as for celebrations such as Mother's Day, birthdays and Christmas... Frankie had endured them rather than enjoyed them, wondering all the time what life might have been like had her mother stayed and what type of mother Freya would have been. For Frankie, this knowledge sat between them like an eight-foot wall, a lifetime of hurt and loss, of wasted love and simmering resentment. Could they ever make up for that? Frankie sincerely doubted it and the knowledge made her feel as awkward as a teenager standing in front of school assembly.

'Shall we go shopping then?' Freya asked, saying words Frankie had dreamt of hearing for almost thirty years.

She shook herself, trying to clear her head of the obstacles that could prevent this relationship from getting off the starting blocks. If she didn't even try, then what was the point of being here?

'Yes, I'd like that.'

'Me too.'

Freya was efficient and experienced, guiding Frankie around the appropriate shops and telling her exactly what she'd need for the trip, and Frankie was really grateful because she wouldn't have thought of half the things she'd need. In the past, on skiing trips and cruises, personal shoppers had whizzed around stores such as Harrods and Selfridges, then arrived in the private VIP rooms and placed whatever Frankie would need right in front of her. It had been effortless, too easy in fact, and although the items provided had been lovely – and always expensive – Frankie had missed being able to select things for herself. She loved browsing the rails of the department stores, running her hands over the different materials of dresses, trousers, jackets and lingerie. It was a pleasure to combine colours and textures, to create whole outfits that would mix and match. But her shopping trips had to be done without Grandma's knowledge, because Grandma was of the opinion that ladies of their class didn't need to trail around shops; that was what the personal shopper service was for. Grandma would have been even more horrified if she'd found out about Frankie's penchant for vintage clothing. She loved having the chance to scour the charity shops and small emporiums that smelt of leather, mixed washing powders, fabric softeners and mothballs. Finding a vintage garment was a secret thrill that would never die for her, and she loved the fact that those clothes had a history; they weren't brand new and soulless. Someone, somewhere, had also worn the clothes – possibly twenty, thirty or fifty years ago – and it made Frankie feel connected to the past. Of course, she suspected it could have something to do with her need to feel that she belonged somewhere, to connect with her mother in some way, even if it was just by wearing something that had been fashionable when she had been younger. Frankie always hid the vintage clothes from her grandmother or claimed that they were new but retro, as Grandma would never have empathized with wearing a second-hand garment.

Within two hours, Frankie had wool underwear, hiking boots with thick insoles, a pair of arctic boots, thick woollen socks, two hats, two pairs of gloves, a scarf, a wind- and waterproof coat – that was even warmer than the one she'd bought already – and down-padded overalls. According to Freya, layering was key. The clothes weren't exactly glamorous but they were practical. Frankie wondered if anyone had ever thought to make an outdoorsy range that was more aesthetically pleasing. She knew that some of the surf and skateboard style brands did some ski wear but surely there was a whole market available here for the right range?

Before they'd gone to the counter to pay in the first shop, Freya had asked Frankie if she was all right for money, and Frankie had replied that money wasn't an issue. If Freya wondered why Frankie was able to spend money without worrying, then she didn't show it. Frankie did earn money from her job and didn't just spend her father's and Grandma's.

'Shall we go for coffee?' Freya asked.

'That's a great idea.'

They found a coffee shop, went in and found a table.

'I'll just pop to the loo.'

Freya got up and Frankie was left alone. She pushed her bags under the table to make sure that no one passing would trip over them then took her mobile out of her bag and swiped the screen. Every time she did that at the moment, she held her breath, wondering if there would be an unpleasant text message or missed call from home. Thankfully, it was clear, but she had alerts from Facebook on the app, so she opened it and scrolled down.

And there it was; even more evidence that Rolo had moved on very quickly indeed. Photo after photo of him and Lorna, tanned and grinning, in the villa, on sun loungers, in the sea and even in the king-size bed with the white-muslin canopy as he fed Lorna chunks of pineapple. A twinge of something flickered through her and she paused, trying to work out what it was, but she couldn't pinpoint if it was jealousy, anger or relief. It was likely a combination of the three.

Rolo and Lorna looked so… right together. As if they fitted.

Frankie exited the app then opened her photographs and scanned them until she found one of her and Rolo. It had been taken in the spring. Months ago! She couldn't recall having a more recent one done and Rolo's mother had taken this. They sat together at a table in a restaurant and Rolo had thrown his arm around her shoulder. They smiled at the camera but something about her expression suggested that her smile was forced. She thought of the easy smile on Rolo's face when he was with Lorna, then examined his smile on the photo with her. It was clearly different. Rolo didn't look relaxed or happy and neither did Frankie.

Had their relationship been such a strained charade then? Were they trying to find something that wasn't there, as if a personal shopper had paired them up like a jacket and trousers, because they were a good match, making them push their personal preferences aside?

How sad it would have been for them both if they'd got married. They could have spent years together living a half life, never knowing fulfilment.

'Looking at anything nice?' Freya asked when she returned to the table.

'Oh… no, not really.'

'No? I'm not prying but it looked like a photograph of you and a man. Do you have a boyfriend then?'

Frankie turned her phone to show Freya.

'He's handsome.'

'I guess so.'

'Boyfriend?'

'Fiancé. *Was* my fiancé, I mean.'

Freya was frowning. 'You were getting married?'

'Yes. Last Saturday.'

'What happened?'

'I couldn't go through with it.'

'I'm sorry. That must have been a hard decision to make.'

'It was. But it was the right one.'

'How did your… family react?'

'Well, my father told me to do what was right for me but my grandmother…'

'Was furious?'

Frankie nodded. 'I saw her as I was heading down the driveway, basically running away from my fiancé's family home, and she said a few unpleasant things. Then I spoke to her last night and she gave me a more severe dressing-down.'

Freya reached across the table and patted Frankie's hand. 'I'm sorry. Sometimes, people can be difficult.'

Frankie gazed into Freya's eyes. There was under-standing there and it comforted her. Freya knew Grandma and would have an idea of how formidable she could be, although in this case she didn't know that Frankie was talking about Helen Ashford. Of course she didn't, because as far as Frankie could tell she had no idea who Frankie was. And that was the way it was going to stay. For now. Until Frankie felt certain that she could tell her who she was. Until she felt that she could trust her.

'Shall we order some lunch as well?' Freya asked.

'Yes, please.'

And in spite of the fact that a secret sat between them, a secret that could send Freya running for the hills, Frankie felt a bit closer to her. Even if their relationship would never be what she had longed for, at least she had this moment, a moment when she sensed an understanding between them. It was a step in the right direction.

Chapter 16

Friday morning, Frankie was packed and ready to go. She'd managed to get all of her new clothing into the rucksack Freya had suggested she purchase after they'd had lunch, and although it was heavy, she could manage it more easily than her Versace suitcase. The latter wouldn't have been at all practical for an expedition.

She walked through the hotel lobby, then through the automatic doors. Outside, the morning air was chilly so she pulled the feather-filled jacket closed over her chest and stuffed her hands into the deep pockets. Jonas had told her that he'd collect her in his car then they'd head to the airport.

The thought of seeing him again was exciting, even at six in the morning. He'd sent her a text yesterday, telling her to rest as much as possible, because the next three days would be busy. She'd tried to take his advice, flicking through her ereader and trying to lose herself in a fictional world, but her mind was too restless to focus for long. So she'd tried to watch a movie but that hadn't worked either. She just hoped that getting away from everything as she headed to the largest city of northern Norway would be what she needed to clear her head.

A dark grey Volvo pulled up in front of the hotel then Jonas got out, so she hurried towards the vehicle. He took her rucksack and hefted it into the boot.

'Morning, Frankie. You OK?' he said once they were sitting in the front seats.

'Yes, thank you. Are you?'

'All good, yes. Looking forward to the tour?'

'Very much.'

He started the engine then drove them through the quiet streets.

'We just need to stop and collect Freya.'

'She mentioned she was hoping to come along but she wasn't sure. I take it she was able to get her friend who occasionally works at the gallery to step in for a few days?'

Jonas nodded but kept his eyes on the road.

So her mother was definitely coming on the trip too, which meant she'd get to spend more time with her and with Jonas. It just got better and better.

They picked Freya up from the gallery then Jonas drove them to the airport.

'Who's looking after Luna this weekend?' Frankie asked.

'My mother. She loves Luna and the feeling's mutual.' He laughed.

'I'd have loved a dog growing up.' The words slipped out before Frankie had really thought about them.

'Would you?' Freya asked from behind her; she'd insisted on taking the back seat.

'I was away a lot though, so it wouldn't have been fair, I guess.'

'Away?'

'At boarding school.'

'Boarding school?' Freya's voice had hardened.

'Yes. I went from the age of six to eighteen.'

'Your father… sent you away?'

Frankie turned so she could see Freya. 'It wasn't just my father. It was more my grandmother. She said it was character building... and for the best.'

'Oh, Frankie. Didn't you get homesick?'

'Sometimes, but to be honest, because my mother wasn't around, it was kind of easier to be away. Then I could pretend that she was at home waiting for me to return.'

Freya broke eye contact and stared out of the window, so Frankie turned back around.

'That's... very sad.' Freya's voice was almost a whisper now. 'I'm sorry for what you went through.'

Frankie nodded but didn't trust herself to speak. Freya might be sorry now but where was she when Frankie had needed her? She hadn't cared then if Frankie was sent away to school or if she'd been missing the presence of her mother in her life. And why had the comment affected Freya so much that she'd had to look away?

She knows who I am...

Of course she did.

Frankie spent the rest of the car journey fiddling with her nails, picking at what remained of her bridal manicure, fighting the urge to tell Jonas to stop the car so she could confront Freya for what she'd done. Now wasn't the time; she needed to wait until the moment was right.

At the airport, Jonas took care of everything and soon they were seated on the flight. They had two seats together and one three rows behind, so Frankie insisted that Jonas and Freya sit together, telling them that she'd snooze for the short flight anyway.

She had closed her eyes but hadn't been able to sleep. Instead, she'd played Freya's words over and over in her mind, wondering if her mother had any idea at all of what she'd done by leaving. And now she would have the chance to find out, because once they were out there in the wilderness of Norway, Freya wouldn't be able to run away.

But the same went for Frankie too, because she wouldn't be able to run away if she didn't like the answers. It was time for both of them to face the truth.

However painful it might be.

–

Freya was quiet for the duration of the flight and Jonas knew why. He'd been glad that Frankie had suggested that she take the other seat, as he wanted to keep an eye on Freya and wondered if she might need to talk. Finding out that Frankie had been sent to boarding school as a child must have been difficult for her. And it was something unimaginable for him because his own mother would've fought tooth and nail to keep him home with her. His upbringing had been so warm and loving, he just couldn't fathom how it would feel to be sent away to school.

The fine lines around Freya's eyes seemed deeper and she was staring out of the window as if searching for the answers to the questions that haunted her.

Jonas wanted to hug her and make her smile, to see the pain leave her face and find the Freya he'd known for so long. Yet he also knew that Freya had never been free of pain and that, in fact, she had suffered every day since arriving in Norway. Things had a way of coming full circle and it seemed that Freya's past had caught up with her now, so it would be better for her to deal with the situation. Nothing could be avoided for ever but he hoped the outcome would be one that would make her happy. Her heartache was etched on her lovely face and deep in her eyes, and it hurt him to see it.

As for Frankie, he felt for her too. Being sent off to school as a little girl, never knowing a mother's love, that must have been very hard. Freya had reasons for walking away from her life in England and she had told him all of them just a few days ago but Frankie didn't know those reasons and she needed to hear them. There could be no proper healing for either woman until they'd spoken honestly about their pasts and their pain – it was always better to get things out in the open – and Jonas hoped that this weekend would be a good opportunity for them to do so.

In comparison, his life had been relatively uncomplicated. His father had died when he was a toddler, so he'd missed having him around but known that his mother and both sets of grandparents loved him. They'd all gathered around to ensure that Jonas enjoyed a good childhood and he'd grown into a contented and secure young man. They hadn't had a lot of money but Jonas knew that money wasn't the answer to everything. After all, Frankie's father must have money if he'd sent her to what sounded like a prestigious boarding school, but look how Frankie felt about that. Jonas would be fine as long as he could pay his bills and help his mother out whenever she needed a bit extra. He'd never felt the urge to settle down or thought about having children, it had just never been on his agenda, so he couldn't see a time when he'd need to earn more money to buy a house or support a family. If it ever arose, then of course he would make some changes; he would always look out for his loved ones. He just couldn't foresee a wife and family in his future.

As the plane descended, though, he couldn't help wondering what Frankie wanted from life. Did she have dreams of creating a family of her own, or had her experience with her mother leaving left her scarred?

He hoped that the weekend would give him the chance to find out more about her, as well as to ease some of the sadness that hung around her and Freya. That was his priority; helping the women to heal and hopefully to get to know each other. As for him and what he wanted, he had yet to find out what that might be.

Chapter 17

In Tromsø, they were collected from the airport and taken to a central hotel by minibus, where they were able to freshen up and prepare for the next leg of their journey. Frankie admired how friendly Jonas was with the tour operators and Freya told her that he worked with them regularly as he also ran tours for individuals or small parties to see the northern lights. However, in this instance, he'd decided to leave the running of the tour to someone else so he could focus on taking some photographs himself.

In the late afternoon, when darkness had already fallen, a bus arrived to take them into the countryside an hour away from Tromsø. Again, Frankie insisted that Freya sit with Jonas, telling them that she'd appreciate the extra legroom. The journey took them through the countryside, away from the busy city and out to where snow had fallen and where the temperature dropped considerably.

On arrival, they were divided into smaller groups and taken to their own areas with a traditional *lavvu* tent, then shown where they could change into their warmer clothes. Frankie did so quickly, keen to make the most of the evening that lay ahead.

They didn't have much time for conversation, as the guide talked to them about the lights and what caused them, as well as about the three hundred huskies at the camp and how everything they would eat and drink came from sustainable resources. They were told that with November often being quite a wet month, the cloud cover might prevent them seeing the lights, but they might also be lucky. There had been more snow this year as the temperatures had been lower than average, so there was a chance that the sky might clear enough for them to witness the light display.

As the darkness seemed to thicken, and fully enveloped the camp isolating it from its surroundings, they went outside and sat around the campfire where they ate a traditional meal of *bacalao*, consisting of cod and tomato. Frankie enjoyed the simplicity of it, while the guide told them stories about the lights and the area. Toasted marshmallows and coffee followed, then they were told that they could go back to the *lavvu* and keep warm while they waited to see if the lights appeared, or lie outside on the reindeer skins and gaze up at the sky.

'If you two are all right, I'm going to go and scout for some good shots. It'll be better if I'm away from the lights of the camp,' Jonas said to Frankie and Freya.

Frankie tried to keep her disappointment from her face.

'Of course. I'll keep Frankie company and perhaps we can get some more marshmallows.' Freya smiled from under the faux-fur trim of her hood.

'Good luck!' Frankie said as Jonas headed away from them with his camera bag slung over his shoulder.

'Let's grab a reindeer skin and sit near the fire.' Freya trudged through the snow and Frankie followed her.

When they were sitting down again, Freya shuffled around to face her.

'Tell me about your childhood.'

'What do you want to know?'

'I can't understand how it must feel to be sent away to school. And you said that your mother... left. Tell me about that.'

'Really?'

Freya nodded, her green eyes holding Frankie's.

'OK then.'

'But don't hold back.'

'What do you mean?'

'Tell me everything. What was said about your mother and how did you feel? What's the version of events that you know?'

'The version?'

'Yes.'

'Why are you interested?' Frankie knew but she wanted to hear Freya say the words.

'I think you know. I think we both know why. But before we discuss that, I want to hear how things were for you.'

Frankie took a deep breath. She hadn't expected the opportunity to speak to Freya about her childhood to come so soon, or so easily, and now it was here, she actually felt tongue-tied and a bit like jumping up and running off into the woods.

But she wouldn't. She'd waited almost thirty years for this, so it was time to do it.

—

'I did have a good childhood.' Frankie glanced at Freya then dropped her gaze to her gloved hands again where they rested in her lap. 'I had everything money could buy, from music and ballet lessons to clothes... I wanted for nothing material, really.'

She paused, wondering how Freya would take what she was about to tell her.

'Go on.' Freya gently encouraged her.

'But the thing I wanted most was missing.'

'And what was that?'

'A mother's love.'

'Oh, Frankie.' Freya reached out and squeezed Frankie's hand through her glove but it unsteadied Frankie and made her feel awkward, so she gently pulled her hand away.

'Sorry… it's just that I might… unravel if you're too kind at the moment, so…'

'I understand.'

'All through my childhood, I wondered where my mother was. I asked my father and my grandmother and they both gave me versions of the truth. My dad was always kind about her… you, but Grandma, not so much.'

'Your father didn't say anything bad about your mother?'

Frankie shook her head. 'He said she'd, or rather you'd had your reasons for leaving and that he truly believed you'd have stayed had certain… things been different. Really, he seemed to blame himself, as if he felt he hadn't been enough for you or supported you enough so you'd want to stay.'

'The poor man.'

Frankie took a deep breath, pulling the clear country air into her lungs and savouring how cold and refreshing it was. Clarifying. Like a fresh start would feel.

'He's a good man and his heart's in the right place but Grandma has always had some sort of hold over him. It's like she's in control.'

'She's a strong woman.'

Frankie nodded.

'It's not that Dad is weak.' Frankie felt the need to defend him, from Freya but also from herself and the situation. 'It's just that he needed Grandma.'

'To help bring you up?'

'Yes. I think that's it. You know… he never married again or fell in love. Grandma tried to encourage him to go out with other women but his heart never seemed to be in it. He was happier playing hide and seek with me, studying his dusty old books in our library, or out on the golf course. It wasn't that he didn't have plenty of admirers either, you know, with him being – as Grandma called him – "a good catch" but he wasn't interested.'

'When you've been in love and been hurt, it's hard to move on. You carry fear in your heart that can last a lifetime.'

'And he worried that a stepmother might not be good to me.'

'That's understandable. Tell me about you, now. How was life for you?'

'I wanted a mum and I didn't have one. I had cards for birthdays and other occasions, but when I was younger, before I turned sixteen and complained about having my post tampered with, most of them had been opened before they got to me. I wasn't sure if it was Dad or Grandma but I suspect it was Grandma.'

'So you know that I tried to stay in touch?'

'Tried? I guess so, but you never rang or came to see me.' The old pain bubbled inside Frankie and battled to become anger. Being angry was easier than being sad, but she also found that she didn't want to hurt this woman sitting opposite her. After all that Frankie had been told and all that she'd felt about Freya, it was hard to see the woman now listening as the same person who'd hurt her. But she was.

'Why do you think that was?'

Frankie shrugged as the familiar embarrassment and shame made her cheeks flush. 'You didn't love me enough.'

'No, sweetheart...' Frankie looked at Freya. Her eyes were glistening and she'd wrapped her arms around herself, as if she was trying to hold herself together. 'That's not right.'

'Finally, when I turned eighteen you sent that card with your address, telling me that seeing as how I was an adult, I was free to contact you if I wished. However, if I chose not to, then you'd understand and wouldn't bother me any more. That card...' She shook her head. 'It caused some sleepless nights.'

'I felt that it was time for you to make the decision about whether you wanted anything to do with me. But you chose not to?'

Frankie nodded. 'It was one of the hardest things I've ever had to do. But I wanted to put it all behind me, to move on and embrace life. I felt that my pain had held me back for long enough and that as an adult, I could deal with it and leave it in my past with my childish longings to be loved by the woman who gave birth to me.'

'You didn't think of contacting me at all?'

'Sometimes I did but then a week would pass and another one and the more time that passed, the easier it seemed to let it go. Then Rolo proposed and we had the wedding to organize – or rather Grandma did – and I was busy with work and time became a blur.'

'Rolo?'

'Yes, he's the grandson of an old friend of Grandma, Pip Bellamy.' Frankie turned to face Freya and watched her carefully. 'Do you know him?'

Freya's eyes widened. 'Yes. Not very well but I met him once or twice. He and your grandmother used to be quite... close when they were younger.'

'They did?'

'They were once in love.'

'I didn't know that.'

'It's not something Helen would have wanted you to know. I only found out when a mutual acquaintance let slip after too many G&Ts.'

'Did Dad know?'

'I did ask him about it but he laughed it off, said it was a rumour.'

'It's not something I can imagine either... Grandma being in love.'

They smiled then, a moment of relief in a heartrending conversation that felt surreal. A tear suddenly trickled down Freya's cheek and plopped onto her jacket.

'I am so sorry, Frankie. I can never describe to you how hard it was to leave you or how much I have missed you.'

Frankie's throat constricted and she bit down on her lip hard. She didn't want to cry, to lose control. Words were easy to say but deeds said so much more. Freya might say that she was sorry now and she might well even be sorry, but that didn't change what had happened.

'Do you think... that you might be able to forgive me? If I explain everything to you properly?'

'I don't know. It's been the best part of thirty years. How can we ever put that behind us?'

'I don't know that we can, but I see you, Frankie. I see my daughter and the reflection of your father and me in your face, your skin, your eyes, your hair. You are a combination of us both, sweetheart, and that's something that will never change.'

'So do you want to tell me why you left? Why I find myself here in Oslo after twenty-nine years asking for an explanation?'

'I do and you're right. It's high time.'

Chapter 18

Jonas had left Freya and Frankie alone deliberately, to give them a chance to talk. He could get the photographs he needed around the camp or further out but making himself scarce had been part of his plan as soon as he'd known Freya was definitely coming on the trip.

So far, the skies had been cloudy and he wasn't sure if they'd have any luck with the lights, but as long as the women had the opportunity to speak candidly, then he didn't even mind. Although, he would like Frankie to have the chance to see the lights first-hand. It was such an amazing experience and it would be something she could take with her when she returned to England. No doubt she had a whole life back there waiting for her, but he hoped she'd stay in touch with Freya.

Not that he expected her to stay in touch with him, even though she'd given him her number for the delivery of the photograph. But she might want to maintain contact, just in case she wanted more of his work in the future. It wasn't entirely impossible.

He trudged back towards the camp, keen to check that Freya and Frankie were OK, when he spotted them sitting away from everyone else on one of the reindeer skins by the fire. They were both gazing into the flames, their faces so similar with their serious expressions and yet so different. There were years between them, and not just in terms of age. Freya had been away from her daughter for a lifetime and it had affected them both.

Jonas hoped that they could find something here this evening, something to carry them through the years ahead. If it wasn't a full-on mother–daughter relationship, then he hoped it could at least be a friendship of sorts. That would surely be better than nothing at all, better than the emptiness that haunted them both.

He stepped backwards and crept away, not wanting to intrude until they'd cleared the air between them. He just hoped the sky would clear too.

-

'Frankie, I just want to make it clear to you that I would never want to influence how you see your father or grand-mother. That has never been my intention and was one of the reasons I waited until you were an adult to give you a way to contact me.'

'I could have tried to find you sooner. In fact, I did Google you a few times when I was younger and I imagined employing one of Grandma's private investig-ators, but I knew that Grandma would be furious and so I never pushed things. But… I was also terrified that if I did, you would turn me away.'

Freya shook her head. 'I would never have turned you away. I dreamt of opening my door to find you standing there, but I also knew what it would cost you with Helen and I never wanted you to go through that. I know how persuasive… or rather manipulative, your grandmother can be.'

'She told me you never loved me.'

'I thought she might have. However, that's not true and never was. I loved you deeply from the moment I knew you were growing inside me but I was also scared.'

'Because of Grandma?'

'Because of lots of things.'

Around them, people stamped their feet and chatted as the guides told them stories in soft voices, gently lilted with the Norwegian accents that were becoming so familiar to Frankie now. Just like Jonas's lovely voice.

'But yes, your grandmother did intimidate me. She never thought I was good enough for your father or to marry into her family.'

'Grandma rarely thinks people are good enough.'

Freya gave a wry laugh. 'Some things don't change. It doesn't excuse me leaving you but there was more to it than that. You see, after I had you, the pressure of trying to be good enough to fit into the Ashford family, combined with a lack of sleep and a particularly traumatic birth, all made me quite unwell.'

'You suffered from post-natal depression?'

Freya nodded. 'It was awful. I couldn't wait to hold you in my arms and when I finally did, after a forty-eight-hour labour, it wasn't at all how I expected it to be.'

'Why not?'

'You were so perfect, so tiny and beautiful and I just looked down at you and felt... inadequate.'

Frankie watched her mother as the light from the fire played across her features, highlighting the pain of the memories she was sharing.

'I know that post-natal depression can be dreadful. A woman I know had it and she walked off and left her baby in Harrods one day. Her family helped her to access some treatment though and she's now a mother of three. But she told me once, at a dinner party, that it was horrendous. She said she felt detached from everything around her.'

'Exactly how I felt. As if I was looking at things from far away, like through a telescope. One day, you were in your cot gurgling and I sat on the rocker next to you. I looked down at my hands and it was as if they didn't belong to me. I felt so distant, as if my head was full of cotton wool. It scared me, because I thought, what if I picked you up and dropped you? Or what if I left you somewhere unattended, like in the bath or somewhere you could hurt yourself by rolling once you got a bit bigger?'

'Did you have any help?'

'It wasn't so widely recognized back then. Or so openly discussed. Now, you can have a thread on Twitter and share your feelings without stigma but back then, it was something to be ashamed of. Especially in Helen's eyes.'

'Grandma made you feel ashamed?'

'As I said, I don't want to influence you negatively about your grandmother.'

'You said you'd be honest so you need to tell me the truth.'

Freya nodded but she was worrying her bottom lip in a way that suggested this was extremely difficult.

'One day, Frankie, when you were a few weeks old, I made a big mistake and there was no turning back.'

'What happened?'

'I was getting weaker and weaker. My breasts hurt, my nipples were so sore from trying to feed you that they chafed against my clothing, and there was a fog around me that I couldn't shake. I just wanted someone to come along and rescue me but, of course, no one did. Your father was back at work and I'm pretty sure that Helen was keeping him busy with extra tasks in order to keep him away from home as much as possible. I overheard her telling him that I needed to learn how to take care of my baby and that he should stay out from under my feet. It was, she said, how things were done and mothering was a woman's job, not a man's. I was exhausted. I hadn't slept because you had cried all the night before. You finally settled about eight o'clock in the morning. The house was quiet, your father at work, and, as far as I knew, Helen was somewhere nearby. I caught sight of myself in a mirror and I looked so awful, like some kind of ghoul. Something inside me snapped. I'd given up my old life as an artist, surrendered my independence and become a shadow of who I used to be. I didn't blame your father or you, of course I didn't, but I did blame Helen. She was like a vampire, bleeding me dry and making me jump whenever I encountered her. I went downstairs, got the car keys off the hook and went outside. I got into my little Mini and started the engine. It was like I was on autopilot as I drove away.'

Frankie's mouth had fallen open. She hadn't known about this and hearing it was painful. Her mother must have been in a terrible state to walk out of the house and leave her baby.

'I stopped the car at the end of the road and just broke down. I cried and cried and cried. It was as if being free of that house allowed me to let go. I was only gone about five minutes and when I headed back, it was as if I'd unburdened by releasing some of the built-up strain. But when I entered the house, Helen was waiting for me.'

Freya's tears flowed down her cheeks now, unfettered. She made no attempt to wipe them away, so Frankie pulled a tissue from her pocket and dabbed at her mother's cheeks gently.

'She was standing in the hallway, her face like thunder when I walked back inside.'

'I can just imagine. I've faced that look myself.'

Freya nodded. 'She's a scary woman when she wants to be. I tried to get past her but she blocked my way and told me to go into the drawing room. I said I needed to get to my baby but she told me the housekeeper was seeing to you. I did as she ordered and sat on the sofa. It was one of those bloody uncomfortable things that you couldn't settle on because it was designed to keep people upright and respectable, and I resented it in that moment, just as I resented her. Then Helen told me exactly what she thought of me and how it was going to be.'

'She does have a harsh tongue.'

'Helen said that after what I'd just done, she could have me arrested for child abandonment. I was crying, devastated at the fact that I'd left you and I felt like the worst mother in the world. She said that at best, social services would be involved and they'd question me and assess my mental health and fitness for parenthood. She had enough to get me sectioned anyway, she said, for at least two days and longer if she used her contacts.'

'She said what? I can't believe how horrid that is and when you were so vulnerable.'

Frankie's anger towards Freya, an anger that had had no flesh and blood target to aim at for so long, now wavered. The anger had been because of what Freya had done, because of the pain she had left behind her, but Grandma had fuelled it. Now it turned out that Grandma was responsible for making Freya's illness worse. Freya had needed kindness and understanding, compassion and support. At her lowest ebb, she had been subjected to threats and recrimination. How many people would be able to withstand that?

'I'm so sorry, Frankie, but I was broken. I believed her. She did have a lot of contacts and could easily have me put away. She told me to pack my bags and go. I was allowed to leave a note for Hugo but I wasn't to say much in it, just that I felt compelled to leave and that it was for the best. I tried to argue with her but the threat of being put away, and what that would mean for me and for you, was enough to force my hand. I was weakened, distressed and... I believed her.'

'So you left?'

'I did. And it has been the big regret of my life.'

They sat in silence for a while as Frankie digested everything. She'd known Grandma could be harsh, cold and even cruel but this was beyond that. Helen Ashford had robbed her daughter-in-law of her right to be a mother and her right to proper support and care, and she had also robbed her granddaughter of a mother's love. If Freya had been given love, patience and medical support, she could have got through her depression and perhaps they would have been a proper family. No wonder her father had grieved so badly if his wife had left with barely an explanation, and then he'd had his mother harping on about what a bad person his wife had been. Helen was responsible for a lot of pain and sadness. Helen was the true villain in all of this.

'I'm so mad at her.' Frankie finally spoke. 'How could she do that to you... to us all?'

'In some warped way, I'm sure she believed she was doing it for the best. I knew she never liked me but I tried so hard to get on with her. However, when you came along, it strengthened her resolve to get rid of me. I think she wanted you and Hugo for herself, to be the main woman in your lives, and I was weak, Frankie, because I let her push me out. I'm so sorry for that.'

'I understand why you felt forced to go, I really do, and I don't think it was weakness on your part. You were ill and needed help not cruelty. But I have one more question.'

'Ask away.'

'Why did you never try to get in touch once you felt better? You could have come back for me.'

Freya pushed her hat back on her head and rubbed her eyes with the heels of her gloved hands.

'I have asked myself that a million times and there is no good answer. I felt so worthless after I left that it took me a long time to even get out of bed. I had some savings and I lived off those then I bought a plane ticket to Norway. I'd always yearned to visit the country and to see the northern lights and in some strange way, I hoped that they would fix me. And they did… over time. I began to paint again and built up a client list then managed to save enough to open a small gallery. I was busy but not a day went by when I didn't think of you and wonder how you were getting on. I had counselling and that helped me enough to contact your father and ask about you.'

'You contacted him?'

Freya nodded.

'What did he say?'

'Not much. He was too ground down himself by that time.'

'When was this?'

'You'd have been about three.'

'It took three years?'

'The darkness took a long time to lift… even longer because I was grieving so badly. I was up and down; my moods were so unpredictable.'

'Dad never said.'

'Your grandmother had convinced him that I would crumble again if I came back and he said it was too great a risk to take. He couldn't let me hurt you again. He said…' She gasped as a sob escaped her throat. 'That… you asked for Mumma every night at bedtime.'

Pain surged through Frankie and she ground her teeth together.

'I begged him to let me see you but he told me that it wasn't wise and that Helen would have her lawyers on the case before I even knocked on the door. He said I should let it be, wait a while longer. So I did.'

'Dad was to blame too.'

'We were angry with each other too and that didn't help. I was angry that he hadn't fought for me and he was angry that I'd walked away. But please, Frankie, don't blame your father. Helen threatened him that if he allowed me back into your life, then social services might take me away from him too and that would have been too much for him to bear. In fact, I don't want you to blame your grandmother either. Formidable as she is, she did what she thought was right. It's too late for blame and recriminations now, Frankie. We have to let go of the anger and the sadness or it will destroy us all.'

'How can you be so forgiving?'

'I've had a long time to think. All I ask, Frankie, is that you consider letting me into your life. I know you'll never see me as a mother but I would love to be here for you, to see you now and then, and to—'

'Oh my God!' Frankie pointed at the sky. 'Wow! I just saw something when the clouds parted.'

They scrambled to their feet and gazed at the sky, searching for a gap in the clouds so they could see the northern lights.

Freya reached out and took Frankie's hand then squeezed it tight.

'I love you, Frankie. I always have.'

Frankie couldn't reply. Her heart was aching and emotion welled in her throat, cutting off her ability to speak. But as she gazed at the dark grey clouds, hoping to see the ethereal light show she'd come here for, she mouthed the words...

I think I love you too.

Chapter 19

Jonas made his way back into the camp. He'd seen Freya take her daughter's hand and even though they were searching the sky for a sign of the lights, his gaze had been glued to the two women. Years had passed since Freya had fled her life in England and there had been miles between her and her daughter, yet here, under a Norwegian sky, those years and miles fell away and what remained was beautiful.

It was love. A mother's love for her daughter and a daughter's love for her mother.

He knew it was too soon to hope that this would be the start of an easy relationship for them, because all relationships took time and effort, but he hoped it was the start of them communicating and spending time together. Time was so precious that it had to be treasured.

One of the guides broke into his thoughts with a cheer and the chorus of *oohs* and *aahs* that followed from the fireside made him smile. It seemed that the husky pups had arrived.

He approached Freya and Frankie. 'Did you see?' he asked, referring to the short glimpse of the lights.

Frankie turned watery eyes his way. 'We did. It was brief but beautiful.'

He nodded. 'Sometimes it just works out that way. Different times of the year are better but at least you had a taste of how amazing they can be.'

'Did you get many photographs?' Freya asked.

'A few.' He'd been too distracted wondering how things were going between Freya and Frankie, so he hadn't been as focused as he usually was. It was funny the way he cared what happened between them. Freya was his friend and had been good to him but he also cared about Frankie. He saw a lot of Freya in her and also something else. She was a good person, he could tell, but she'd been lost. Whether that was entirely down to the fact that her mother had been absent all her life, because of other factors, or a combination of them all, he didn't know for certain, but she had a radiance about her that shimmered like the northern lights. Things couldn't always be explained in detail; they just were as they were.

'Is everything all right, Jonas?' Frankie asked and he realized he'd been staring at her.

'Yes! Absolutely. Look...'

He gestured at the puppies that were rolling around on the ground in front of them.

'Aren't they adorable?' Frankie crouched down and removed her glove then petted two of the pups, running her fingers through their thick fur.

Jonas stepped closer to Freya. 'How are you?' he whispered.

'Good.'

He hugged her with one arm then knelt down next to Frankie.

Soon, the puppies were taken back to their enclosure and the guides brought round sweet rich hot chocolate. Jonas sat in front of the fire in silence, with Freya and

Frankie either side of him, enjoying the hot drink, the warmth from the fire and the cold night air.

It was a perfect moment, and when Frankie shuffled closer and smiled warmly at him, he knew it was one he'd never forget. Something in him was reaching out to something in her and he realized that he really wanted to help.

—

'Frankie?'

'Hmmmm…'

'Wake up.'

She blinked to find Freya gently shaking her.

'We're going back to the hotel now.'

'My hotel?' She realized that she was leaning on something and bolted upright when she saw that it was Jonas. 'Oh! I'm sorry I must have drifted off…'

He smiled. 'Apparently my shoulder made quite a good pillow.'

'The hot chocolate, the puppies and the fire all made me sleepy.' *As well as the emotional roller coaster.* She was glad of the darkness to hide her blushes.

'It's fine.'

'The bus is ready.' Freya smiled at them both before standing up.

Frankie cast a glance around the place where she'd spent the evening, the place where she'd found out the truth about why her mother had left, and she knew that whenever she thought about Norway in the future, it would have a very special place in her heart. It was the first step in what might well be a long journey for them, but it was one that they now had the chance to walk together.

They made their way through the snow to the bus then took their seats, and as they travelled through the darkness, Frankie played Freya's words in her head, allowing herself to fully absorb what she'd learnt.

When they arrived back in Tromsø, Frankie couldn't wait to get to bed. She ached with exhaustion and the idea of closing her eyes and drifting off was incredibly appealing. She said goodnight to Freya and Jonas then they went to their rooms, agreeing to meet at seven for breakfast.

She was too tired to even shower, so she stripped to her thermal layer, pushed back the duvet, snuggled into the clean sheets, and allowed sleep to claim her.

–

When she woke, it was still dark, so she checked her mobile. It was six-thirty, so she had time to shower before breakfast if she got up now. The hotel room was cold, so she hurried to the bathroom and turned the shower on then waited for the steam to warm the room. She'd slept heavily and didn't recall dreaming, but then she had been drained after an eventful evening. So she'd freshen up, dress warmly then she'd be ready for the day.

But as she stepped into the shower and the hot water caressed her skin, an image flashed through her mind. She had dreamed last night after all! She'd been outside with Jonas, standing on a reindeer skin as snow drifted around them. They'd suddenly been naked, in that strange way that happens in dreams, but she hadn't felt the cold. He had cupped her face gently then kissed her mouth before showering sweet kisses down her neck and over her shoulders, turning her round and lifting her hair to kiss her nape. She hadn't felt vulnerable; she'd felt safe, aroused and alive. Then Jonas had lifted her in his arms and carried her into a *lavvu* tent and the dream had, frustratingly, ended.

What did it mean?

Probably nothing, she tried to convince herself, as she soaped her skin then rinsed, stubbornly refusing to let the thought of what might have happened inside the tent distract her from getting ready.

When she headed down for breakfast, she found Jonas and Freya already seated. She joined them, admiring how comfortable they were with each other and how that made her feel relaxed around them, even though she'd only known them for a short time.

'We were just talking about what to do today,' Freya said.

'How'd you fancy an authentic Norwegian experience?' Jonas asked.

Heat seared in Frankie's cheeks. Thank goodness he didn't know what she'd dreamt about.

'I thought that was what we had last night.' Frankie giggled inwardly at her private joke then accepted a coffee gratefully; she needed the caffeine this morning.

'It was one of the experiences on offer, yes. But I thought today we could see some more of the countryside.'

'Isn't it a bit late notice to book something?' Frankie scanned his face, wondering how his eyes sparkled even at such an early hour. He always seemed so full of life, so eager to leap into the day and to savour everything that it brought his way. He was a force of nature and it made her want to match his energy and enthusiasm. It was as if she was waking up, opening up to all that life had to offer, and it was wonderful.

She glanced at Freya and wondered what she was thinking and feeling this morning. They had a long way to go to make up for the years that had passed but if Freya wanted to make their relationship work as much as Frankie did, then the future looked very bright indeed. Knowing that Freya had left because she was ill and because she'd been pushed to by Grandma had freed something inside Frankie. Her mother had not run away because she didn't love her but because she'd been ill, broken and full of self-doubt. They had lost so much, years they would never get back, memories they would never make, and yet… there was time now to fill with new memories and years ahead that they could enjoy together.

How could she fail to be happy about that?

'It's never too late,' Jonas replied as she met his eyes, and he held her gaze until she felt that heat creeping up her neck and back into her cheeks. How did he do that to her? 'I know people.'

'Of course.' She dropped her eyes to her coffee, but she couldn't suppress the smile that played about her lips or the fluttering in her belly. 'What were you thinking?'

'Dress warmly and I'll surprise you.'

–

'Jonas! You really did surprise me.' Frankie laughed later that morning as she snuggled up in the sleigh with Jonas and Freya. Sitting between them, Jonas tucked the fluffy blankets around them then they set off, following a train of identical sleighs pulled by wild reindeer.

She gazed at the snow-dusted landscape as the sleigh glided through the forest. The trees were dark shapes against the flawless white background and the mountains rose majestically towards the sky where their peaks disappeared into the clouds. The breeze on her cheeks was cold and fresh and it felt so clean compared to the London air she was used to.

'Isn't it just wonderful?' Freya asked as she leaned forwards to see around Jonas.

'It's perfect.' Frankie smiled.

After about forty-five minutes, they arrived at a camp made up of traditional Sami tents.

'Now you can feed the reindeer.' Jonas smiled.

'Feed the reindeer?'

He helped Frankie and Freya out of the sleigh and they walked towards the guide who was dressed in traditional Sami clothing.

'He's wearing a *kofte*,' Jonas explained as they approached him. 'That one is probably made of wool but traditionally they were made from reindeer skin.'

'It's very colourful,' Frankie said as she eyed the bright-blue long-sleeved tunic with its high collar and red, yellow and green embroidery. It was cinched in at the waist with a brown belt adorned with silver buttons.

'He's a married man.' Jonas nodded.

'How'd you know that?'

'The buttons are square. If he was single, they would be round.'

'Ahhh.' Frankie smiled. 'Kind of like a wedding ring.'
'Kind of.'

She shuddered as she realized how close she'd come to wearing Rolo's wedding ring.

'Are you cold?' Jonas stopped walking. 'I could go back and get one of the blankets from the sleigh.'

'No, I'm fine, thanks. I was just remembering something.'

'As long as you're sure.'

The guide led them to a gate and they stepped into a large enclosure where reindeer roamed freely then he demonstrated how to feed the animals. Freya went first, scooping up a bucket of feed and sprinkling it on the ground. The reindeer followed her around, snuffling at the feed.

'Do you want to have a go, Frankie?' Jonas asked. 'Here, Freya, take my camera.' He took it from his bag and handed it to her.

'I don't know. I'm a bit nervous around large animals.' Frankie chewed her lip.

'Like Luna?' His eyes twinkled.

'She's a big dog.'

'She's a big softy. Come on, I'll stay close.'

Jonas handed her a bucket and she dipped it into the feed trough as Freya had done then walked into an open space. Two large reindeer approached her slowly, so she shook the feed onto the ground, but one of them tried to stick its head into the bucket. In order to avoid its antlers, Frankie stepped backwards and lost her balance as she tripped over a rock.

'Frankie!' Jonas was at her side in seconds, helping her up, which wasn't easy with all the layers of clothing she was wearing.

'Thank you.' She leant on him, grateful for his size and strength. Even though she knew the reindeer weren't aggressive, she still felt nervous about their antlers, but with Jonas holding her, she knew she'd be safe.

'Shall we try again?'

'We?'

'I'll keep hold of you.'

'OK.'

They walked to the trough and he filled the bucket then handed it to Frankie. He stood behind her, one arm wrapped around her waist, while she held the bucket out and sprinkled the feed. She left a small amount in the bucket and one of the reindeer came and stuck its nose inside, but she didn't panic this time because Jonas was right there with her.

He made her feel protected and… something else. He didn't try to dominate her as Rolo had done. Rolo's possessiveness and need to control everything had been stifling at times. Jonas was a true free spirit but he was also masculine in a quietly assured way. Frankie felt empowered by his help, not overwhelmed by it, and she also sensed that something else could be happening. The dream she'd had about him last night came rushing back with breathtaking clarity, teasing her with how much she had wanted him in that moment, and she turned in his embrace and gazed up at him.

Had they really…

She giggled and he cocked his head.

'What is it? Has my beard frozen or something?'

'No. It's not that.'

'Then what?'

'Smile you two!' They jumped apart as they realized Freya was not only watching them but taking photographs.

'I'd forgotten I gave her the camera.'

'Did you get me falling over on film?' Frankie shook her head.

Freya smiled broadly, her green eyes wide, as she peered over the camera at them.

'Maybe!' she teased.

And Frankie wondered if her mother had also captured the way she'd looked at Jonas, because she knew she wasn't doing a very good job of hiding how much she liked him.

–

'I was ready for this,' Freya said as they sat in the warm *lavvu* cradling bowls of *bidos*, the hearty Sami soup. It consisted of slow-cooked reindeer meat with onions, potatoes and carrots, garnished with herbs, and the rich flavour reflected the pastures that the reindeer roamed. Flatbread and a cranberry jelly that was both sweet and tart accompanied it. This was followed by a fermented milk and angelica dessert served with sugar, that reminded Frankie a bit of rice pudding, then tea and chocolate biscuits. The meal was hearty and satisfying and seemed suited to their surroundings.

Frankie ate well. She was really hungry after the time outdoors and enjoyed the simple but tasty meal. The Sami guide performed a *joik* that he asked them not to record because he said it was a very personal experience, and then they relaxed in the warmth on the wooden benches provided, as the guide told them stories about his people and the landscape.

All too soon, it was time to return to Tromsø. Frankie was sad to leave the camp behind but it had been a wonderful cultural experience. On the bus back to the city, she sat next to Freya and Jonas sat with one of the tour guides he knew well.

'Thank you, Frankie.'

'Whatever for?'

'Out there... seeing you smile and just being able to spend time with you means the world.'

'I've waited a lifetime for this too.'

Freya took her hand and they sat together, watching as the landscape passed in a dark blur, until the bulky shapes of the buildings of Tromsø became the landscape once more.

Chapter 20

As they disembarked from the bus in front of their hotel, Frankie was aware of a buzzing from deep in her bag, so she rooted around inside until she located her mobile.

She had five missed calls from her father and three from Jen. They'd both left vague voicemails asking her to call home as soon as possible.

Her heart dropped like a stone. Something had to be wrong back in London. She couldn't risk leaving it, so she held up her mobile.

'I've got some missed calls from home so I'd better find out what's wrong.'

'Is it your grandmother again?' Freya asked, her face etched with concern.

'I don't know. They're from Dad's number and my friend Jen's.'

'I suppose you'd better call them,' Freya said. 'But don't let them upset you.'

Frankie nodded but she couldn't make that promise.

'I'll go to my room and ring them.'

'Let us know, won't you?' Freya asked.

'I will.'

She hooked her bag back over her shoulder then went inside, feeling the dark clouds of disappointment and anxiety gathering. Today had been wonderful and she'd felt free, that she had left all of her worries behind her and was building something new here in Norway. But, of course, she couldn't run away from reality and that life she'd lived for twenty-nine years in England. It just wasn't possible. Freya had run away but with good reason, believing that she had no choice, but Frankie had ties there. Ties that she couldn't just sever, because too many people would be hurt, and for all that her father might have flaws, she loved him dearly. She loved her grand-mother too, in spite of all she'd done. She just hoped she'd be able to forgive her.

—

Jonas watched Frankie hurry into the hotel then he turned to Freya.

'You want to go straight to your room or grab a drink?'

'A drink sounds good.'

They went through to the hotel bar and Jonas ordered two glasses of red wine, then they found a table away from everyone else.

'Quite a day, huh?'

Jonas could tell that Freya had something on her mind and it was no wonder after the day they'd just had. A day that had followed an eventful night.

Freya took a sip of her wine then licked her lips.

'I'm scared, Jonas.'

'What of?'

'That I could lose her again.'

'That's understandable.'

'What if… this all comes to nothing? What if I'm a disappointment?' She held up her hands and her bangles jangled.

'You could never be a disappointment, Freya. You're an amazing and inspirational woman.'

'But I don't know what Frankie wants from me. I wasn't there to wipe her nose, to put antiseptic cream on her knees when she grazed them. I wasn't the one who wiped away her tears when she cried over friends and boyfriends and I wasn't there to hold her when she needed me.'

'But you are here for her now.'

'What if it's too late?'

Jonas ran his finger around the base of his wine glass and pondered her words.

'It's not.'

'How do you know?'

'You both want this. You need Frankie and she needs you.'

Freya nodded.

'So go with it. Be her mum now. You can't change the past and Frankie knows why you left. She understands.'

'I hope so, although sometimes when I look back I can barely understand myself. I hate that I left her.'

'I know that but you can't spend your life regretting the past. It would be such a waste. What you need to do now is to grab today and look forward to tomorrow.'

'You're very wise, Jonas.'

He shrugged then smiled. 'I try.'

'I'm also afraid that Helen will get her claws back into Frankie and persuade her to return to London and cut me out of her life.'

'I don't think that's going to happen.'

'You don't know Helen Ashford.'

'No, but I'm starting to know Frankie and she has your spark. She won't be pushed around, I'm sure of it.'

'I wish my spark had flared twenty-nine years ago.'

'No regrets, remember?'

She grimaced. 'Sorry, I'll try harder.'

'Glad to hear it.'

'And what about you and Frankie?'

'Sorry?'

'Well, I've seen the way you look at each other.'

Jonas took a drink of his wine to give himself time to think. He couldn't deny that Frankie was a beautiful young woman, that he liked what he'd seen of her so far, but she was from a very different world and their lives were poles apart. She was also Freya's daughter, another reason why he couldn't view her as anything other than a friend. And she would return to England. There were many reasons why nothing would ever happen between them, even if the thought of kissing her pretty mouth had passed through his head more than once since they'd met.

'I... uh... I don't really know how to answer that, Freya.'

'It's OK. You don't need to. I love you both, you know?'

He raised his glass. 'Skol! To new beginnings.'

'Skol, Jonas!'

—

Frankie dropped her rucksack onto the bed then perched on the end. She held her mobile tight, trying to summon the courage to return her father's call. Or her grand-mother's call, of course, if Helen was using her son's mobile again.

She had two options: have a shower and delay but worry about it, or get it over with then have a cry in the shower if Grandma was being overbearing again.

'Get it over with, Frankie.' She pressed redial.

Fifteen minutes later, she found herself staring into space. It hadn't been a good phone call. But it had been her father. She had to get out of the room or she'd break down completely and that wouldn't achieve anything.

In the hotel lobby, she looked around. She could go out for a walk, but in her current frame of mind and in the thick Norwegian dark, she might get lost, so perhaps she'd go and sit in the bar. At least then she'd be around people and she felt the need for some human company.

The bar was quiet, with just a few couples and one group of women in there, so she went to get a drink, thinking she'd sit quietly in the corner as she digested the news from home.

'Frankie?'

'Oh, hi, Jonas.'

'How did it go?'

'What?'

'The phone call.'

'Not well.'

'Let me get you a drink and you can tell me about it if you like.'

'Are you sure?'

'Of course I am. Your mother is over there.' He pointed at the far side of the bar where Freya was sitting at a table by the window. Outside, the streetlight glowed and flakes of snow swirled, sparkling as they caught the light then disappearing into the impenetrable darkness.

'Right.'

'Red wine?'

'Please.'

She waited for him to order the drinks then took her glass and they went over to Freya.

When they were sitting down, Freya asked, 'How did it go?'

Frankie took a sip of wine and tried to focus on the rich berry flavour and the floral bouquet. Anything to stop the tears from falling.

'It was Dad and he had some news. I'm... I have to go home.'

'Oh no! I knew this would happen. What has Helen done now?'

'She collapsed.'

'She what?' Freya's eyebrows rose.

'Dad said it's not my fault and I mustn't worry or feel guilty but in light of what I've done recently, it's hard to believe I'm blameless.'

'I'm pretty sure it's not your fault.' Freya pressed her lips together.

'Dad said that Grandma is eighty-one and she still smokes and drinks and the doctor said he's surprised she hasn't collapsed before, the way she abuses her body, and because of how she still rushes about. But it's likely this was brought on by stress.'

'She never was very good at relaxing or letting things go.'

'I'll need to try to get a flight from Oslo tomorrow.'

'So soon?' Jonas asked.

'I have to go and see her. If I didn't and she... she died, I'd feel awful. For all her faults' – she reached out and took Freya's hands – 'and they are many, I need to see her even if it's to say goodbye. I know that she did love me in her own way. What she did to you, and to us, is unforgivable but—'

'I already told you, Frankie, that you have to let that go or it will eat you up. Anger is so destructive. You're young and free and you have a life ahead of you to enjoy.'

'I never thought about it like that before.' Her stomach churned as she mulled over the words. She was free now, really free. She wasn't Rolo's fiancée or in Grandma's debt and she could do anything she wanted to do.

'Of course you are. It's your life, my angel.'

'Will you come with me?'

Freya dropped her gaze and toyed with her bangles, pushing them up her arm then letting them fall back to her wrist.

'Oh, Frankie, I don't know if I could.'

'I know it won't be easy but I'd really like it if you did. We've only just found each other and I don't want to leave you. Come with me and spend some time in London.'

'There's the gallery though…'

'We can sort that out, Freya,' Jonas said.

Freya looked at Jonas. 'Would you be all right there for a few days or longer?'

He shook his head. 'I'm coming with you.'

'What?' Frankie and Freya blurted the question together.

'Well… I'm concerned about you… both. So I'll come too.'

Frankie looked from Jonas to her mother and back again. 'You both want to come to London?'

'I've never been there and have always wanted to see it.' Jonas nodded. 'Now's as good a time as any. Besides, after everything, I think Freya could do with the moral support. And don't worry about the gallery, Freya, I'll sort something out.'

'Jonas, you really are an angel.' Freya smiled.

'That's settled then. Shall we see if we can book some flights?'

Frankie pulled out her mobile and scrolled down to the search engine. As she flicked through the flight times leaving Oslo the next day, she couldn't help feeling a sense of hope. Grandma was ill and that was devastating, but she'd also been saddened at the idea of having to leave her mother behind. That idea hurt and if Grandma's health declined, it would be some time before Frankie would be able to return to Norway. But, thankfully, Freya wanted to come with her, so they could continue getting to know each other.

And the bonus was that Jonas was coming too. For some reason, that warmed her through, and she realized that she hadn't wanted to leave him behind either.

Chapter 21

As the black cab pulled up outside her London home, Frankie's heart grew heavy. Bringing Freya and Jonas here had seemed like a good idea in Norway, but now that they were back in the grey winter drizzle of her home city, she wondered at the wisdom of her decision. Freya had suggested that she and Jonas book into a hotel and give Frankie a chance to speak to her father first, but Frankie had been nervous about letting them out of her sight. She was afraid in case she never saw them again, as if she'd conjured them in Norway and they would disappear behind the clouds, like the northern lights had, if she wasn't holding onto them.

In spite of these feelings, it was nice to be home. So much had happened since she'd last been here that she could imagine years had passed. She glanced at her mother, wondering how she felt, because it actually had been years since she'd been there. Did it feel like home to her at all, or just a place she'd prefer to forget?

She paid the driver then opened the door and got out, breathing in the familiar scents of London. The four-floor grade II listed Victorian buildings hadn't changed in the time she'd been away, but she had, and in a strange way she felt as though they should have too. But they stood there, white and solid as ever, stucco-fronted with their porticoed entrances and first-floor balconies. They were truly beautiful and Frankie imagined how impressive they would likely seem to a stranger.

Jonas got their luggage out of the boot then stood on the pavement gazing around him.

'You live here?'

'Yes.'

'It's… enormous and very grand.'

'I'd forgotten how impressive it is.' Freya came to stand next to them. 'Are you sure this is a good idea, Frankie? I'm sure that the last thing your father needs right now is his… me and a strange Norwegian man turning up on his doorstep.'

'He's not here at the moment because he's gone to the hospital – a text came through just after we landed. Besides, there's plenty of room. Dad spends so much time at work or playing golf that this is more like a hotel to him.'

'Poor Hugo.' Freya shook her head.

They climbed the stone steps and Frankie retrieved her key from her bag and pushed it into the lock. The door opened and they went inside.

The airy hallway smelt of lilies and beeswax furniture polish, as it always did, and Frankie swallowed the lump in her throat, realizing that Grandma usually greeted her whenever she returned home. That might never happen again.

Approaching footsteps alerted her to the presence of Annie, their housekeeper. She'd only been with them for about six months. None of their housekeepers lasted long because of what she thought of as 'the Helen Ashford Effect'. Her grandmother's harsh tongue and demands always proved too much for the housekeepers over time, and one had even walked out after two days. It meant that

Frankie had never had the chance to get to know any of them very well and that the opportunity of having another female role model around never happened.

'Ah, there you are, Miss Ashford! Mr Ashford said you'd be back today. How was your flight?'

'It was good, thanks, but obviously I wanted to get home as soon as possible.'

'Of course.'

'Any news?'

'About Mrs Ashford?'

'Yes.'

'Nothing as yet. Mr Ashford has gone to see her and will be speaking to the doctors.' Annie smiled at Frankie then eyed Freya and Jonas. 'We have guests?'

'Yes, Annie. They'll be staying too.'

'Of course, Miss Ashford. Welcome to you both. I'll go and make up two of the guestrooms, shall I?'

'Thank you.'

When Annie had gone upstairs, Frankie turned to her mother and Jonas. 'I thought it best not to tell her who you are just yet. I'd rather speak to Dad first, as I think it's better coming from me, although I'm sure he'll be fine.'

'I hope you're right. I do feel a bit awkward.' Freya's face was pale and her eyes darted about as she took in her surroundings. 'In fact, Frankie, on second thoughts, this wasn't a good idea at all. It would be better for Jonas and me to stay at a hotel. Would you call us a taxi and we'll find somewhere suitable?'

'Please don't do that.' Frankie's heart squeezed. 'I want you to stay here.'

Freya looked at Jonas and he shrugged, clearly unsure what to do for the best, and Frankie held her breath, waiting for her mother to make a decision. It was strange how things worked out. The last time she'd stood in this hallway, she'd been on her way to Rolo's family home to get married. Since then she'd run away from her wedding, fled to Norway, met her mother and Jonas, briefly seen the northern lights and fed a reindeer. And now, the woman who'd dominated her life – and her father's life – for years was critically ill in hospital and Frankie's ex-fiancé was on their honeymoon with one of her friends.

Who knew how things would work out?

What she did know, however, was that bringing Freya and Jonas here was a bit risky, because her father wasn't expecting them. Frankie had brought friends home over the years and they often had guests staying, but in this case, one of the guests was Hugo's ex. But she also knew her father's generosity of spirit would have made him sad to think that he couldn't offer accommodation to Freya and Jonas, especially in light of the fact that Frankie wanted to keep them close.

'No. We really should go.' Freya nodded as she came to a decision. She picked up her case and walked to the door. 'We'll find a hotel as close as possible.'

Jonas met Frankie's eyes and she could see the uncertainty there.

'Come on, Jonas.'

Just then, the front door swung open and a tall figure stepped into the hallway, causing Freya to gasp.

–

'Freya?' Hugo's eyes widened and he raised his hands as if to hug her then dropped them to his sides. He looked so awkward that Frankie had a flash of regret for bringing her mother here without warning him.

'Hugo.' Freya was frozen to the spot, still holding her suitcase, ready to walk out the door.

'Hi, Dad.'

Hugo tore his gaze from his Freya and met Frankie's eyes. 'Darling, you're home.'

He crossed the hallway in three strides and enveloped Frankie in a hug. His familiar woody cologne washed over her and she hugged him back, glad to see him even though it had been just days since she'd left.

'It's good to see you, Dad.'

'You too.' He released her then stood back. 'What a week, eh? Well, slightly more than a week but... oh, I don't know, I've lost all concept of time. And we have guests?'

He turned and eyed Freya and Jonas, then, seeming to remember his manners, he shook Jonas's hand before walking back to Freya.

'Freya. It's... so good to see you. How are you?'

Frankie watched as they evaluated each other, taking in how the years had changed them yet left them the same. Finally, Hugo opened his arms and leant forwards to hug Freya. At first, she stiffened, but as Hugo whispered something to her, she visibly relaxed and hugged him back. Frankie felt awkward now, as if she was intruding upon a private moment, and she picked up her suitcase to carry it upstairs.

'I'm OK, thanks, Hugo. But we were just leaving. I'm sure you and Frankie have things to talk about,' Freya said, moving back from his embrace.

'Where will you go?' Hugo frowned. 'You're very welcome to stay here.' He smiled at Freya then at Jonas. 'We have plenty of bedrooms.'

'Actually, we were just going to go and find a hotel.' Freya nodded at the door.

'No, no. I won't hear of it.' Hugo shook his head. 'Why waste money on a hotel when we have such a big house?'

'But what about… I mean, won't your mother…'

'She won't be back for some time.' Hugo's face dropped and Frankie's stomach churned. It didn't look like the news was good.

'How is she, Dad?'

'The doctor said she'll make it through – hopefully! But she won't be dancing any time soon.'

'So she's all right?'

'Yes… and no. She had what they describe as a minor heart attack. I wasn't aware that a heart attack could ever be mild, but apparently it can. She's been left with some arrhythmia in the form of tachycardia, which means that her heart keeps beating too quickly and it's making her dizzy and breathless. She's also, as would be expected, exhausted. But try not to worry, Frankie, she's in the right place, has excellent care and they're working out the best treatment plan for her. For now, let's get our guests settled then we can catch up properly.'

'I'm quite happy to find a hotel.' Freya tried again.

'No, please stay here.' Hugo held up his hands. 'After everything that's happened, it's the least I can do.'

Freya looked at Jonas and he nodded.

'OK then, but just for a few days.'

'Wonderful. Right, uh…' He glanced at the staircase where Annie was descending in her practised quiet way. 'Annie! Show our guests to their rooms, please.'

'Of course, Mr Ashford. Your rooms are ready, so if you'd like to follow me…'

Freya looked around her once more, as if wondering if this really was a good idea, then pushed her shoulders back and headed for the staircase. This clearly wasn't easy for her, but then it wasn't easy for any of them.

Jonas carried his and Freya's suitcases up the stairs and once they were out of earshot, Frankie took her father's arm.

'Sorry if that was a bit of a surprise.'

'It was a huge shock, actually, Frankie, but not a bad one. I mean, I didn't expect to walk in and see your mother standing there but it wasn't unpleasant at all. Gosh, she looks good; as good as she did thirty years ago.' He gazed up the staircase as if hoping to catch another glimpse of Freya.

'Are you sure you're OK about it?'

He nodded. 'Yes, I'm sure. Besides, I suspect that now you've managed to get your mother to come home, you'll be keen to spend some time with her. And you can do that if she stays here.'

'Thanks, Dad.'

'What else could we do? Mother's not here and won't be for some time and to be honest... I'd quite like to have some time to speak to Freya myself. If she'd be happy to speak to me, that is.' His eyes flickered around and he seemed agitated.

'I'm sure she will be, Dad. I expect you both have things you want to say.'

'I'm sure we do.'

'But for now, can you tell me how Grandma's doing?'

'Of course. Shall we put the kettle on?'

Frankie followed him though the hallway and off the short corridor that led to the kitchen. It was certainly a strange feeling having both her parents under one roof, and she realized she was looking forward to spending time with them both. Something she hadn't done since she was very young indeed.

Since she was too young to remember. Now she had the chance to make some lasting memories. She hoped they would be good ones.

Chapter 22

Jonas sank onto the edge of the enormous bed and gazed around him. He couldn't get over his luxurious surroundings. Frankie actually lived here, but to him it resembled a fancy hotel or a house out of one of those period dramas that his mother liked to watch. Frankie's home was huge and they even had a housekeeper, and a gardener judging by the garden he had seen from his window, and no doubt an army of cleaners. He'd gathered that Frankie came from money from things Freya had told him, but he hadn't imagined it would be to this extent.

His room was decked out in red, gold and cream. The plush vermilion carpet was so thick that his soles sank into it every time he stood up. He'd felt terrible wearing his boots when he'd entered the room, and had removed them as soon as possible and put them on top of his suitcase for fear that they would taint the flawless expanse.

The king-size four-poster bed resembled one that he'd expect a royal to sleep in, with its rich mahogany frame and cream and gold bedspread. It even had a bolster pillow, and a wooden chest at its foot that featured carved animals and trees in some sort of Elizabethan scene. He had no doubt that it was an antique. The sash windows were framed by heavy gold and red curtains currently held back with golden-fringed ropes, and there wasn't a fingerprint to be seen on the glass.

The furniture was just as grandiose. There were two mahogany wardrobes, a heavy-set chest of drawers and a dressing table, all so shiny that he could see his reflection in them. The aroma of beeswax polish hung in the air, a sign that the room had likely been dusted just that morning.

There was even an en suite bathroom with a deep roll-top tub, a double shower and a bundle of Egyptian cotton towels that looked brand new.

Did Frankie actually live like this? It took his breath away. It also made him feel like a fish out of water. Jonas wasn't used to this level of opulence and he couldn't imagine living like this. Frankie came from this world and would no doubt be accustomed to all its trappings. If there had been any doubt in his mind about the possibility of dating someone like her, then it now disappeared altogether. Jonas lived for the outdoors, for the fresh air in his lungs and the open skies. He could never live like this; he wouldn't want to. He was used to a different lifestyle, one where he slept on sofas, bunk beds and in tents. As he'd travelled around, he'd been happy just to have a roof over his head some nights, on the nights that were especially cold. His mother's apartment in Oslo was modest and although comfortable, it could never be described as luxurious, yet it was perfect in his eyes. He was proud of his mother and how hard she worked and of where he came from.

Freya had walked away from all this, and while Jonas could see that it might be nice to live in such luxury, it also unsettled him. He had never cared for material possessions, rarely thought beyond tomorrow, and valued things like friendship and nature's beauty far more than towel thread count and lavish surroundings.

It was clearer than ever that Frankie came from a very different world.

But was it a world that Freya would ever dream of returning to?

Was it a world where Freya could ever fit in?

It certainly wasn't the type of world Jonas had associated her with; she was as free a spirit as he was. But her move away from this lifestyle had been forced. He couldn't imagine Frankie leaving it as her mother had done.

He checked his mobile and realized he'd been sitting there musing about true wealth for twenty minutes, and it was time to shower and change then head downstairs to see what the afternoon had in store for them all.

–

'Annie's prepared us a light lunch in the dining room.' Hugo gestured towards the doorway. 'I'm sorry though, I forgot to check if anyone had any allergies.'

Jonas and Freya shook their heads.

'That's a relief.' Hugo smiled. 'I know you never used to, Freya, but things change.'

'Luckily I haven't developed any.'

'I'm glad to hear it.'

In the dining room, Hugo sat at the end of the long table and Freya took the seat to his right, as if it was something they did every day. Seeing her parents together fascinated Frankie. It was clear that they'd once been close, as they seemed to anticipate what the other would do, yet they also had an awkwardness about them that told of years apart.

Frankie sat next to her mother and Jonas stood next to her, not quite sure what to do.

'Take that seat next to my father,' she told him. 'See... Annie has set a place there.'

Jonas nodded then went and sat down.

'Help yourselves to whatever takes your fancy.' Hugo gestured at the platters of cold meat, cheese, salad and pasta. 'There's plenty more in the kitchen should you want it and if you want something that's not there, let me know and I'll go and get it.'

While they filled their plates, Hugo poured wine from the bottle in the cooler next to him then they tucked in. The wind howled around outside, skittering brittle leaves across the patio slabs, and through the glass, the sky was an ominous shade of grey. It was an English winter and as cold and grim as every one that Frankie could remember. And yet... it was different. She'd eaten so many meals in this room, gazed out at the changing landscape through the cycle of the seasons and dreamt of how different things could be. Today they were different, very different indeed. Instead of Frankie and Grandma flanking her father at the table, he had Freya and Jonas, and instead of Frankie imagining how it would be to have her mother here, she actually was.

Hugo was a good host; years of practice had perfected his skills at small talk and filling silences. He asked Freya about her business and her life in Oslo, yet avoided referring to the past or any topic that could make things uncomfortable. He asked Jonas about his photography and his family, enabling Frankie to find out things about the handsome Norwegian that she hadn't heard so far. Then he added in his own details, making them laugh with tales from the golf course and the boardroom. It opened Frankie's eyes to who her father really was. She'd always known him as Dad, businessman and golfer, subordinate to Grandma but with a warm heart and perfect manners. Yet here he was, a practised conversationalist, a generous and attentive host, funny and bright, calm and confident.

Was this what happened to her father when Grandma wasn't around but Freya was? Did Hugo Ashford blossom in the presence of her mother? Did he become a better version of himself?

It was as though her father had been set free by Grandma's absence and Frankie's heart filled with love for him. Then it fluttered with sadness. If her father had been this man consistently, if he had shown this side of himself to her mother and Grandma had not been around, then perhaps Freya would never have become ill and left, and life would have been so different for them all.

She raised her glass and cleared her throat.

'I'd like to make a toast. To good company and to family.'

They clinked glasses and Freya smiled at her, understanding deep in her eyes. It was as if they'd been given a fresh start, a brand-new opportunity, and Frankie hoped that it was the beginning of something very special indeed.

–

After lunch, they made their way into the lounge to relax and have their coffee. Annie brought in a tray of chocolate cake, cherry pie, cheese, crackers and olives. Frankie watched as Jonas's eyes widened and she wondered what he was thinking. Did he find her home pleasing or too lavish? Did he think she'd grown up spoilt or lucky? He'd been polite and amiable during lunch and smiled often, but she sensed that he was holding something back. She was so used to this lifestyle, to the variety of food on offer, to buying whatever she wanted and to living in such a pleasant location. She'd never had to worry about money, even if she'd worried about many other things, but she'd have traded it all in just to have her mother around. A lot of people she knew would struggle to understand that, some who didn't live as she did would struggle to believe it. But for Frankie, as nice as wealth was, it didn't make for happiness; it didn't make up for not having a mother.

'What are your plans for this afternoon?' Hugo asked as he poured cream into his coffee.

'Well, I thought perhaps I should go and see Grandma.' Frankie tried to suppress her shiver of reluctance.

'I wouldn't, not today anyway. I'll take you in the morning. She'll be tired this afternoon and probably sleeping.'

'OK, that makes sense.' Relief loosened the tension in her shoulders that she hadn't even noted until now.

'I wondered if you'd like to take a walk with me, Freya.' Hugo kept his eyes on his coffee and Frankie knew that he was nervous about asking.

'That would be lovely.'

Hugo looked up. 'Really?'

'I'd love to see some of the old places... See how things have changed around here and what, if anything, has remained the same.'

'Wonderful.' Hugo's smile was so broad that it reached his ears. Frankie had never seen him smile quite like that.

Freya smiled too.

'How about you, Jonas?' Frankie asked him, hoping he realized that her parents wanted some time alone.

'I don't mind. I could take a nap... or read a book.'

'What about taking your camera out and getting some shots around here? There are plenty of interesting sights to capture,' Frankie suggested.

'That also sounds like a good plan.'

'Great. Well, let's have coffee then I'll get my boots on and show you around my home city.'

Jonas nodded and Frankie felt that strange warmth flooding through her again, that only he seemed to cause. It was as though he had woken something inside her and it lifted her spirits and stirred excitement in her belly.

'I can't wait,' he replied.

I can't wait either.

Chapter 23

'Your home is lovely,' Jonas said as Frankie pulled the heavy door closed behind her.

'That old place.' Frankie giggled. 'I grew up there and I suppose I forget how nice it is sometimes. Although…' She paused, not wanting to sound ungrateful.

'What?'

'Well, it's not particularly cosy, is it?'

'It's big.'

'Exactly. I've always pictured myself living in a cosy log cabin or a barn conversion out in the countryside. Perhaps it's me being ungrateful or silly but I sometimes find the house a bit… well, I feel… a bit lost.'

'I can understand that.'

Frankie pulled her hat down to keep her ears warm and tucked her hands deep into her pockets. The late November day was cold and bright as the wind rushed through the London streets, the grey clouds from earlier now blown away.

'When I was younger… a lot younger… I used to create a den in my walk-in wardrobe. I'd put up blankets and take pillows and my stuffed animals in there just to feel more secure.'

Jonas watched her intently, his blue eyes seeming to reach down into her soul. She imagined that he could see her as she was then, at six years old, a small girl with her long brown hair in plaits, her pink teddy bear clutched under her arm and her tiny feet in fluffy slippers, as she crept into her wardrobe and snuggled in the corner. It certainly hadn't been like the adverts she'd seen on TV where children ran into their parents' rooms after they'd had a bad dream and jumped into their bed before falling fast asleep. For Frankie, there had been no night-time cuddles, no words of reassurance. She'd been left to her own devices, hiding herself away from the darkness and the creaking of the old house as it settled throughout the night, comforting herself with toys and dreams of a mother who was out there somewhere thinking of her too.

'Are you OK, Frankie?' Jonas asked.

She nodded. 'Just got sidetracked thinking about my childhood for a moment there. Come on, let's take a walk.'

They strolled along, through streets that were familiar to Frankie yet strange to Jonas. She pointed out the places where she'd played, drunk wine taken from her father's cellar and tried a cigarette. She didn't show him the corner of the immaculate communal gardens belonging to the inhabitants of Royal Crescent Gardens, where she'd had her first kiss, or the garage she'd crept into to throw up after the wine she'd taken had made her head spin. There were some things worth sharing and some best forgotten. Jonas snapped constantly, clearly spotting plenty of sights worth capturing on his camera. Frankie didn't even need to point things out to him because his eye for detail was instinctive.

'Your nose is red.' Jonas smiled at her as they stopped at a crossroads.

'It's really cold.'

'I'm surprised, actually. I didn't expect it to be so cold here.'

'Do you fancy a coffee?' Frankie pointed at a small pub on the corner.

'Good idea.'

As they opened the pub door, the warmth from inside greeted them like a hug and Frankie sighed with relief. She hadn't wanted to cut their walk short, as Jonas had been interested in his surroundings, but the cold had been making her eyes water and her nose run. Neither of which were pleasant, or her best look. Not that what she looked like mattered right now; she was merely showing an acquaintance around London, but even so, she didn't want his memories of his guide to be of a red-nosed block of ice.

They sat in a corner booth opposite the log burner where logs crackled and the flames glowed orange. It was cosy and intimate, and Frankie became fully aware that they were alone. They browsed the drinks menu and Frankie snatched a few glances at Jonas. He really was very handsome and so big, filling the booth with his large frame and his quiet confidence.

He would make someone a good boyfriend…

She shook her head. Where had that thought sprung from? The last thing Frankie wanted was to tie herself down to another man.

A waitress arrived at their table and took their drinks order. Frankie asked her to add two of the pub's mince pies to it, as they were the best she'd ever tasted.

'Do you come here often?' Jonas asked.

'To this pub?'

He nodded.

'No, not that often. I've been in here a few times, but in all honesty, I don't spend a lot of time in pubs and clubs.' She looked around. 'I'm not sure why I haven't come here more often though. It is very pleasant.'

'It's very cosy.' He smiled and his eyes crinkled at the corners.

When the waitress returned with their coffees and mince pies, Frankie noticed her eyes lingering on Jonas. She wasn't surprised, but did think it was a bit rude, as he could well be Frankie's partner.

'I'm sorry to ask but...' the waitress chewed her bottom lip, 'I don't want to be rude, but see, behind the bar, we were debating whether you're an actor.'

'An actor?' Jonas's eyebrows rose.

'Yes. I promise we won't hassle you or anything... the manager would kill us... but you look so familiar.'

'I do?' A smile played on Jonas's lips and he winked at Frankie. 'Who do you think I am?'

The waitress's cheeks had turned scarlet now and she glanced at the floor before meeting his eyes again. 'Chris Hemsworth.'

Jonas let out a deep booming laugh that made the waitress jump.

'Thor?'

'Yes.'

He nodded. 'You think I look like him?'

'Well... yes.'

'I'll take that.' He rubbed a hand over his golden beard.

'So... are you?'

He shook his head, his shoulders still shaking with laughter.

'No, I'm not Chris Hemsworth.'

'Oh...'

'But thanks for the compliment.'

'It's OK.' The waitress turned to go then paused. 'Are you sure? Because you look an awful lot like him.'

'I'm positive.' He nodded.

'Right... OK... sorry to have troubled you.'

'Perhaps Hollywood beckons?' He directed the question at Frankie but the waitress turned around again.

'Oh definitely. You should go into acting.' She glanced at Frankie. 'Sorry... I didn't mean to sound like I was hitting on your boyfriend or anything. I was just settling a bet with my colleagues.' She nodded at the bar where two men and a woman were staring at them.

'It's OK. He's not—'

'She doesn't mind, do you?' Jonas took Frankie's hand and squeezed it. 'We get this quite a lot.'

'We do?' Frankie watched his face.

'Yes, angel.' He raised her hand and kissed it.

'Enjoy your coffees.' The waitress smiled then scurried away.

'Angel?'

Jonas laughed. 'I was just playing along. It was easier to let her think we're together.'

'It was?'

'Yeah, why not?'

She shrugged, sensing there was more to this than Jonas was letting on but not wanting to go any deeper into it right now.

'Have you ever tried a mince pie before?'

He shook his head. 'Freya has offered them but I don't know... I never fancied one.'

'Try it now. They're delicious.'

She watched as he dug his fork into the crumbly buttery shortcrust pastry then scooped some of the brandy butter up on the edge of the fork. The mince pie was gone in three bites.

'You liked it then?'

'Delicious.'

'I've always enjoyed them. We used to have them at boarding school in December and it meant that I'd soon be heading home for the holidays. Every year I'd make a wish on the first one I ate.'

'What did you wish for?'

She sighed. 'Can't you guess?'

'Uh… toys or expensive gifts? New shoes or a laptop? A horse?'

'No.' She shook her head, sad that Jonas seemed to think she might be that materialistic. But then, didn't most children wish for the things he'd named at Christmas? 'I wished that my mother would come home.'

He held her gaze then, his eyes clear and kind. 'Of course. I'm sorry. I understand because even though I had my mother and grandparents around, I used to wish that my father could come home too. But that was impossible because he died when I was very young.'

'I'm sorry. It's hard growing up without one of your parents.' Frankie nodded, strangely comforted by knowing that another human being understood how she felt. Even though Jonas's circumstances were different, he'd still lost a parent so he knew how that left an empty space.

They drank their coffees then ordered more and Frankie began to relax. Jonas was so easy to be with and unlike when she'd been with her peers, she didn't feel judged or as though she had to act a certain way to impress him. They chatted easily about London and Norway, what they felt was similar and different, and he talked about her mother and how kind she was to everyone she knew. Frankie was hungry to hear more about Freya, so she listened attentively as he told her about how Freya supported local charities and anyone she knew who was in need.

The woman he spoke about was nothing like the woman her grandmother had described, and not for the first time Frankie questioned her grandmother's motives in painting Freya the way she had done.

–

Jonas finished his second coffee then placed the cup in the saucer. He was having a great time with Frankie and found her company refreshing. There was more to her than an upper-class socialite from London's aristocracy. She spoke very well, pronouncing words like a news reporter on the BBC, just as they'd tried to teach him and his classmates to do back in school, but on her it seemed natural. Cute even. He liked to listen to her and could have sat there and done so all day. He also liked looking at her, she was beautiful and every day she seemed to grow more beautiful, as though having Freya in her life was healing her from the inside out. Nothing could come of their acquaintance but he would enjoy being with her while he was in London.

When Frankie excused herself to go to the toilet, he felt someone watching him. He looked up to find the waitress who'd served them their coffees and the other woman behind the bar gazing at him. He looked away quickly, not wanting to acknowledge their attention. What was it with them? He'd told them he wasn't that famous actor and that he was with Frankie.

He'd actually felt quite uncomfortable when the waitress had been questioning him, even though he'd tried to hide it behind laughter. He'd been mistaken for Chris Hemsworth in the past, and he did find it amusing, but he didn't enjoy the attention that often came with it. Jonas didn't want to pose for selfies with strangers, or to make polite conversation with the drunken female tourists who sometimes accosted him in his homeland; he was a private person with a small group of close friends and he didn't want any fuss. So, even though he hadn't said as much, the idea of being famous was one of the worst things he could imagine. Why anyone would want the media, hell, the whole world, watching their every move, he had no idea. He hadn't really got into the whole social media thing and had a Facebook account but that was kept private and mainly used to stay in contact with fellow photographers, clients and friends. He never accepted friend requests from strangers, and the message requests he always denied often made him blush with their proclamations of love as well as the dirty things that the women and men who sent them told him they'd like to do to him. And all because they mistook him for a famous actor.

He'd also laughed off the waitress's questions because he didn't want Frankie to think he was hostile or unfriendly. Laughing was one way he dealt with embarrassing situations. And, of course, telling the waitress he was with Frankie had two motives: he wanted the woman to go away, and he'd seen something flash across Frankie's face when the waitress had interrupted them, something he thought might have been hurt or irritation. He didn't know her well enough to read her properly. But it had been instinctive for him to say that she was his girlfriend. In fact, he had been quite proud to do so. Even though it had no roots in the truth…

Frankie returned to their table and sat down just as 'White Christmas' started to drift from the speakers.

'Do you ever have a white Christmas here?' he asked her.

'Sometimes. Although it's nothing like you get in Norway. Snow causes utter panic in the UK. We're just not equipped to deal with it like you Norwegians.'

'I love the snow.'

'I do too. I'd love to spend a winter in a snowy climate, to know that every day I'd get up and find a flawless white landscape just beyond my window.'

'You should come back to Oslo with Freya and me.'

She met his eyes.

'That would be lovely, but I don't know what's going to happen yet. I need to visit my grandmother in the hospital and to see how she does over the next few days.'

'Of course.'

'How long will you stay in London?'

He shook his head. 'I'm not sure yet. It kind of depends on Freya but obviously we will… or at least *I* will need to get back to the gallery.'

Frankie nodded, causing her brown hair to slide forwards. Without thinking, Jonas reached out and tucked it behind her ears then gently cupped her face. His heart pounded, making blood rush through his ears. The sounds of the pub, the music and the conversations of other people faded away and it seemed that they were the only two people in the world.

'Frankie, I—'

She gasped then pulled back slightly and he dropped his hands. What the hell was he doing? Had he gone completely mad? This hadn't been planned. He hadn't even thought about it. Not in any detail anyway.

'Jonas…' She frowned.

'Sorry.' He rubbed his eyes. 'I don't know what happened then.'

Frankie appeared to be dazed.

'Excuse me for a moment.' He got up and made his way to the toilets where he ran the cold water over his hands and splashed it over his face. He stared at his reflection in the mirror, took in his flushed cheeks and wide eyes, and it confirmed what he already suspected. He was, for reasons beyond his own comprehension, very taken with Frankie Ashford. She was beautiful and sweet, easy to talk to and he felt comfortable with her, that he could be himself, but there was more to her than that. Jonas rarely felt a connection to anyone, other than some of his close friends, Freya, and his mother. And now he seemed to be developing a connection with Frankie.

But he had no idea if she felt the same.

It was a new situation for him and he wasn't sure if he liked it, because it made him feel vulnerable. It was also hard to admit this to himself, especially after he'd internally reiterated the fact that they were too different to ever be anything other than friends. His mother had always told him that the heart wants what it wants, and therefore it often refuses to listen to reason. He'd repeatedly teased her for being a romantic, but now he was starting to wonder if she had a point.

When he returned to the booth, Frankie was buttoning her coat.

'Are we going back to the house?'

'Yes, it's probably best if we do. Dad might have news about Grandma and much as I'd like to sit here all afternoon, I probably need to get a few things sorted.'

He nodded and pulled on his own coat.

Frankie sighed then sank onto a chair. 'Jonas, there's something I haven't told you. My life and my emotions are rather complicated right now.'

'You don't have to tell me anything, Frankie.'

'Sit down for a moment.' She patted the seat next to her. 'Please.'

He sat down and watched her face carefully.

'Jonas, I came to Norway to find Freya but it wasn't planned. Well, not until that point in time anyhow. See… I was running away from something.'

'Your grandmother.' He nodded.

'Yes, but see I was running away from her because I walked out on my wedding.'

'You were getting married?' His heart plummeted.

'I was. To the grandson of a family friend. We were due to marry at his ancestral home. It was a big affair and was going to be covered by the high society magazines and everyone Grandma knew had been invited. But when the day came, I just couldn't go through with it. So I ran away.' She dropped her gaze to her hands and he watched as she wrung them in her lap.

'Well, if it was wrong then it was wrong, Frankie. Better to walk away before the ceremony than after.'

She looked up. 'Do you think? That's what I told myself. Grandma wasn't of the same mind.'

'She'll be OK about it in time, I'm sure.'

'I hope so.'

'And it's your life, anyway, so you have to live it the way you want to.'

She nodded. 'I didn't love him. It was all wrong and if I had loved him, then I'd have married him and been Mrs Rolo Bellamy now. He wanted me to take his name,' she added.

'You didn't want that?'

She shrugged. 'I didn't love him so the thought of being his wife was bad enough as it was. But I feel awful for the upset I caused by walking away. So much money and time wasted.'

Jonas gently placed his hand on top of hers. 'You have a right to be happy. No one should ever tell you that you don't.'

'Thank you.'

They stood up and Jonas smiled at Frankie, trying to offer some reassurance. It must have taken great courage to get to her wedding day then call a halt to proceedings. It would have been easier to keep her head down and go through with it to save face. Yet she hadn't, and he admired her for that. Frankie was stronger than he had realized and it made him admire her even more.

They paid the bill then went back out into the wintery afternoon. The sky had darkened now and was positively leaden, as if at any moment it would throw down freezing rain or possibly snow. Jonas didn't know which, as he was used to the skies of Norway and not accustomed to reading this British sky, just as he wasn't accustomed to reading Frankie. Something he wished he could remedy, and soon. If only he knew how she felt about him...

Chapter 24

On the walk back to her house, Frankie couldn't banish the image of Jonas cupping her face in his big hands from her mind. It was emblazoned there, as was his touch, imprinted upon her skin. Frankie had never been a hopeless romantic, remaining unconvinced by her girlfriends' claims that they were madly in love and that they had found 'the one'. Love like that only existed in books and movies and she had never expected to feel anything like it or to even want to.

Until now…

She glanced sideways at him as they walked. With his long-legged strides and imposing height, he was impossible to miss. She actually had to walk faster than was comfortable in order to keep up with him.

His gesture, brushing her hair from her face and tucking it behind her ears, was innocuous enough but it had been so gentle, and when his hands had then rested on her cheeks, something inside her had somersaulted and she'd pulled away quickly before she flung her arms around him and kissed him the way they kissed in fiction.

She bit the inside of her cheek to stop herself smiling. This was all a bit silly and romantic and she knew that it probably had roots in what she was going through with her mother, her grandmother and breaking up with Rolo. No doubt a psychologist would explain it clearly and tell her to take care, as she was likely to regret any impulsive actions linked to Jonas. Frankie was not impulsive.

But around Jonas she wanted to be.

They climbed the stone steps outside her house and she slid her key into the lock. Once inside, she paused. Something was… different.

Music was playing. Her father had never played music for as long as she could remember. Sometimes Grandma would have her radio stations on in the dining room, as she listened to opera or a radio play, but now uplifting pop music filled the hallway, making it seem more positive and alive than ever before.

She shrugged off her coat and hung it on the coat stand then kicked off her boots.

'Are you all right, Frankie? You looked shocked just then.'

'It's the music. Dad never plays music even though he has lots of records in the cellar from… from before.'

'Before?'

'Before Freya left.'

'Ah…' Jonas nodded. 'Freya loves music. Anything and everything. Sometimes I've even seen her cry as she listens to it but she refuses to turn it off.'

'I think that's why Dad never plays music. He doesn't want it to stir his emotions up.' Frankie shook her head. She was learning more about her parents all the time, even her father who had been there as she'd grown up. 'Let's go and see what they're up to, shall we?'

Jonas nodded.

In the kitchen, they found Hugo and Freya side by side at the marble-topped kitchen island. They had glasses of red wine in front of them and were laughing as they spooned food into serving bowls and chopped and stirred bubbling pans.

Frankie stood in the doorway watching them. It was a scene she'd long ago stopped imagining as it was far too painful when it didn't materialise. The idea of united parents was a childhood fantasy, although Freya's face had always been hazy in those daydreams, but now she was here. Standing next to her father. And they looked… happy.

Jonas cleared his throat and Freya and Hugo both looked up.

'Oh, hello. I didn't hear the door go.' Hugo grinned at them.

'We went to the deli and got dinner and Hugo's making his mushroom and basil risotto.' Freya gestured at the spread in front of them.

'Where's Annie?'

'We told her to take the night off.' Freya waved a hand. 'That girl works far too hard.'

'How about a carpet picnic?' Hugo asked.

'A carpet picnic?' Frankie stared at her parents.

'Yes, sweetheart. Have you never had one?' Freya came around the island and Frankie could see that she was wearing one of the housekeeper's aprons.

'No.'

'Well, you are in for a treat!' Freya clapped her hands. 'Here, you two take the wine through to the lounge and find a movie to watch. Your father and I will bring the food in a bit.'

Jonas accepted the bottle of wine from Hugo and two clean glasses, and Frankie led the way into the lounge. She couldn't speak; she was unable to formulate the words that were spinning around her head into coherent sentences.

She sank onto one of the plush sofas and curled her feet up under her as Jonas filled the two glasses then handed one to her.

'I'll look for a film, shall I?'

She nodded.

Jonas sat next to her as he scanned the channels, occasionally asking her if she'd seen this or that movie and if she fancied it. She didn't have the heart to tell him that she didn't care what they watched as long as they were all together. But she really didn't. She was overwhelmed by what she'd just seen and terrified of doing or saying anything that might upset it, so she sat still as a statue, waiting to see what would happen next.

When her father entered the lounge, he had two large patchwork quilts under his arms. He pushed the other sofa back and spread one quilt out on the floor, then gestured at the sofa Frankie and Jonas were sitting on. Jonas got up and pushed the sofa back effortlessly, even though Frankie was still sitting on it, then Hugo spread the other quilt out in front of her sofa.

Freya came in with a large tray of food.

'I'll go and get the rest,' Hugo said.

'Frankie, darling, you need to sit on the floor.'

'What?' Frankie had a vision of Grandma's reaction when she'd found Frankie sitting on the lounge floor when she was about eight. Grandma had told her that the floor was for pets and not for humans and that she should sit as she'd been taught to do, on the sofa, back straight and legs to one side, crossed at the ankles. She'd barely been allowed a childhood at all, Grandma had been so caught up with the importance of appearances and what was right and proper.

'Come here.' Jonas took her hand and helped her stand up then he sat down on the quilt and she sat next to him.

'Now, help yourselves to whatever you want.' Freya handed them plates. 'We got cheeses, breads, meats, dips, olives, sun-dried tomatoes, Hugo's risotto… and so on.'

'It looks delicious.' Jonas nudged Frankie.

'It does. Thanks.'

'My pleasure.' Freya held her gaze and Frankie saw a flash of uncertainty there. For all that her mother seemed confident and happy, beneath the surface she was just as vulnerable as Frankie was. They were both trying to navigate their way around this new situation, as was her father. Thank goodness that Jonas was here to relieve the tension that would otherwise have been unbearable, because if he'd been absent, then they might have felt compelled to discuss everything that had built up over the years more quickly, and sometimes certain topics required a gentler approach, to be dealt with softly and slowly.

Once Hugo had brought in the rest of the food, as well as another bottle of wine from his well-stocked cellar, Jonas ran through the movie options.

'I think we should go with that new Marvel one.' Frankie smiled.

'The Thor one?' Jonas frowned at her.

'Oh yes, let's watch that one!' Freya said. 'I always think that Jonas is a bit like that Chris what's-his-name.'

Jonas shook his head, but he was smiling. His lovely, open and honest smile that Frankie was growing quite fond of.

–

As the final credits rolled, Frankie drained her wine glass then placed it on the coffee table. She'd been absorbed in the movie but not so much that she hadn't noticed the glances her parents shared or how they laughed at the same scenes and lines of dialogue. She'd also been conscious of Jonas at her side – how could she not be when he'd offered her food, topped up her wine and smiled at her now and then, lifting her heart and making her feel that everything would be OK?

Jonas was so reassuring, just by being there, and it made her aware of what a good guy he was. Not many men could pull off caring and supportive like that. She had a feeling that whatever happened, he might be a part of her life from now on, even if remotely, as Freya's friend. Frankie suspected she would still want to know how he was, what he was doing, and to see him again.

I will want to see him again.

The thought ricocheted around her mind, the idea of never seeing him once he returned to Norway seeming too awful to dwell on. So she wouldn't. For now… even though he had a whole life she knew nothing about and came from a different world to the one she had lived in.

Yet hadn't she often heard the phrase 'opposites attract'?

—

Hugo had gone and got another bottle of wine and the four of them were lounging around the fire now, gazing into the flames as they enjoyed the dark ruby vintage Chianti.

'Did you always want to be a photographer, Jonas?' Hugo asked.

'Pretty much. I tried painting when I was at school but I wasn't very good and it frustrated me because I saw so much beauty in the world that I wanted to capture. So, when I was twelve, one of my teachers suggested photography and from there, my enthusiasm for it escalated. Every birthday and Christmas, I'd ask for money to save for the perfect camera. I started with a very basic model but when I got a job at sixteen, helping out at a building firm with stocktaking and the like, I was able to invest in better equipment.'

'I bet your parents are proud.' Hugo smiled.

'My mother says she is.'

'What about your father?'

'Oh… he's not around. He died when I was very young.'

'Gosh, I'm sorry. I'd just assumed from how you spoke about your family and friends before that you had both parents around.' Hugo grimaced.

'Don't be. It's not your fault. I don't really remember him because I was a toddler when he had a heart attack. He was older than my mother by twenty years. She tells me good things about him and says I remind her of him and that's a comfort. I wish I had known him but it just wasn't meant to be and Mum always made me feel as if he was still there, which might be what you picked up on. He was a part of my life even though he wasn't there physically, if that makes sense.' He looked at Frankie and she nodded. She understood. Jonas didn't feel robbed of his father because his mother had more than compensated for his loss. Sure, he'd have liked to have had him around but from what his mother had told him, his father had been ill for years and it was a miracle that they'd conceived Jonas. So she'd always told him that he was her gift from her husband, his way of making sure she had a reason to go on when he was unable to stay with her any longer.

Frankie's situation had been different. She'd known her mother was out there somewhere, and from what he'd been told she had believed her mother hadn't wanted or loved her. None of it was true but that was what she'd been led to believe. Not by Hugo, apparently, but by her grandmother, and Jonas wondered what sort of woman her grandmother was. Who did that to a child?

'What about you, Frankie?' Freya asked. 'Did you always want to go into management consultancy?'

Frankie sat up and crossed her legs.

'Not really.'

'I'm afraid that Frankie was kind of… directed into her career.' Hugo hung his head and stared into his wine glass. 'It's all quite beastly now that I look back at it.'

'I wanted to do something creative, to follow a career in the arts in some way. I wasn't really sure how but I did know I wanted the freedom of working for myself.' Frankie sighed. 'However, Grandma said I needed to do something sensible and to follow a career that would earn me a decent wage and reputation. She suggested a few things like law and accountancy and I knew it wasn't worth putting up a fight. After some work experience with an acquaintance of hers, I decided to go into management consultancy because there seemed to be a gap in the market.'

'Do you enjoy it?' Jonas asked.

'It has good days and some that are… not so good.'

'If you'd done what you wanted to, what would you be doing now?' Freya asked, her eyes fixed on her daughter.

'I'd be… designing clothes.'

'Really?' Freya's eyes widened.

'Yes. I love fabrics and colours and matching them up and I would have loved to have been a fashion designer.'

'It's not too late.' Jonas inched his hand sideways until he could brush her hand with his. He wanted to reassure her, to encourage her to continue to open up to her mother… and to him. 'You could still do this.'

Frankie shook her head. 'I don't know. I mean… I have clients and people relying on me. I have—'

'You have time, Frankie. Plenty of time and you should do what makes you happy.' Freya raised her wine glass. 'Here's to new beginnings.'

'Cheers.' Hugo clinked his glass with hers and Jonas did the same with Frankie.

'Frankie, I'm so sorry. I feel that I've let you down terribly in so many ways.' In the firelight, Hugo's face looked haggard and he seemed much older than his fifty-eight years.

'No, you haven't, Dad. You did your best.'

'I didn't. I should have done so many things differently, starting with going after your mother when she left.'

'Hugo, you couldn't have.' Freya shook her head. 'She wouldn't have let you.'

'I could have stood up to her.'

'And she'd have carried through her threat.'

'I don't think she would have. Mother wasn't that foolish. She'd have lost me too.'

'And you might have lost Frankie. At least you were there for her.'

'I'll never forgive myself for being such a coward.'

Freya took Hugo's hand. 'You are, and have always been, a good man. You don't have a bad bone in your body. I wish things had been different, that Helen hadn't been so… overpowering, but I also know why you did what you did. I wish I had acted differently, but I can't change it now. It ate away at me for years and that kind of guilt rots you from the inside. But finally…' Her voice thickened and she took a few deep breaths. 'Finally, Hugo, we have a chance to put things right.'

'Aren't you at all angry with me, Freya? You're perfectly entitled to be.'

Freya sighed softly. 'Over the years, I've been through a whole range of emotions. I often lay awake deep into the night wondering why you didn't fight for me, why you didn't try to find me. You had my address. You could have come after me, brought Frankie and we could have been together again. But you didn't.'

'The absolutely biggest regret of my life is that I was such a cowardly ass. All I can say in my defence is that Mother was always so domineering and I lost sight of how things should have been, of how I should have protected you and put you before all others. Things between you and me hadn't been… well, we weren't as close as we'd once been, and I know now that it was because of a combination of factors, including my mother's interference, me being weak and not as supportive as I could have been, and you being unwell. I also… I worried that you left because I'd already let you down and that if I followed you, you might not want me. Then I'd have been in a right old pickle.'

'I don't think that would have been the case, Hugo, but I was very unwell for quite some time. None of us know what we'd have done back then and even with hindsight, we can't turn back the clock. It's a shame but it's the way life goes. What we can do now is look forwards and appreciate what we have. Look at our beautiful, perfect daughter, for instance.'

'We made her.'

'We did.'

'But *she* has made herself into the amazing woman she is today. I never want to leave your life again, Frankie.'

'Please don't.' Frankie shook her head then pulled her knees up to her chest and hugged them, and Jonas saw a flash of how she would have looked as a little girl. Afraid. Lonely. Confused. And the urge to comfort her grew even stronger.

'Right… shall we get some dessert, Hugo? We did buy a delicious-looking strawberry gateau.'

'Indeed we did! It looks rather marvellous, in fact.'

Hugo and Freya left the lounge and Jonas turned to Frankie.

'You OK?' he whispered, running his gaze over her pretty profile, from her chin that was set at an angle that suggested a permanent display of strength, to her rosebud mouth, her thin straight nose and her large expressive green eyes.

'Yes, I'm fine. It's just that so much is happening and I'm trying to digest it all. Seeing my parents like this is… well, it's just…'

He took her hand. 'I can imagine. I want you to know, Frankie…' He paused, wondering if it was the effect of the good wine and the cosiness of their surroundings where only the orange glow of the fire provided any light now, or if it was something else that was making him bold. 'I'm here for you. Anything you want to talk through or… if you want a shoulder to cry on… I have broad shoulders.'

Frankie couldn't help running her eyes over his shoulders, and yes, they were broad and strong. She met his eyes. 'You really do.'

'At your disposal.'

'Thank you. I'll keep that in mind.'

Then they sat back, watching as the flames danced and flickered in the spacious hearth, while the wind howled around outside the window, and snowflakes swirled from the sky dusting the frozen ground.

Chapter 25

The next morning, Frankie sat in the passenger seat of her father's Range Rover as they made their way to the hospital. They'd woken to find the outside world covered with a dusting of snow that sparkled in the bright morning light. It was already beginning to thaw but she couldn't deny that it made London seem clean and fresh, reminding her of a Dickensian scene on a Christmas card.

When her father drove them into the hospital's underground car park, the knot in her stomach tightened. She wished they could have stayed at home with her mother and Jonas and enjoyed a lazy morning, the four of them talking and laughing and learning more about one another. Last night had been a night of revelations in more ways than one, what with her finding out more about her father's regrets and seeing how well her parents got on. Her mother and father could have been angry with each other, resentful of how the one had not been strong and supportive and the other had run away, but she didn't see any of that between them at all. Instead, there was a sadness, a mutual awareness of years lost and love wasted, of pride in their daughter and regrets that things hadn't been different. But when it came down to it, neither of them was fully to blame, if at all. Freya had been ill and done what she thought was best. Hugo had been afraid of losing his child as well as his wife, so stayed and allowed his mother to take control. He'd also been fearful of being rejected by Freya if he did go after her, and that would've meant he'd have been a single father without any other support, because if he'd crossed Grandma by leaving to follow Freya, she'd never have forgiven him. Perhaps her father would have coped alone, but Frankie could see how it would have been a daunting prospect, especially after the upbringing he'd had. It was a sad tale indeed but, as her mother had said, they all had a second chance to try to put things right. Of course, there was also the fact that Frankie hadn't contacted Freya when she turned eighteen. Had she done so, then the lost years might have been fewer. So when it came down to apportioning blame, perhaps she had to accept some of it herself.

And now she had to see her grandmother for the first time since she'd run away from her wedding to Rolo. She was trying to prepare herself for a barrage of recriminations and hostility, because Grandma was good at hurling verbal abuse, but even better at coldness that could penetrate your bones and hang around you for weeks at a time. The coldness was something Frankie had dreaded even more than the rows, because she always longed to be loved and accepted, to have her grandmother be proud of her, even if she didn't seem to love her. But nothing had ever seemed to be enough to merit Grandma's pride or affection.

Once her father had parked, they got out of the car and crossed the car park in silence that was only punctuated by the click-clack of Frankie's low-heeled boots. They took the lift to the first floor then Hugo led her to a ward where they were greeted by a nurse with a warm smile and a very white outfit of tunic and trousers.

'How is she today?' Hugo asked.

'Well, Mr Ashford, she's stable now and improving steadily but she shouldn't tire herself or become agitated in any way.'

He nodded.

'Perhaps me visiting isn't a good idea then?' Frankie asked, looking from the nurse to her father and back again.

'Are you Frankie?' The nurse displayed a set of small square teeth as white as her uniform.

'Yes.'

'She'll be delighted to see you. We've all heard so much about you.'

'You have?' Frankie shivered, imagining what Grandma might have said to them about her only grandchild, the one who'd fled her wedding and run off to Norway without a second thought for her poor, loving grandmother. She'd heard her grandmother on the phone many times when she was younger, and usually Frankie didn't sound like the perfect granddaughter in Grandma's eyes at all.

'Oh yes. She talks about you all the time. Come this way.'

She ushered them along the ward and to a private room at the end of the corridor. The whole place smelt clean, a mixture of antiseptic and lemons. It was also very quiet, as if the staff moved around in a permanent state of hush, not wanting to agitate or alarm the patients who paid handsomely for the privilege of private health care.

'She's in here. Now remember, try not to tire her or give her any... bad news.'

'Of course.' Hugo nodded, then the nurse walked away. 'We'd better...' He gestured at the hand sanitizer sitting in a holder on the wall.

'Of course.'

Hugo placed his hands under the bottle and it auto-matically squirted the clear astringent liquid onto his open palm. He rubbed his hands together vigorously. Frankie copied his actions, rubbing her hands until they were dry again.

'Dad… I don't know if I can…'

'I know, darling. I felt the same when I first came here. I was nervous about seeing her, about how she'd be and what she'd say. I was also afraid she'd be abusing the staff and even get herself thrown out.'

'Can they throw you out if you're paying for your healthcare?'

He shrugged. 'If you're hostile enough, I suppose, although Mother has always been jolly good at putting on a public face. Be prepared though, as you'll see some changes in her. She's not her usual feisty self, so just be ready for that.' He squeezed her shoulder.

A passing patient's slippers whispered over the tiled floor as he walked past pushing his IV stand. He gave them a cursory nod, then disappeared into the room next to Grandma's.

'OK. Let's go in then.'

As they entered the hospital room, she wondered how she could prepare for something like that, especially when she found it hard to imagine the severe matriarch of her childhood as anything less than fierce. The aromas that Frankie had encountered in the corridor were stronger in the confined space of the hospital room and she wondered how Grandma could bear it. Even just inside the doorway, she already felt as though she would choke on the heavy air. She took a few steadying breaths, aware that her tightened throat was probably more to do with anxiety than the smells; in fact, it had probably heightened her senses, making everything seem far stronger.

The room was shadowy, as the blinds were drawn, but over near the window she could make out a bed with a monitor next to it and an IV stand. The green light from the monitor filtered through the gloom, creating an ethereal atmosphere.

They approached the bed, Frankie on her tiptoes to avoid the click-clacking from her heels, and her breath caught in her throat, because the tiny form curled up under the blankets could not possibly be her grandmother. They must have entered the wrong room.

'Hugo? Is that you?'

A shock of white hair above a thin wrinkled face peered over the blankets at them, ghostly in the unnatural light, and Frankie took a step back. That wasn't Grandma; it looked nothing like her. Grandma usually reminded her of the Queen with her coiffed white hair in a style she hadn't changed since the Fifties. She had beady slate-grey eyes that could bore right through you and her flawless make-up was worn from dawn until dusk; she was never seen without it.

'Yes, Mother, I'm here, and Frankie is too.'

'Open the blinds.' The faint voice issued an order and Frankie did as she was told, her instinct to obey Grandma still strong.

Morning light flooded the room, banishing the shadows and revealing the white hospital sheets and the shining floor tiles. They were so clean she could see her hazy reflection in them when she looked down. At least Grandma was in a place she couldn't find fault with in terms of cleanliness, although Frankie supposed she'd likely find fault in other ways.

She turned back to the bed and watched as the sheets were folded down and her father helped Grandma sit up against her pillows. When she was comfortable, she looked at Frankie, causing her to swallow hard.

If Grandma was going to have her say, Frankie had just as well let her crack on, because it was, surely, inevitable. So she sat on the chair next to the bed, tucked her legs to the side and crossed her ankles, folded her hands in her lap and waited for the onslaught to begin.

–

But it didn't come.

Grandma really was much changed. She seemed so tiny propped up against the bright white hospital issue pillowcases, her white hair blending in with the material. Her skin was transparent, the veins in her bony hands standing out, blue and purple roads that bulged then disappeared beneath the long sleeves of her lilac nightgown. The skin on her face was stretched tightly over her cheekbones but it gathered in wrinkled folds around her eyes and mouth, as if the fat beneath had been sucked out while she slept. Her eyes were dull, their grey diminished without the usual steeliness behind their slate, and without her fuchsia lipstick, her lips were thin and pale.

'Thank you for coming, Frances.'

'Of course I'd come, Grandma. Why wouldn't I?'

'Well... I wasn't even sure you'd return to London.'

Frankie had to lean forwards to hear her grandmother because she spoke so quietly, as if every word took great effort.

'It's my home.'

'That may be but you left it, left us, and ran away.'

'I didn't really run away, so much as take a break.'

Her grandmother's lips curved slightly.

'Was it all that bad then, Frances? Rolo. A country estate. The chance to be someone.'

Frankie dug her nails into her palms and counted to ten before replying.

'To be "someone"?'

'Yes. To be Mrs Rolo Bellamy. When his parents passed on you'd have had that whole estate at your disposal. You'd have been wealthy and comfortable for the rest of your life.'

'Grandma... I am "someone". I'm me. Frankie Ashford. Your granddaughter, Dad's daughter and... Freya's daughter.' Her grandmother winced when she said her mother's name. 'I'm sorry, Grandma, I don't want to upset you but Freya is my mother. She always was.'

Helen gave a small cough then reached up and rubbed her throat.

'Are you OK, Mother?' Hugo stood up, pushing his chair backwards with his legs so he could get closer to the bed.

Helen nodded but gestured at the bedside table. 'Some water...'

He filled the plastic cup from a jug then helped her to take a drink.

She nodded when she'd had enough, and he sat back down heavily, as if his knees would have given way had he stood any longer.

'I only ever wanted the best for you, Frankie. I'm sorry if I did wrong... I've had time to think since I... collapsed and I know I could... I could go at any time now.'

'Don't say that.' Frankie shifted in her seat.

'But it's true, darling girl. I'm eighty-one. The doctors say I could live another twenty years… if I quit smoking and drinking, but as I said to them, where's the fun in that?' She started to cough, so Hugo gave her some more water. When she'd caught her breath again she said, 'I'm too old to change my ways now.'

'You could and you should. None of us want to lose you.' Frankie reached out and squeezed her grandmother's hand, trying not to wince at how thin it was. She seemed so fragile that a breeze could snap her.

'Who's "us"? Frances, when I go you and your father will be free. Apart from you two, no one else cares.'

'Your friends care.'

'Friends?' Grandma shook her head. 'The people I know are acquaintances rather than friends. They have their own lives and reputations to think of. One or two might shed a tear, but they'll move on, as they should do. I don't want anyone to grieve for me. We're all alone in this life.'

'Mother, you're not going yet so please don't talk like this.'

'And we're not alone.' Frankie shook her head. What an awful way to think. Had Grandma felt that way all her life? No wonder she had been so harsh and unsentimental.

Frankie looked at her father and her heart sank. Since she'd returned to London, she'd seen a different side to him, one that smiled and laughed freely, that ate and drank and sang. And it had all been because of her mother. So really, Grandma was right; Hugo would be freed when she passed away. It was tragic. But true. Her father could only be himself when his mother wasn't around. How sad that some families ended up in such awful situations, that the people who should be there for them could be the ones who hurt and oppressed them the most.

'Oh, Hugo, always the pacifier. Time for you to grow a set, isn't it?'

'What?' Hugo's eyebrows shot up his forehead.

'Come on, Hugo, darling, you've let me rule you all your adult life.'

'But… but… I didn't want to upset you, Mother.'

'And look where that got you. Your wife walked away and your daughter was sent off to boarding school.'

'Mother, really, I—'

'Let me speak candidly now, Hugo, please. It's about time.' She licked her lips then sucked in a breath. 'If I'm not going to be around… then some things need to change. I won't be like one of those voice-automated devices that you can put in every room so you can ask it questions, will I? There's no link to heaven… or hell… or wherever I'm heading.'

She paused again, her lips tinted blue, and Frankie stood up.

'Shall I call the nurse?'

Grandma shook her head. 'Be OK… in a minute.'

They waited, the tension in the room palpable, and Frankie could see that it was taking a lot of effort for her father to stay in his seat. He obviously wanted to call for the nurse but he was torn between obedience and concern, as he had, apparently, always been.

'You loved Freya and she loved you,' Grandma finally continued, 'but I didn't think she was good enough for you. At first I thought you'd grow out of your fascination with her, but as time wore on I realized it would take a seismic shift to separate you from that… from Freya. I had high hopes that you would marry from your own class, but no, soft romantic that you are, you fell head-over-heels for her. That was where the problems started.'

Hugo hung his head and Frankie's heart went out to him. This would be hard to hear but if Grandma was right, and this was the last chance she'd have to speak candidly, then she should have that opportunity. Besides, Frankie was still shocked that Grandma hadn't launched into a reprimand that would have made an army general look like a fluffy bunny.

'Actually, I've been fibbing. In truth, it all started with Pip Bellamy.' Grandma sighed.

'Pip Bellamy?' Frankie asked.

'Yes, dear. I loved him very much.'

'You loved Rolo's grandfather?' Her mother had mentioned something about this but Frankie hadn't thought it could have been this serious, had wondered if it had in fact been a rumour as Freya told her Hugo had said.

'Oh yes. Before your dear grandfather came along, Pip and I fell madly in love. I was sixteen and he was eighteen when we met. He was a junior clerk at my father's firm in London and I met him there one day when I'd gone to see Papa. I fell for him instantly with his handsome face and his twinkly blue eyes. He seemed so much older, so worldly wise, rather marvellous, in fact. We managed to exchange notes and to accidentally on purpose bump into each other when he was on errands, and soon I knew I wanted to be his wife. He said it was impossible but we were a bit like Romeo and Juliet; everything was so passionate, intense and painful. It was terribly thrilling and back then I had such a thirst for excitement and adventure. However, someone saw us together, only talking... but it was enough in those days to raise eyebrows and my father hit the roof. He fired Pip and told him that if he ever came near me again, he would make sure he regretted it. My father was a powerful man in certain circles and back then, as now in many ways, money equalled power.'

'Sorry... I can't get my head around this.' Frankie had abandoned her ladylike pose and was now hunched forwards on the chair with her hands on the bed. 'You and Pip actually were in love. Like... properly in love?'

'We were. Is it hard to imagine as you look at my wrinkled old form now?'

'No. That's not what I meant. I just find it so sad that Great-Grandpa would have done that to you.'

'My mother agreed with him, of course. Marrying into another class was frowned upon then, even though we'd been through two world wars and lost so many of our young men. Some things never change.'

'I hadn't realized you loved him, Mother.' Hugo shook his head. 'I'm so sorry Grandpa did that to you.'

'If I'd married Pip, I'd never have married your father and had you, Hugo, so don't feel sorry for me. It was all a very long time ago and look at Pip now! He's done so well for himself.'

'So Pip started out... poor?'

Grandma nodded. 'After my father fired him, he went away for a while and when he came back, he had money and a new confidence. It was as if my father had given him the push he needed, and he built his business from scratch, starting small with buying a few residential properties and warehouses and renting them out, then he kept on going. Now, as you know, he has an extensive property development portfolio. Money breeds money, eh?'

Frankie nodded. She knew a lot of people who'd made their money from investing in property, especially in areas like Belgravia and Mayfair.

'Then, he married Henrietta Walford, whose father had long since passed and whose mother was far too interested in her gin bottle to care. Henrietta was wealthy too, having already been widowed, and together they built their empire. So, Pip did pretty well out of it all. Sometimes, my dears, things happen the way they're meant to.'

Frankie nodded, but something wasn't sitting well with her.

'Grandma, I can understand all of that but what about my mother and father? You pushed Freya away when she was ill. Why did you do that? Did you... hate her that much?'

Helen smoothed out the quilt cover and when she opened her mouth, her lips trembled slightly.

'I never hated Freya. It wasn't hate, more disapproval. She was so arty-farty and—'

'Arty-farty?' Hugo's voice rose. 'What the hell is that supposed to mean, Mother?'

Helen waved her hands around as if searching for the words. 'You know... she was a painter and had no solid income or aspirations and I didn't believe she was good for you. Either of you. And her... her weakness irritated me.'

'Weakness?' Frankie's jaw dropped. 'Grandma, she had post-natal depression. That's an illness not a weakness. She was low enough as it was and you offered her no support. Instead, you kicked her when she was down.'

Grandma nodded but she didn't seem smug about it. Her eyes were sad when they met Frankie's, her shoulders hunched forwards as if the knowledge was a weight around her scrawny neck.

'So you forced my parents apart because of social class.'

'I did.'

'You thought it wouldn't work?'

'Yes. I suspected she might have been after his money and the security of marrying into our family… that she was a scrounger.'

'But you've already admitted that you wanted something like that for me… by marrying me to Rolo.'

'I did, Frances, but you are from the same class as Rolo and you have a good career. You're not living off pennies you make from selling your paintings.' Hugo coughed so Helen turned to him. 'Oh come on, Hugo, she wasn't exactly raking it in, was she? You, Frances, had much to offer Rolo in return. There was no inequality between you. Freya was from a council estate and from… hippy parents. They'd both died by the time I met her and she seemed so… lost and needy. Your father has such a big heart and I feared he'd give her everything, or that at some point she would tire of him and take him to the cleaners, as they say.'

'I wanted to give her everything, Mother.'

'I regret what I did now… seeing the hurt it has caused you two, but it was almost thirty years ago. Things change. People change.'

'Are you saying you'd do it differently now, Grandma?'

'Who knows? Maybe I would. But hindsight has a lot to do with that. At that time, when I found you all alone, a tiny baby abandoned by her mother, I thought I was doing the best for you. What if she'd done it when I wasn't there, Frances? As it was, you were in your cot, but if you'd been a bit older and toddling around and she'd walked out, you could have wandered into the garden and fallen in the pond or down the steps. You could have trotted out onto the street and been abducted by someone or mown down by a car. Anything could have happened and you were far too precious for that.'

'But if you'd got my mother some help, it wouldn't have happened. She needed help. She was a member of your family too.' Frankie's throat was tight and she swallowed hard. She didn't want to lose her temper, or to start crying, because she wanted to hear Grandma out. But this was incredibly difficult. 'Anyway... if I was so precious why did you send me away to boarding school when I was six?'

Grandma winced then rubbed her eyes. 'As you grew, you started to remind me of Freya. It was like being haunted by a spectre that increased my guilt. Your eyes were like hers, the way you sang when you were in the garden, the way your little nose wrinkled up when you were sad. It all reminded me of how I'd pushed her away from you and awareness of what I'd done started to gnaw at me. Not seeing you every day was a way of trying to forget.'

'You could have sent me to my mother.'

'That couldn't have happened. As far as we knew, Freya had moved on. I thought Hugo would move on... I was wrong.'

The three of them sat in silence as Grandma's words drifted around them, a tale of loss and heartbreak, passion and class. Frankie's chest was tight, heavy with sadness and grief, for what had been lost and for what was to come if Grandma didn't recover.

'I hate my job.' Frankie blurted her confession, the silence in the room had become imposing and she needed to be honest too.

'Pardon?' Grandma frowned.

Hugo's face, already pale, blanched completely.

'I need to say it now, while we're sharing candidly.'

'But why, dear? It's a good job.'

'I find it boring. I find no satisfaction in it at all. It is a good career for some, but it's not for me.'

'Then change it now, Frankie.' Her father nodded. 'Do it.'

'And do what instead, now you won't have a wealthy husband to support you?' Grandma asked.

'I want to design clothing.'

'Oh no, not that again.' Grandma sighed dramatically.

'Mother!' Hugo's tone was sharp and his mother gasped then buried her face in her hands.

'I'm sorry. Old habits are hard to break.' She looked up again. 'Frances… you must do what makes you happy, and if that means finding your mother too, then do it. I am sure that she will be glad to see you.'

Frankie met her father's eyes and his widened.

'Actually, Mother, there's something I need to tell you. Frankie didn't return to London alone…'

Chapter 26

On the drive back from the hospital, Frankie felt drained. Her whole body ached with exhaustion and she wanted to crawl into bed and sleep for a week.

It had been a day of revelations.

Grandma had taken the news about Freya being in her house better than expected and even reassured Hugo and Frankie that she'd be in the hospital for some time, so they should spend some quality time with her estranged daughter-in-law.

Something occurred to Frankie.

'Dad?'

'Yes.'

'When did you get divorced? I realized I never asked before. I just assumed you'd done it when I was small.'

He cleared his throat but his knuckles whitened as he tightened his grip on the steering wheel.

'Actually, we never did.'

'You're still married?'

'To my knowledge and I don't think she could have divorced me without my knowing.'

'What do you mean... to your knowledge? How did Grandma let you get away with that?'

'I might have told her that I took care of it all.'

'She didn't demand to see the papers?'

He shook his head. 'I'm not sure why. Perhaps she knew deep down, perhaps she felt guilty enough as it was, or perhaps she didn't want to push me with that one. It might have been a step too far.'

'You think you would have stood up to her on that?'

'I do. When I married your mother, I felt it was binding. Not in a religious sense but because I loved her deeply. I'd never met anyone like her and I couldn't imagine ever wanting to be with another woman. Besides, I thought that if anything happened to me and she came back for you, then at least she'd have some money to support you both.'

Frankie nodded then released a deep sigh.

'What a complicated history.'

Her father glanced at her. 'I'm sorry, angel. I let you and Freya down.'

'Dad, it's what we do from here that matters.'

He flashed her a smile.

'Do you think Grandma will be OK?'

'I don't know. I hope so, because whatever she's done, she's still my mother. I still love her, even though she was never the warmest of women. I think that's another reason why I fell for your mother. Freya is the warmest woman in the world. She lights up a room when she enters it and she has a way of making you feel better about everything.'

'Sounds to me like you still have feelings for her.' Frankie gazed out of the windscreen but from the corner of her eye, she saw her father's cheek darken.

'Between you and me, Frankie, I never stopped loving her. Never will. She's the only woman for me, even if she doesn't feel the same. I wouldn't expect her to care for me after what happened.' He adjusted his grip on the steering wheel then cleared his throat, as if embarrassed to admit that he could understand why Freya could never love him again.

And Frankie wondered, how did Freya feel? Was it possible that she still had feelings for Hugo or would that be too much to hope for? It was rather a lot to hope for.

'I love you, Dad.'

'I love you more.'

―

Jonas and Freya had walked for miles. They'd taken the Tube into central London and Freya had shown him around the city she used to live in, keen to distract them both from where Frankie and Hugo had gone. It wasn't for Jonas to worry, of course, because Frankie wasn't his girlfriend, but he couldn't help it. Freya had spoken to him that morning after Frankie and Hugo had gone, telling him more about Helen Ashford and how she'd made Freya feel she wasn't good enough for her son. From what Jonas could gather, Helen Ashford was a hard woman and she had a sharp tongue. He hated the thought of her upsetting Frankie and Hugo but he was also worried that Frankie would be upset at seeing her grandmother in a hospital bed. It was all very complicated indeed.

'Where shall we go next?' Freya looked at her watch. They had just grabbed a sandwich and coffee in a small cafe and were back out on the street. He pulled his beanie down over his ears and tucked his hands in his coat pocket.

'Do you think they'll be home yet?'

Freya met his eyes and he could see how worried she was too.

'Maybe.'

'Shall we head back and find out?'

'OK.'

She tucked her arm into his and they headed for the nearest Tube station, the wind making their eyes sting and goose pimples rise on his skin. Norway could be cold but the way the wind howled around the streets of London made it like a freezer.

Jonas chatted on their journey home, about the landmarks they'd seen and how impressive they were. His favourites had been the cosy pubs and the markets where you could buy just about anything. He had enjoyed himself but knew he'd have enjoyed it more if Frankie had been with them. The more time he spent with her, the more he liked her, and the more he saw of her, the more he wanted to. She was a fascinating woman and he was growing increasingly fond of her.

Too fond perhaps, seeing as how they were going back to Norway in two days. Freya said she'd have liked to stay longer but they couldn't leave the shop indefinitely and Jonas didn't like to leave Luna with his mum for long periods. She loved Luna but found her hard to walk at times, and Jonas knew it was because his mum was too soft with her. Luna was an angel on the lead for him, so he knew she took advantage when she stayed with his mum. At least they'd be having lots of cuddles.

When they arrived back at the house, Freya walked up the steps first and knocked on the door. Hugo opened it almost immediately, and the smile that spread across his face made him appear twenty years younger.

'You're back!' His voice sounded relieved, as if he'd suspected they might not return.

Inside, Freya shrugged out of her coat and scarf.

'How did it go, Hugo?'

'All right, actually. Better than Frankie and I had anti-cipated, I think.'

Jonas looked around, wondering where Frankie was.

'She's gone for a nap,' Hugo said, nodding at the stairs. 'It was quite draining.'

'Are you tired too?' Freya asked.

'No, I'm fine. I'll go and put the kettle on.'

'Great idea.'

Freya followed Hugo through to the kitchen.

Jonas hung his coat and hat on the stand then paused. Freya and Hugo might want some time alone to talk, so he would go up to his room and read for a bit. He didn't want to be in the way and he had so been looking forward to seeing Frankie that he had to fight off the disappointment.

Yes, he'd go and lose himself in a book then possibly take a nap himself. At least when he woke up, Frankie would be up and about too.

He climbed the stairs, two at a time, enjoying the feel of the plush carpet beneath his soles and trying to work out how many people would fit on each stair at a time. They were so wide that he estimated fifteen people could stand on one stair if they turned sideways and were squashed together. When he reached the first landing, he turned right to go to his room but he heard a noise from the next floor, so he looked up.

'Jonas?' Frankie leant over the banister, her long hair falling either side of her face.

'You OK?'

'Yes… and no. Are you?'

'Freya walked my legs off.'

She giggled.

'Come up.'

'Up there?'

'Yes. Come on.'

'OK.'

When he reached the next landing, he made his way to the open doorway and entered the room that was directly above his own. It was the same shape and layout but clearly well lived-in. The curtains, bedside lamps and rugs were a deep, luxurious shade of purple and the wooden floorboards gleamed. Apart from the huge bed, that was draped with a large patchwork quilt in shades of pink and purple, there were two chests of drawers and an ottoman.

'Hello.'

Frankie smiled up at him. Her hair was messy, as if she'd only just woken up, and she had a slight crease on one cheek from the pillowcase. But she had colour in her cheeks and her eyes were sparkling, as if she'd rested and was recovering after a difficult time.

She was truly and utterly beautiful and desire shot through him, taking his breath away.

He broke eye contact. This was so awkward. He was in her bedroom, alone with her and thinking about making love to her. And... as he lowered his eyes again, he saw that she was wearing navy blue silky pyjamas that clung to her slender curves and that would feel delightfully soft to the touch.

He ran a finger under his shirt collar and looked around him.

'What's that door for?' He frowned. He'd seen the door to the en suite when he'd come in but there was another in the far wall.

'That's my cupboard.'

'Is it one of those walk-in things?'

'That's right. The one I used to sleep in when I was younger. Come on, I'll show you.'

She crossed the room and opened the door. A light came on in what appeared to be a small room. Jonas followed her and had to grit his teeth to stop his mouth from falling open.

The room was longer than it first appeared and must have taken up the rest of the length of the corridor. And it was full... of things. There were clothes, arranged in colour, style and designer. There were bags, at least fifty of them, in all colours and sizes. Then there were shoes. So many shoes that it made his head spin. None of the women he'd dated over the years had possessed this many clothes, bags and shoes. None of them had possessed this kind of wealth. He'd known from the house and things they'd said that Frankie came from money but this was insane. Frankie didn't act like she was privileged or spoilt but she clearly had everything, every material thing, she could ever want. Jonas lived in a small rented apartment where his clothes lived in a bag or on hangers on the back of the door. He had his winter clothing and boots for his expeditions and his photography gear, but apart from that, he slept in a single bed and his room would have fitted into this cupboard five times over.

It hit him like a brick between the eyes.

As much as he liked Frankie and wanted her, it could never happen; they were just too different and from such different worlds. He wondered what she would think if he took her back to his mother's apartment, and the thought that she might look down on him, look down on his mum and her simple existence, hurt him. He couldn't allow that to happen. He couldn't subject his mum to that or face being a disappointment to Frankie. Jonas was proud of his roots, of his hardworking mother and of how she had brought him up, but he couldn't see how Frankie would appreciate his home or his lifestyle.

Her hand on his arm startled him.

'Jonas.'

She was so close he could have slipped his arm around her waist and pulled her against his chest, run his hands over her silky pyjamas then lifted her and carried her back to the bed. It was what he wanted to do, to shower her with kisses, to let her know how special she was and how beautiful.

He coughed then tucked his hands into his jeans pockets to stop them misbehaving.

'Jonas, are you OK?'

'Yeah…' His voice came out squeaky so he cleared his throat a few times. 'I'm fine. I was just wondering how things went for you today.'

'I'll tell you all about it. Come on, let's go and sit down.'

Jonas turned but something caught his eye. 'Where does that lead?'

Between the rails at the back of the cupboard he could see another door.

'Oh… uh, it's just another cupboard.'

'These old houses are like mazes, aren't they? What's in there?'

'My clothes.'

'*More* clothes?'

'No, not MY clothes but clothes I've designed.'

'Wow! Can I see them?'

'Really?'

'Well, of course.'

'All right. But… bear in mind they're just things I put together from my own designs. I haven't had any proper training and I used a sewing machine I bought and stowed away in here.' She pointed at a box tucked under one of the rails.

'Why is it hidden?'

'Grandma didn't approve. So I used to come in here to sew when I knew she was out.'

'But... you're a grown woman. She couldn't have stopped you, surely?'

Frankie shook her head. 'No, but she would have expressed her disapproval so it was easier to indulge my "little hobby" privately.' She air-quoted little hobby.

'That's a shame.'

'I could have moved out, set up on my own. I was going to, but then I started seeing Rolo and there didn't seem any point moving twice. In fact, I think living here meant I had a way of getting out of seeing him as much as I would have, had I had my own place.'

Jonas nodded, not sure what to say.

'Anyway, go sit in my room and I'll bring my designs through, so you can see them properly.'

'I can't wait to see them.'

'Well, no laughing.' She wagged a finger at him.

'Absolutely no laughing at all.' He flashed her a smile then walked through to her room and sat on the purple chair in front of the window.

Waiting for Frankie to share her secret designs with him, he hoped he would have the strength not to fall for her, because there could never be a future for them, and walking away if he did fall for her would be enough to break him. He'd never been in love before and he didn't want to be now. If only his heart realized that too.

Chapter 27

Frankie's belly flipped as she stood back and surveyed the array of garments on her bed. She'd never actually set them all out like this before, so hadn't realized how many she'd made. It was laying her dreams bare in front of the first and only man who had shown interest in what they were. No one in her life had ever asked her to do that before, not even her father and certainly not Rolo. In fact, Rolo had laughed when she'd once told him about her fashion designer aspirations, so she'd downplayed it and never broached the subject with him again. She'd doubted that she was good enough, told herself that it was just a hobby and that other people would probably think she was mad when she earned so much from her 'real' job. It had meant that for years, she'd created in secret, designing and making garments from dresses to tunics to playsuits to pashminas.

She raised her eyes to look at Jonas, wary of his reaction. If he laughed, just as Rolo had, then she'd put this dream well and truly behind her.

But his expression made something inside her shift. It was like an uncoiling, as if something had been tightly wound for a very long time and now, kind-hearted Jonas was gently freeing it with his compassion, teasing it out and encouraging it to fly.

He got up from the chair by the window and walked to her side, then gazed down at the clothing. His Adam's apple bobbed and he whistled long and low.

'You made all of these?'

She nodded.

'I'm no expert, Frankie, but I'm pretty certain that these are incredible.'

'Really? You don't have to be kind.'

'I wouldn't do that to you. If I thought they weren't that good, I'd say so... well, words to that effect. But you have talent, Frankie.'

He leant forwards and picked up a sleeveless layered dress that she'd created a few weeks earlier. It was made of pale-blue silk and as he held it up, the dress fell like a waterfall to the floor. The fishtail hem drifted across the wooden boards of her room and the front seemed to billow as if in a breeze.

'This could be a wedding gown, Frankie, or a prom dress. It's so soft... I feel bad touching it with my big old hands. You should show your parents. They'll be really impressed.'

'Oh... I don't know.'

'I do. Wait here.'

He gently laid the dress back on the bed then disappeared and she heard his heavy tread as he went downstairs.

Jonas thought she had talent and had told her he wouldn't mislead her. However, as he'd also said, he was no expert. But it was nice to have someone see her designs and comment on them.

She picked up the dress and held it against her then walked over to the full-length mirror in the corner of her room. It was beautiful, and as she moved, the light made the dress shimmer, reminding her of Jonas's photographs of the northern lights.

Something occurred to her. She'd created garments in a range of colours and fabrics but blues, purples and silver were her favourites to work with. What if…

She could call it her Northern Lights range.

'Frankie?' Her mother entered her room. 'Jonas said you've got something to show us.'

'Yes—'

'Oh my goodness.' Freya was standing in front of the bed gazing at the clothes. 'Did you make all of these?'

'Yes.'

She crossed the room to stand next to her mother.

Freya raised watery eyes to meet Frankie's. 'My darling girl, you are so talented.' She reached out as if to touch the clothes, then withdrew her hand and walked around the bed looking at everything instead.

'So much beauty.'

'What's all this then?' Hugo came in. 'Frankie! You made these?'

His expression mirrored Freya's as he looked at the clothes.

'Where's Jonas?' Frankie looked behind her father.

'He's gone to get something.'

'Oh…'

'Isn't she clever?' Freya said, as she held up a long-sleeved tunic in deep purple linen. The cuffs and collar were decorated with a silver trim and Frankie had embroidered tiny stars from the V-neck right down the centre to the hem. 'I would wear this!' She turned the tunic around, causing her silver bracelets to jangle, and pressed it to her front then went to the mirror.

'It's yours.'

'What?' Freya turned around. 'Oh no, darling. I couldn't take it. Unless I paid you for it.'

'I don't want payment. I'm thrilled that you like it. No one's ever seen these before and I didn't think anyone ever would.'

'That's nice, Freya,' Jonas said as he entered the room. 'It suits you. Why don't you put it on? And Frankie, why don't you put that dress on? I have an idea.'

'You do?'

He nodded.

'Mother and daughter photo shoot.'

Frankie and Freya looked up at the same time and smiled.

'Uh, I don't know. I'm not really a fan of being photographed.'

'I think you could sell this range to a boutique owner I know in Norway. But she'll need to see pictures of it first.'

'Sell it?'

Jonas nodded, his face brightened by a big grin.

'I think he's right.' Freya walked back to the bed and picked up a silver wool pashmina with purple swirls. 'And it would be unique, not mass-produced. Who wouldn't want a range like that?'

'Go on, girls, why not?' Hugo beamed at them. 'And, Frankie… I'm sorry for not asking to see what you'd made before. It's another area where I was remiss, I'm afraid.'

'It's OK, Dad. I didn't exactly push for you to take an interest in it, did I?'

'That's not the point. I chose not to get involved with it and I should have done.'

'No more regrets, Dad. Just living for here and now and for the future.'

He nodded then sniffed before turning and walking over to the window, clearly needing a few minutes to compose himself.

'OK, let's do it,' Frankie said.

'Try them on?' Freya asked.

'Yes. An impromptu fashion show.'

'Tell you what, why not use the staircase?' Jonas pointed at the doorway. 'With the chandeliers, it's nice and bright and it'll give the shoot a dramatic old-house feel.'

'You're the photographer.' Frankie smiled at him, appreciating his enthusiasm, even if the thought of posing for photographs wearing clothes she'd designed did give her butterflies.

An hour and a half later, she sat on the bottom step next to her mother, with her right arm draped around her shoulder as they modelled the last two dresses in the range. Freya's was a silver Jane Austen style dress that was gathered beneath the bust and fell to her ankles. It showed off her mother's slim figure and the silver shimmered as she moved. Frankie was wearing a purple tie-dye playsuit that fell to mid-thigh and had spaghetti straps. Under it she wore a silver camisole. She'd paired it with purple PVC and suede Manolo Blahnik mules that had sat in her wardrobe for years and never seen the light of day. They'd been a gift from Grandma for snagging an important client, but for some reason, Frankie had never worn them. Guilt flashed through her; she had so much she'd probably forgotten they were there. She'd certainly try to ensure that she made more of an effort to go through her wardrobe in future and not to just buy more. She had so many beautiful things, probably far too many for one woman to wear in a year – and that was with three or more outfit changes a day – so she should have a good clear-out too and take some to the charity shop.

Jonas was a wonderful photographer. He made her and Freya relax and giggle as he coaxed them into different poses, including hugging, gazing off into the imaginary distance and even jumping in the air together.

'I think that's it then, ladies.' Jonas looked up from his camera. 'Well done.'

'Well done, indeed.' Her father appeared with a tray of champagne flutes and a bottle of Veuve Clicquot. 'Thought we should celebrate.'

He popped the cork then poured them all a glass and they headed into the lounge. Dusk had fallen and Frankie could see her reflection in the large windows, so she went over and closed the curtains. It heightened the sense of cosiness in the room and when she turned around, seeing her parents on one sofa and Jonas on the other, as the fire flickered in the grate and Ella Fitzgerald crooned from Hugo's old record player about the man she loved, heat warmed Frankie's chest then emanated throughout her whole body. Moments like this were to be treasured.

If only things could stay this way.

But that was the problem.

Jonas and her mother had lives in Norway and she and her father had lives in London. They had Grandma to care for and the house to maintain and she had her job…

Her job.

She'd been on leave because of the wedding and the thought of returning to her role as a management consultant made her throat tighten, as if invisible hands were choking her. How would she be able to do it?

She went over to the sofa and sat next to Jonas. He smiled at her then handed her his camera. 'Take a look. You and Freya are naturals.'

She placed her champagne on the side table then started to flick through the photographs. He was right. They did look as though they'd done this before but it was all down to Jonas; he was the talented one. She darted a glance at him, her pulse racing as she tried to focus on the photographs.

'I do wish that wasn't the case.' Her father's words snapped her back to their conversation.

'What case?' she asked.

'Your mother and Jonas have to go back to Norway on Thursday.'

'So soon?'

'There's the gallery, my mother and Luna to think of.' Jonas cleared his throat. 'I wish we didn't have to go yet but... well...' He let the silence hang between them but Frankie replayed his words *I wish we didn't have to go yet* over and over.

He wanted to stay?

'Can't you stay a bit longer?' She looked at Jonas then at her mother.

'I wish we could, Frankie, but with Christmas coming, I can't leave the gallery for long.'

Frankie nodded then lowered her eyes to the camera and continued pressing the button that scrolled through the images, barely seeing them because of the tears blurring her vision.

They had to go; she knew that. She'd known it from the moment they'd got on the plane to London with her, but now... now that it was about to happen... she wished with all her heart that they could stay.

The next morning, Frankie woke when it was still dark. She tried to fall back to sleep but her mind wouldn't stop racing, so she decided to get up and make a cup of tea.

She padded quietly down the stairs and through the hallway, keen to avoid making any noise that might wake anyone else. The grandfather clock in the hallway struck five just as she passed it, causing her to jump. She clutched a hand over her pounding heart and hurried by, realizing that it was so early that even Annie wasn't awake. She pulled her baggy cardigan tight over her pyjamas because the central heating hadn't come on yet and the large house was cold and draughty.

In the kitchen, she filled the kettle then switched it on before dropping a teabag into a mug. She crossed the room to fetch the milk and peered into the large fridge, wondering if she was hungry. Nothing appealed, so she grabbed the milk then closed the door.

And gasped when she realized she wasn't alone.

'Sorry, Frankie, I didn't mean to startle you.' Her mother rubbed her arm gently. 'I couldn't sleep so I came down to get a drink.'

'Me too.' Frankie held up the milk. 'Tea?'

'Yes, please.'

Frankie went over to the door and turned the lights on, closing the door carefully to avoid waking anyone else, then she got another mug from the cupboard and made the tea. In her big slipper boots, she shuffled across the kitchen and handed Freya her mug.

'Shall we sit down or are you going back to bed?' Freya asked.

'No, I won't be able to sleep.' Frankie shook her head. 'Shall we sit in here?'

They pulled out stools from under the kitchen island in the centre of the large room and sat down, both nursing their mugs.

'Why couldn't you sleep?' Frankie asked.

'Too many thoughts swirling around in my head.' Freya rubbed her eyes. 'It's so strange being back here, in this house. At every turn I'm being assaulted by memories and ghosts.'

'Is it awful?'

'Not awful… some of the memories are good but because of how things ended, it's also a bit unsettling. It makes me wish that I could go back in time and change things.'

'I know.' Frankie sipped her tea, finding comfort in the familiar act. She could understand how it must be odd for her mother to be in the house after so long, and how the past must be ever present here. 'I guess when I asked you to stay I didn't really think it through properly. All I could see was that I wanted you to stay.'

'It's fine and I'm glad we came. It's been lovely to spend time with you and Hugo again.'

'Are you all right with Dad now? I mean, I know that must also be very strange but you two do seem to get on so well.'

Freya chewed her bottom lip then sipped her tea. As she exhaled, steam drifted from her tea and disappeared into the air. If only hurt and regret could do the same, Frankie thought, then it would be a lot easier to move on.

'It's a complicated situation for Hugo and me. There's a lot of hurt there and we definitely need to talk a lot more. We're both sorry for the past and for the pain and sadness that we caused each other, and you, of course, but even with all the anger and… the rest, I don't hate him. I can see how sorry he is that he didn't do more to protect me from Helen and I know now why he didn't come after me. If only we had spoken more then, we might have been able to save things, to find a way to be together as a family. But, as with all things, people can be stubborn, they can be angry and they can run away to avoid any more confrontation. Hugo and I did both, and we know that we should have spoken sooner. However, we were a lot younger then and life was… more intense because of your grandmother and because of our different backgrounds. Love can work between people from different classes, even different countries, cultures and religions, I'm sure of it. But back then, it seems that neither of us was one hundred per cent convinced of that, and insecurities, along with my illness and Helen's interference, all seemed to be insurmountable.'

Frankie reached out and took her mother's hand. 'So what happens now?'

Freya smiled. 'Now, we get on with our lives but we keep talking. We see what we can fix, mainly to make your life as good as it can be, and… to be honest, I'd like to have Hugo in my life again, even in the capacity of friend. We were friends before we fell in love and I have missed him.' She squeezed Frankie's hand. 'Whatever happened between us, we will always have you and that means we have a bond that exists through you.'

Frankie nodded. 'I'm glad. I'd like you to be able to get on because I want to see more of you and if you hated Dad, it would be quite difficult.'

'We don't hate each other. We never did, Frankie. Life just got in the way, as it sometimes does.'

'Do you want more tea?'

'Yes!' Freya frowned. 'Do you know... I used to do a lot of baking in this kitchen when Hugo and I were first married.'

'What did you bake?'

'Oh, all sorts of things. I loved this kitchen and how much space there is to move around. The oven is new, of course, but look at it. I bet you could make cakes and pies and scones all at the same time with the double ovens.'

Frankie looked at the oven and a wave of sadness washed over her. It was something she'd often thought of as a child, being able to bake with her mother, to do all those normal things that families did. But that time had passed and she couldn't get it back.

'Frankie, darling, would you like to make something with me?'

'What? Now?'

Freya nodded. 'Why not? We're both awake and soon we'll be hungry. Why don't we see what's in the cupboards then whip up some scrummy delights to surprise your father and Jonas?'

'I'd love to.'

Frankie's stomach fizzed with delight as she located some aprons and washed her hands at the sink. She didn't know if Freya realized how wonderful her suggestion was, but for Frankie it meant a great deal.

One by one, her dreams were coming true...

–

Jonas descended the stairs slowly, yawning as he reached the ground floor. He'd woken from a deep sleep and felt quite rested, even though it had taken him a while to drop off the night before. He'd had a lot of fun taking photographs of Frankie and Freya as they modelled Frankie's fashion range and it had been a good evening, but later on, when Freya had told Frankie that they had to return to Norway, he'd seen sadness settle in Frankie's features.

It had hurt him to see it. Strangely. As if their connection had deepened further. He'd been glad to go to bed, hoping it was the effect of the champagne and the fun they'd had, that he was just getting carried away with everything because of that and because he was in a foreign country. Back home in Norway, with his mother at hand, he'd feel differently, he was sure.

At least he hoped he would. Otherwise, leaving Frankie behind when he went home was going to prove to be tough. He hated to think of her here alone, except for her father, rattling around in this big old house, wondering whether her grandmother was going to make it home from hospital and when she'd be able to see Freya again.

Never before had life seemed so complicated.

Or so… exciting. It was strange, this rolling in his stomach that thinking of Frankie created, but it was there and he couldn't deny it. He liked being with her, seeing her smile and even though he knew that she was from a very different background to him, he couldn't suppress the way he desired her. He didn't want to suppress it because it was so different from anything he'd experienced before. And yet… surely this was just a one-way street to heartbreak for both of them, that was if Frankie even saw him that way, of course.

He crossed the hallway, the grey light of a winter's morning making him shiver, and just as he reached the kitchen door, the grandfather clock chimed seven o'clock and made him jump. What was it with clocks like that? Why did it have to be so loud? His internal body clock was pretty accurate, so he'd never feel the need for a huge clock like that to remind him what time it was, even with the time difference.

The kitchen door was closed and he stood outside it, wondering if there was some upper-class custom that said you couldn't enter when it was closed.

Then he heard laughter from behind it so he pressed his ear to the wood.

And listened.

He could hear Frankie and Freya, chattering away, as well as pots and pans clattering and clunking. What were they doing in there?

'Can I help you?'

A voice from behind made him turn quickly and he lost his balance. He flung his arms out to steady himself and grabbed the kitchen door handle, which swung open under his weight, sending him flying into the kitchen.

He closed his eyes for a moment, willing what had just happened to undo, but when he opened them he found three women staring down at him: Freya, Frankie and Annie the housekeeper who'd startled him in the hallway.

'Jonas!' Freya knelt at his side. 'Are you all right?'

Frankie knelt next to her and placed her hand on his arm. 'Jonas? Can you hear us?'

He smiled then nodded. 'I'm fine. I just slipped as I went to open the door.'

'Hmmm.' Annie's noise of disapproval made him blush.

'I wondered what was going on in here and didn't want to come in unless it was OK to do so.' He sat up and rubbed his shoulder, the part of him to hit the floor first. 'I didn't want to disturb you.'

'It's fine,' Freya said as she stood up and held out a hand to him. 'Frankie and I were making breakfast.'

There was a gasp from Annie as she entered the kitchen and looked around her at the mess. There were pots and pans on every surface, cracked eggs, bags of sugar and flour littered the island and Frankie and Freya were covered in flour too, as if they'd been throwing it up in the air then dancing around as it fell. But they were grinning broadly and the kitchen was filled with the most delicious aromas of cakes and pastries.

Jonas allowed Frankie to lead him to a stool at the island and to help him to sit down, even though she was much smaller than he was and even though he didn't really need her help; his pride was a bit bruised but the rest of him wasn't hurt at all.

'Don't worry, Annie, we'll clean it all up.' Freya gestured at the mess.

'Yes, Annie, why don't you go and relax?' Frankie said. 'In fact, take the day off.'

Annie frowned. 'Oh, I couldn't do that. Mr Ashford might need me.'

'No, it's fine. Go and have a nice day. Grandma's not here and I'll make sure your wages aren't affected.'

Annie looked at the mess once more, then at Freya and Frankie, then she smiled briefly, as if she was unaccustomed to being given extra holidays.

'Well… if you're sure.'

'I am! Bye!' Frankie ushered the older woman from the kitchen then turned back to Jonas and Freya.

'Are you sure you didn't hurt yourself, Jonas?'

'I'm fine, honestly. I take it that you two have been having some fun?'

'Oh yes.' Freya opened the oven door and lifted out a tray of enormous muffins. 'We've been baking together.'

'For the first time.' Frankie smiled then went and got a tray of pastries out of the other oven.

When she placed them on the island in front of Jonas, then met his gaze, there were tears in her eyes.

But Jonas could tell that they were happy ones.

—

Frankie finished loading the dishwasher then closed the door.

'All done?' Freya asked as she folded a cloth over and placed it next to the sink.

'I think so.' Frankie scanned the kitchen, looking for flour, utensils or crumbs that they might have missed during their big clean-up, but she didn't spot any. Her eyes landed on Jonas who was sweeping the floor around the island in the middle of the kitchen. He was wearing a white T-shirt and baggy grey jogging bottoms that sat on his slim hips. He looked too big for the room, as if he was some kind of giant better suited to the wilds of Norway than an English kitchen. But he did look good, with his blond hair tied back from his face and his golden beard shining in the electric light.

'Well, in that case, it's time to eat!' Freya announced.

'Thank goodness for that. I'm losing weight as I sweep. And I can't help drooling… over the food you've baked, I mean.'

Pink spots appeared on Jonas's cheeks and Frankie wondered why he'd felt the need to mention the food. What else would he have been drooling over? Unless…

Surely it couldn't be her in her silky pyjamas and apron, sleeves rolled up and covered in flour with her hair in a messy bun? She was hardly picture-perfect this morning but she didn't care. She'd had a blast baking with Freya, and they had made muffins, cherry tarts, sultana scones and cheese scones. The kitchen smelt glorious, homely, and as Freya taught her how to rub butter into the flour for pastry and scones and how to rest the pastry before rolling it out, Frankie had felt the bond between them deepen. It was such a simple act, that of baking, but it could be so much fun. Freya had proved to be a patient teacher, evidently as keen to teach as Frankie was to learn, and Frankie had experienced a shifting inside, as she accepted that although they'd never be able to turn back the clock, they could build on their relationship from now on. Maybe even spend more days like this, waking early and enjoying a mug of tea as the sky outside turned from black to grey, as the house warmed up and the wind outside howled around, as the sky threatened more wintry weather. During the past few hours, even when Jonas had come down, Frankie had felt warmer than she ever had done before, as if the only thing that mattered was the here and now, right here at the heart of her home.

And it was all because of Freya. Her mother had come home. At last.

Of course, she was leaving the next day, but Frankie knew that they'd stay in touch now. As for Jonas, who knew? She really hoped so.

'Jonas, help yourself now.'

'He already has.' Freya giggled. 'But we do need more tea and perhaps someone should wake your father.'

'No need.' Hugo entered the kitchen, freshly shaven, showered and dressed. 'The delicious aromas drifted up the stairs and woke me up. Looks like we're in for a treat, eh, Jonas?'

Jonas nodded, pointing at his mouth to show that it was full of muffin.

'I could get used to this,' Hugo said quietly, as if to himself.

'To having cakes baked for you in the morning?' Freya asked as she switched the kettle on.

'That…' Hugo nodded. 'And to having you all here, to having a family.'

So could I, Frankie thought. *So could I.*

Chapter 28

The drive to the airport on Thursday was quiet, as the previous day had been following the enjoyable morning of baking. Frankie and her father had visited Grandma in the afternoon, and when they'd returned, Jonas and Freya were packed and ready to leave early the next day to catch their flight. They ate dinner around the dining room table and talked about Christmas plans and the music charts, about art, science and photography. Then they'd all gone to bed before ten, agreeing that an early start would require an early night, but knowing that they wouldn't sleep well.

Sadness gnawed at Frankie as Hugo pulled into a space in the short-stay car park. She'd only just got Freya back and saying goodbye to her was going to be painful. And there was Jonas. Her feelings for him were so conflicting. She was physically attracted to him but there was more to it than that. Something inside her seemed to recognize something inside him, as if they were kindred spirits, drawn together by something she couldn't explain. But, of course, she was probably being overly romantic even entertaining such thoughts. Frankie wasn't a starry-eyed dreamer, never had been at any rate, but the handsome Norwegian made her want to be.

If she was a hopeless romantic, if she had that wonderful sense of abandonment and wasn't hindered by her upbringing and by social awkwardness, then she'd fling herself into his arms at the airport and kiss him as if tomorrow would never come. She'd give her heart to him, even though she didn't know if he really wanted to take it. She'd…

'Are you coming, Frankie?' Her dad had opened her door and was smiling as he held out his hand.

'Oh! Yes.' Her cheeks burned as she got out so she made a show of tucking her skinny jeans into her brown ankle boots to give them some time to cool.

Some time to get a grip!

She shook her head as they walked towards the airport terminal. Frankie Ashford needed to sort her life out, not lose her heart to unrequited love. Jonas had only ever been kind to her and besides, he lived in Norway, she lived in England. It might even be why she found herself attracted to him: because she could never have him; this could never work. Perhaps Jonas was the perfect man for her to yearn for because nothing could ever come of it. The automated doors swished open and they passed through, entering the airport terminal. Even though it was early, the airport was busy, with people arriving to collect relatives coming to London for Christmas shopping and celebrations, and those jetting off to foreign climes for the holidays. Frankie couldn't help wishing that they were collecting her mother and Jonas rather than dropping them off.

They walked further into the building and the aromas of coffee and pastries filled the air. Frankie's stomach grumbled, reminding her that it was empty. Her father had made plenty of toast but she'd been unable to force a mouthful down, even declining some of the melt-in-the-mouth muffins they'd baked the previous day, although she had drunk two mugs of coffee in an attempt to wake herself up after a restless night.

'I guess we need to check in,' Freya said to Jonas.

He nodded. His face was pale in the false lighting of the airport and he'd tied his hair back which showed off his manly beard.

'Well, uh… it's been really good seeing you, Freya,' Hugo said awkwardly. This was the man Frankie knew and recognized, as if saying goodbye to his wife had turned him back into his regular self.

'Oh come here, you fool!' Freya opened her arms and hugged Hugo. He stiffened then relaxed and hugged Freya back. They stayed that way for a while, as if afraid to finally let go.

'I'll let you know once I've shown the photographs to my friend.' Jonas adjusted his bag strap up his shoulder. 'Hopefully it'll be before Christmas but if not, very soon after.'

'Thank you. I still can't quite believe you thought the range was good enough.'

'Believe me, it's very good indeed.'

His blue eyes roamed her face and she gazed into them, wanting to remember exactly how beautiful they were. She was worried that she'd forget as soon as she left the airport, that he was a part of something she'd never be able to fully hold onto. And that applied to her mother too. Letting them go was one of the hardest things she'd ever done.

'What will you do now?' Jonas asked.

'Go home.'

'No… I mean, over the next few days.'

'Try to deal with my clients and to sort them a suitable replacement… if I'm really going to do this, that is. Make some serious decisions about my future. Start shopping for Christmas, which I'll spend quietly with Dad. Visit Grandma some more.' Weariness overwhelmed her. It all seemed insurmountable, challenging and exhausting.

A woman squealed then ran past them before flinging herself into the arms of a man in uniform. A soldier home for the holidays. They hugged then leant back and eyed each other, oblivious to everything else as he tenderly took her face in his hands and they kissed.

Frankie dragged her gaze away. Why was it that she was saying goodbye when other people were welcoming the people they cared about home?

The people they cared about…

She cared about Freya, of course she did, and now… it seemed that she cared about Jonas too.

'Speak soon then.' Jonas leant forwards and she moved into his embrace, lifting onto her tiptoes to wrap her arms around his neck. She made to kiss his cheek but he turned his head and her lips brushed his instead. They both gasped and pulled away then gazed at each other. His pupils were large and dark, his lips parted. She wanted to kiss him again, to see if she'd really felt that powerful jolt of electricity, or if she'd imagined it. If it had been created by the friction between her soles and the airport tiles.

'Jonas,' she whispered.

He shook his head then took her hand and kissed it.

'But…'

'I can't.' He sighed. 'I'm so sorry. I just can't.'

'Frankie?' She turned to her mother and saw that she was holding hands with her father.

'Yes?'

'I'll phone every day and we'll get together very soon.'

Frankie nodded then embraced Freya, breathing in her floral perfume and hugging her tight. Her heart felt as though it had cracked and would shatter into a thousand pieces as soon as her mother let her go. She couldn't let go…

'Freya?' It was Jonas. 'We'd better check in now.'

'Of course.' Freya nodded then squeezed Frankie hard before releasing her. 'I love you so much, my darling daughter. I am so proud of the beautiful, bright, strong woman you have become. I have always loved you and I always will. Look after your dad, won't you?' She kissed Frankie's cheek then Hugo's. 'And you look after our baby girl.'

She went to say more, but her eyes glistened and she shook her head then mouthed *Speak soon*, before allowing Jonas to guide her away.

Hugo wrapped an arm around Frankie's shoulder and they watched as Freya and Jonas were swallowed up by the airport, dragging their cases behind them.

'Come on, Frankie. Let's go home.'

She nodded, unable to reply, and when she met her father's eyes, she saw that they were filled with tears too.

–

On the plane, Jonas flicked through his mobile, looking at the photographs he'd uploaded to his iCloud from his camera.

He'd told himself he was going to choose the best ones to show his friend with the boutique, but in reality, he needed to look at Frankie again. He came across the ones Freya had taken of him and Frankie as they fed the reindeer, and one in particular made his breath catch in his chest. Freya had captured them gazing at each other in the intense way that lovers might do. They'd only said goodbye a few hours ago but already he felt as though she was slipping away, that if he didn't see the green sparkle of her eyes, the luminescence of her skin and the shine of her silky brown hair, he would lose her for ever.

And what had happened at the airport? They'd hugged, then accidentally kissed and something had shot through Jonas, something he was pretty certain he'd never felt before. Frankie had jolted his very core with a gentle brush of her lips. He'd yearned to pull her close and kiss her properly, to lift her into his arms and carry her off somewhere quiet so he could truly appreciate her and show her how wonderful he thought she was. But, of course, they'd been in a busy airport, not far from her parents, and he was about to check in for his flight home.

She'd tried to speak to him but he'd had to tell her he couldn't. Couldn't speak about it. Couldn't do it. Couldn't allow himself to fall for her. Couldn't vocalize the confusing mass of thoughts and emotions swirling around inside him. How was it even possible to feel this way about a woman he barely knew?

It had been a strange two weeks. Frankie had arrived in Oslo to find her mother, and Jonas had met her in the process. She'd seemed damaged, vulnerable and in need of tenderness and reassurance. At first, he'd thought she might just be rich and spoilt, and after seeing her enormous, and clearly expensive, home, as well as her wardrobe full of things, it would have been understandable if she had been shallow and self-centred. But she wasn't. At all. She was sweet and funny, kind and caring. She worried about other people and clearly wanted to do her best to make them happy.

Yes, she was a bit of a fashionista; she loved clothes and shoes and fabrics and a good lifestyle. But there was nothing arrogant or horrid about Frankie at all. There was an inherent goodness, a desire to create and to express her love of the world around her through her creations. He could see it clearly now; she was an artist with a keen eye, just like him. She saw things that many others wouldn't even notice, whether it was a shade of colour that matched another, or a texture that gave a garment an extra layer, an extra dimension. Frankie could, if she returned his fondness for her, give his existence another layer, another dimension.

And yet... Jonas lived a simple life. He could never offer her all the things she would want. Jonas took his pleasure from nature, from a beautiful sunset or a freshly fallen blanket of snow. There was purity in the natural world that humankind often lacked, and he wondered how far Frankie might have been corrupted by her affluent upbringing, innocent as she still seemed to be. Jonas knew that as much as he loved to travel, he would never want to leave Norway permanently. London was magnificent but it was so busy, so cosmopolitan and so far removed from what he needed on a daily basis to thrive. As fabulous as Frankie's home was, he couldn't live somewhere like that full time; it would suffocate him. He rarely spent more than a few weeks at his mother's apartment, needing the open vastness of the Norwegian countryside, the endless plains and skies that allowed him to really breathe.

Frankie was a city girl. An English woman. Rich beyond his imaginings.

They were very different and even if there was an attraction between them, a meeting of minds, there could never be anything more permanent. Frankie had grown up wealthy and never wanted for anything material. All Jonas could ever offer her would be himself. How could that be enough? Sooner or later, a man from her set would come and turn her eye, steal her away and Jonas would be broken by that. Better not to let it begin…

He gazed at the photograph that he'd zoomed in on, of Frankie wearing the blue silk dress, and ran a finger over her face. What he wanted and what he could have were two very different things.

He switched his mobile off then tucked it into his shirt pocket.

'You OK, Jonas?' Freya asked from the seat next to him. He'd thought she was snoozing; her eyes had been closed when he'd pulled out his mobile. Had she seen him looking at photographs of her daughter?

'Yeah, I guess so.'

'She's very special, isn't she?'

He nodded.

'You'd be good together.'

He turned to her and smiled.

'How're you? I thought I'd never manage to get you away from Hugo.'

She wrinkled her nose. 'That was tough. Almost as tough as leaving him the first time around. However, I now know that we'll stay in touch and who knows…'

'Who knows?'

'What the future holds.'

She smiled then closed her eyes, signalling that it was OK for him to go back to his own musings.

He peered out the window at the bright white clouds. Freya had been through so much and yet emerged from it so positive. She'd suffered for years and lost not only her husband but also her child. And now... she'd reunited with them and there was a chance that there could be more for the three of them in the future.

Freya could have put a thousand genuine obstacles in the way of her and Hugo, easily prevented any sort of attachment from re-forming. But she hadn't. She'd gone with the flow, allowed Hugo to explain, and even when his explanation had been about his guilt and what he saw as his weaknesses, Freya had not judged him. She was prepared to give him – to give them – a chance. At what, it wasn't yet clear, but it seemed that she wasn't ruling anything out.

Jonas, on the other hand, was repeating to himself all the reasons why he could never be with Frankie. Another one being the fact that Freya was his friend and if it didn't work out with Frankie, then he might ruin things with Freya too. It wasn't like him to be negative and to harden his heart to his desires, but his desires had never included a beautiful Englishwoman before. A woman who reached inside him and made his heart squeeze.

It hit him like a blow to the jaw.

Jonas was afraid.

He'd always analysed his feelings and behaviour, finding it fascinating to consider why he did what he did as well as why other people behaved as they did. When he allowed his mind to mull over things, he usually came to a conclusion that told him more about himself and others.

And now, it seemed, he was searching for reasons why he couldn't be with Frankie. For reasons why he couldn't pursue her as his heart wanted him to.

He needed to get back to Norway and to head out into the countryside.

Only then, when he was at one with nature, would he be able to free his mind and heart and to think clearly about what it was that he really wanted. Without hindrance, without excuses and without hesitation.

Chapter 29

Frankie entered the cafe and looked around. Jen waved at her from a booth, so she made her way over, carefully weaving between tables and chairs, trying not to fall over people's shopping bags and small children.

'It's so busy!' she said when she'd returned her friend's hug.

'Christmas is almost upon us, Frankie, what do you expect?'

Just over three weeks had passed since Freya and Jonas had returned to Norway. In that time, Frankie had moved her client list on to colleagues, tied up the loose ends from her business and dealt with all the paperwork with the bank and solicitors. It felt good to free herself from the career she'd never wanted, if terrifying letting go of the security it had given her.

Jen flicked her long blonde hair then ran her fingers though it before pulling it over her left shoulder. She was, as always, flawlessly made-up from her smoky-grey eyes to her plumped-up pink lips.

'What is it? Why're you staring? Have I got a rash from the threading?' Jen's eyes widened as she ran a long finger over her top lip, the tiny diamond on her manicured nail glinting in the light.

'No, no rash.' Frankie shook her head. 'You look amazing, as always.'

Jen grinned. 'I'm all ready for the holidays. I'm hoping Henry will surprise me with a sunshine break, to be honest. I've dropped enough hints and... just in case he does... I've been waxed, threaded, tanned and bleached, so I am bikini ready, baby!' She flashed her pure white teeth and fluttered her fake eyelashes.

'You've only just got back from Florida, Jen.' Frankie laughed. They hadn't been able to get together until now because Frankie had been so busy with sorting her life out and Jen had been away with her sister in America.

'I know but this would be a holiday for Henry and me to have some alone time. We need to get working on our baby plans.'

'Well, let's hope Santa does leave you a break in the Bahamas in your stocking.'

Jen wrinkled her nose. 'Oh God, don't talk to me about stockings! That's all Henry wants right now... you know... the full shebang.'

Frankie frowned.

'You know... stockings, suspenders, basque. I don't know what's got into him.'

Frankie nodded, hoping the women at the next table had gone quiet because they were eating and not because they were eavesdropping.

'Remember a few Christmases ago when I had a whole load of... leather gear under the tree because he'd seen me reading *Fifty Shades* and thought that was what I'd want?' She rolled her eyes. 'The last book I read was a Mary Berry cookbook, so am I going to find a white wig and apron in my stocking?'

'Probably a new bakeware set.'

They laughed together then, causing one of the women at the other table to cast them a curious glance.

'Ooh I've missed you, Frankie. How are you, darling?'

Frankie gave her a quick rundown about Freya and Jonas and their visit to London. She had spoken to Jen on the phone but not wanted to go into detail about everything because it still felt too raw. Watching them leave at the airport had cut her deeply.

'How're you feeling about everything? It must be amazing to meet your mother after all that time.'

'It was. And she's just so lovely, Jen. She's sweet, kind and beautiful. She has her own art gallery and she's doing really well. When she came back with me and was reunited with Dad… even though it was just for a few days… well, it was just better than I could have hoped for.'

'Why? You don't think they still have feelings for each other, do you?'

'Without a doubt. What will come of it, I have no idea, but at least they can be civil.'

'It must've been strange for them to see each other after all that time?'

'I have no doubt that it was but they also seemed… really happy to be reunited.'

'Wow. Just wow! What about you?'

'What about me?'

'Are you happy to see them like that? Will you see more of your mother now?'

Around them people chatted to friends and loved ones, children squealed, laughed and cried. The noise was comforting, it showed that life continued whatever was happening in Frankie's world, that the emptiness inside her because she missed her mother – and, if she was being fully honest, because she missed Jonas – hadn't affected anyone else. The familiar carols that drifted from the speakers and the hum from the cappuccino machine all added to this belief, and Frankie knew that whatever happened now, she would survive. She was a survivor. She had got this far and surely life looked a lot better now than it had before?

Frankie nodded. 'Yes on both counts. It's far too early to say if my parents have any romantic inclinations, and they have things to sort out – my mother said they need to do a lot of talking – but some contact is better than no contact. And they were just so natural together. I guess it helped that Grandma wasn't around and Dad was more relaxed.'

'It would be like one of those magazine stories if they got back together. You could give *Hello* a call.'

'I doubt *Hello* would be interested in it and even if they were, I think my parents are both too private to want their lives splashed across the pages of a magazine.'

'But you have to admit that it's romantic.'

'I guess so. Or it would be if it hadn't all caused so much pain and sadness over the years.'

'They have lost out on a lot of time, haven't they?'

'Thirty years when they could have been together, possibly had more children and when I could have had a mum.'

'At least she's in your life now.' Jen squeezed her hand. 'How's your grandmother?'

Frankie winced. She hadn't told Jen about her grandmother's role in it all yet; she was still trying to process Grandma's atrocious behaviour herself. 'She's OK. The doctor says she's getting stronger every day but she looks so different in that hospital bed. It's difficult visiting her because she's not the old battleaxe I know so well.'

'How was she about your mother being back?'

'Well... see, she was partly... actually, *mainly* responsible for my mother leaving in the first place.'

'What?' Jen's eyebrows shot to her hairline.

Frankie explained what had happened when her mother left and Jen listened carefully. When Frankie had finished, Jen's eyes glistened with tears.

'That's so sad, Frankie. And yet... does it make you feel better to know that your mother didn't walk out on you... because she didn't love you?'

'Oh yes, a lot better, obviously. But I feel so sorry for her because she was pushed into leaving.'

'So, your grandmother really is a battleaxe.'

'I was so angry when I first found out about it but my mother said I need to let it go. She has. She said that holding on to the grief and anger will just hurt me in the long run, and that even if I can't forget, I need to put it to one side.'

'And you're back together now, so she's probably right. Do you also feel angry towards your dad?'

'For not standing up to Grandma?'

Jen nodded.

'Yes. I wanted to scream at him and ask why he didn't fight for his wife, but now... after seeing them together, I know there's no point. Dad was compromised because Grandma made him believe that she'd take me away from him too. He was also afraid that if he went after my mother she wouldn't want him and he couldn't face that rejection, couldn't cope alone with a young baby and the recriminations that would have followed from Grandma. He might have made the wrong decision but it was the one he thought was right at the time.'

'Poor Hugo.'

'He's a good man but he made a mistake and he's clearly punished himself over the years for it. He never even got divorced, let alone remarried, never even dated as far as I know, and I'm convinced it was because he loved my mother so much.'

'I hope they get back together at some point. It sounds like they should.'

Frankie shrugged. 'I'm just happy to know that they don't hate each other and can be friends. That's all I ever wanted growing up, and to know that my mother was there. I'm looking forward to spending more time with her.'

'Will you go back to Oslo?'

'Hopefully in the new year.'

A pang of longing pierced Frankie's chest as she thought of the beautiful city and the Norwegian countryside, of the possibility of seeing the northern lights properly and getting to know Jonas. If he wanted to get to know her better, that was.

'Anyway, tell me more about this Jonas.' Jen cocked an eyebrow.

'Nothing to tell, really.' Frankie dropped her gaze to the table and toyed with a packet of brown sugar, turning it over and over until Jen stopped her hand.

'I've known you for a very long time, Frankie, and when you say something like that I know he must mean something to you.'

'Jonas is... kind, caring and a talented photographer.'

'And gorgeous?'

'He looks like Thor. Or a Viking.'

'Thor? You mean the actor who plays Thor?'

'Yes. I guess so.'

'Or a Viking?'

'Yes.'

'Do you have a photo?'

Frankie pulled her mobile from her pocket and scrolled through the photographs. She'd taken some in Norway and some while Jonas had been in London, and she looked for the best one of his face. Gazing at him made her heart ache and she hoped it wouldn't show in her expression, so she forced her lips into a smile.

'Here you go. This was when we went to see the northern lights and met some of the huskies.'

Jen took her phone and looked at the screen then enlarged the photo with her thumb and forefinger. She raised her eyes slowly and smiled.

'He's gorgeous. Did you…?'

'Oh no. Nothing like that.'

'Why not? I would.'

'No, you wouldn't. You're married.'

'If I were single.'

'But you're not and I'm only just single.'

'You've always been single in your heart.'

Frankie met her friend's gaze and swallowed hard. Jen had hit the nail on the head; she hadn't really ever fully committed to Rolo and that had been part of the problem. But neither had he fully committed to her.

'Yes, but I have just come out of a relationship where I was engaged. I ran away from my own wedding.' She shook her head, still stunned that she'd done it.

'You did but you did it for the right reasons.' Jen sipped her coffee. 'Have you looked on Facebook recently?'

'Not for a few weeks.' She hadn't wanted to see what people were up to, to read about their joys and to see their edited photographs of perfect lives and families. Usually, she could cope with it but at the moment, she didn't feel she had the strength. Her heart had been too full of her own family and of her uncertainty about Jonas and what she wanted from him.

'Oh… uh…'

'What is it?'

'Rolo's moved on.'

'Yes, I know that. With Lorna.'

Jen shook her head. 'No, he's with someone else now.'

'Bloody hell! Who?'

'Some actress who was staying in the villa adjacent to his and Lorna's.'

'Is Lorna OK?'

'Yeah…' Jen waved a hand. 'You know her, it's probably all a PR stunt anyway. She adores some media exposure, that one.'

'So Rolo's dating an actress and Lorna's newly single?'

'For five minutes. She'll bounce back and be jolly good in no time at all.'

Frankie nodded, knowing Jen was right. Lorna had hopped from bed to bed for as long as Frankie had known her. Men, women, older, younger; it was all the same for Lorna. But Rolo's behaviour had surprised her. Had their relationship stopped him from being the lothario he'd always wanted to be, or had he merely hidden it from her?

'Do you think that Rolo was… seeing other women when we were together?'

Jen's eyes darted right then left and colour rose in her cheeks.

'Jen?'

'I'm so sorry, Frankie. I didn't know for sure and I didn't want to ruin it all for you. I hoped he'd settle down once you were married, that once he put a ring on your finger, he'd be faithful.'

Frankie frowned. 'I wish you'd told me. I could have married him and he'd have been carrying on behind my back. Bloody hell, Jen, I must've been a laughing stock.'

'I don't think many people knew; he was, at least, discreet. But I only found out recently and only knew about one… OK, two… women it was *rumoured* he'd been seeing. I should have told you and I'm so sorry.'

Frankie shrugged. 'It doesn't matter now though, does it? However, knowing he was a love rat does make me feel a bit better about calling off the wedding.'

'Of course it does. It should.'

But where did it leave her and Jonas? Nowhere was where. She'd still just emerged from an engagement and even if her fiancé had been cheating, it didn't change the decision she'd made to take some time for her, to find herself. Jonas was a decent man and he could be a good friend but that was all that lay ahead for them. He'd made that clear at the airport. Frankie needed to take some time to enjoy being with her parents, to get to know them properly and to decide what to do about her life. She had big decisions to make and getting her new career sorted was a good place to start.

'So, what will you do now?' Jen handed her mobile back. 'I do think you'd make a great couple. You with your pretty eyes and brown hair and him with his blond hair and… ooh, that big muscular frame.'

'Jonas is just a friend and it'll never be more than that, Jen. But I do need to make some big decisions about my life and what I want to do from here on in. In fact, remember I told you I'd like to design clothes…'

As the Christmas songs played, the waitress set spiced mince pies and fresh frothy lattes in front of them and Frankie told Jen about her fashion design dreams and how Jonas was going to show the photographs of the range to an acquaintance. And she started to believe that this could be a Christmas wish that might actually come true.

—

Outside the cafe, Jen had hugged Frankie then hurried away to meet another friend for afternoon drinks. Frankie could have gone too, but she didn't fancy drinking and sitting around in a club. She needed some time to collect her thoughts about everything. She also didn't want to go straight home, so decided to have a wander around the shops instead.

Regent Street was packed and she had to weave her way through the crowds of shoppers keen to grab last minute gifts on the final Saturday before Christmas. She made her way to the cream front and red awnings of Hamleys and gazed into the first window that she came to. A snow-covered scene greeted her, where fat fluffy penguins wearing hats and scarves frolicked beneath a large Christmas tree. The lights on the tree twinkled and made the glitter in the snow sparkle. It was beautiful.

The next window showed the inside of a drawing room where Santa Claus sat in front of a roaring fire. The room was decked with gold and red tinsel and a large Christmas tree stood in the corner. Gifts were piled around the tree, wrapped in a rainbow of foil paper and decorated with large golden bows. The window in the room was flung open and outside was the perfect festive scene that spanned London rooftops covered in snow. The full moon glowed in the background and in front of it the silhouette of a sleigh pulled by reindeer could be seen. Goose pimples rose on Frankie's arms as she took in all the details of the scene. It evoked a combination of memories and she remembered how wonderful it had been to snuggle next to Jonas in the sleigh as it had whisked them through the Norwegian snow. She could also recall the excitement of childhood Christmases when she'd wonder if Santa would visit their home and what he would bring. Of course, every year she had wished that he'd bring her mother home, and she could remember promising him – as she sat in front of the fireplace in the drawing room and placed her letter to Santa in front of the grate – that if he brought Freya home, she would wish for nothing else.

She shook her head, sad for the child she had once been. She moved on from Hamleys and breathed in the smells of December, the cold air, the aromas of food cooking in the streets – from hot dogs to crêpes to the rich spices of mulled wine – and watched the people who hurried on by. They were so busy, so focused on their task, that they didn't notice her watching and she felt anonymous, something that she didn't mind at all. She'd spent so much of her life under a spotlight because of her grandmother, always watching her behaviour and thinking of the family reputation, when inside she'd ached for what she didn't have. But now, she had that, she had been reunited with her mother and it was as if all her Christmas wishes had finally come true.

She paused in front of a perfume shop to admire the Christmas lights that adorned the buildings and street lamps, all of them twinkling in the now dark afternoon, then she spotted a Salvation Army band about to start up. In their dark coats and hats with red scarves, they looked smart and it made Frankie smile. All the wonderful traditions and familiar sights of London in December seemed better than ever before, brighter even, as if being reunited with her mother had removed the filters that she'd viewed the world through. As the opening notes of 'In the Bleak Midwinter' rang out, Frankie smiled, her heart gladdened by the music and by life. She fished around in her bag for some change which she dropped into the collection bucket then she stood there and watched them for the next half an hour, swaying along to their musical set and soaking up the atmosphere of Regent Street at Christmas.

And as snowflakes began to drift down from the sky, Frankie appreciated exactly what it was to live entirely in the moment.

Chapter 30

'Can I come out now?' Grandma's voice was muffled behind the bathroom door.

'Ready?' Hugo asked Frankie.

'Ready!'

As her father helped Grandma back to her bed, Frankie turned on the fairy lights that she'd draped around the small Christmas tree in the corner.

'A tree!' Grandma exclaimed, clapping her hands together. Then she frowned. 'The nurse won't like it, mind. They're even funny about flowers.'

'We had a word earlier and got the OK to do it.' Hugo took his mother's hand as Frankie wondered at her grandmother's concerns over what the nurses might disapprove of. Had she turned over a new leaf?

'It's very pretty, thank you.'

'A bit smaller than you're used to.' Frankie thought of the enormous pine trees that were a tradition at the house every December. Grandma would get Hugo to fetch the large boxes of decorations down from the attic and she'd instruct the housekeeper of the time how to decorate the tree. Afterwards, she'd always go back round the tree herself, rearranging until she felt it was just right. Frankie could see now that this was one of the ways she needed to have control; everything had to be just right. Had losing Pip Bellamy when she was so young meant that she needed to have that same control over so many other things? It was very sad that she'd been hurt and forced to surrender the man she loved, and all because of class and wealth. Grandma had suffered, it was true, but Frankie still wished she hadn't felt the need to impress the same regulations upon her own son and the woman he loved.

'But it's beautiful, Frankie, and I'm really grateful.'

'Happy Christmas, Mother!' Hugo kissed her hand.

'Happy Christmas, both. I'm so grateful to you for coming here today. I didn't expect you to.'

'Why wouldn't we?' Frankie asked.

'After everything, you'd be entitled to stay away from me for the rest of my days. I don't deserve your compassion.'

'Now, now, Mother.' Hugo shook his head. 'We wouldn't leave you alone on Christmas Day, would we?'

Helen smiled but her eyes were watery as she looked at her son and granddaughter.

'We also brought your gifts.'

Frankie held up the two glitter-encrusted bags they'd brought with them.

'You shouldn't have. I don't have a thing for you because I've been stuck in here.'

'Not to worry, Grandma. Our gift is seeing you get better.'

At that, Helen buried her face in her hands. Frankie and her father stared at each other in shock. She had never seen her grandmother lose her composure like this and didn't know what to do. Neither, it seemed, did her dad. The medical staff had managed to get Grandma's condition under control with medication and the spells where her heart raced, making her faint, dizzy and sometimes nauseous, had reduced significantly. She still wasn't out of the woods, and because of her age and the abuse she'd given her body through smoking and drinking, they had advised that she stay in hospital over the holidays and into the new year.

'Uh… Mother?' He patted her hand. 'There, there. It's all right. Everything is jolly good.'

Helen sniffled then removed one hand. 'A tissue, please.'

Frankie got the box from the nightstand and handed it to her grandmother.

After she'd wiped her eyes and blown her nose, Helen looked at them both.

'I'm terribly sorry about that. Nothing like a near-death experience to make a woman re-evaluate her life. Gosh, I've made so many mistakes.'

'Grandma, you have to let it go now. We can't change the past; we can only look to the future.' Frankie took her grandmother's hand and gently squeezed it. She thought of what Freya had said about moving on and it hit her how important that was, especially when you reached the age her grandmother had. Every day was precious.

'As long as you know I'm sorry for everything and that I'll do my best to be a better mother and grandmother from now on.'

'Just get well, Mother. That's all we want. The rest can wait.' Hugo nodded.

Frankie handed her grandmother the smaller of the gift bags.

'What is it?' Helen asked.

'Open it and see.'

Inside were three mindfulness colouring books, a large pencil sharpener and a pack of coloured pencils.

'Colouring?' Helen's brow furrowed.

'Yes. It's good for relaxing, apparently.' Frankie smiled. 'And according to the doctor, you need to learn to switch off and relax more.'

'Thank you.' Helen ran her hands over the books then turned and placed them on the bedside table. 'I shall try them later, although I haven't coloured in years.'

'I think it's time for *Carols from King's*,' Frankie said as she pulled a gift from the second bag and handed it to her grandmother.

Helen opened it to find a digital radio inside.

'The batteries are already inside and it's tuned to the correct station.' Frankie smiled.

'Oh, how wonderful,' Helen said as she switched it on.

The hospital room was instantly transformed from clinical to festive as it was filled with the hauntingly beautiful sound of carols from King's College Cambridge.

The three of them sat together, a small family unit, and listened to the service, holding hands and rebuilding bonds. Frankie knew that the past would never be forgotten and the hurts would never completely fade, but lessons had been learnt and because of it, their future as a family looked far brighter than ever before.

–

'It looks beautiful, Dad,' Frankie said as she sat at the dining room table. Her father had taken the seat at the end and she was sitting to his left. Outside, the afternoon was dark but they'd left the curtains of the French doors open, not wanting to shut the remains of the day out. Snowflakes swirled in all directions and occasionally landed on the glass while some fell to the ground where a soft white blanket had begun to form.

Hugo had set the table with gold-rimmed glasses and their best cutlery and cooked them a dinner of turkey crown, vegetables, gravy and stuffing. It wasn't the usual grand spread that Grandma would have organized – paying a catering company to come in and do it – but Frankie was glad. It was a quiet, intimate festive meal that she would share with her father. He'd put the turkey in the oven on a very low heat before they'd left for the hospital and it had been ready for their return. They'd stayed at the hospital longer than they'd anticipated, because it had been so pleasant sitting with Grandma and listening to the radio, and because they hadn't wanted to leave her alone. But when she'd clearly become tired, they knew it was time to let her rest.

'Shall we exchange gifts now?' Hugo asked.

They'd been so busy that they hadn't had a chance to consider gifts all day.

'Good idea.'

Frankie got up and went to the sideboard where she'd placed her father's present. It had arrived a few days before and been so well wrapped that she hadn't taken it out of the packaging but had tied a big red bow around it.

She carried it over to her father and set it down next to him.

'Goodness, Frankie, what is that?'

'Open it and see.'

'Here's yours.' He handed her a small square parcel wrapped in silver paper.

'Shall we go together?' she asked.

'Yes.' Her father smiled.

They tore at wrapping paper that they dropped to the floor between them, something that Grandma never would have allowed, and Frankie sighed as she opened the black box to reveal a pretty silver bangle.

'Thank you, Dad. It's beautiful.'

'Like the ones your mother wears. It was her suggestion, actually.'

'I love it.' Frankie slid the bangle over her hand and admired it.

'And this…' Hugo stood up and lifted the photograph, setting it onto one of the chairs. 'This is incredible.'

'It's the one I bought at Freya's gallery. Jonas took it.'

Her father nodded as they gazed at the photo. Seeing it again made emotion surge through her. So much had happened since she'd first seen it but it was just as beautiful, if not more so. The contrast of the darkness and the northern lights, of the snow and the dark shapes of the trees was so intense that she felt as though she was there. She knew that when she exhaled, her breath would form a cloud in front of her and that her nose would tingle. A longing to see Norway again, along with her mother and Jonas, pierced her chest and she wondered when she'd have the chance.

'Thank you, darling, this is a wonderful gift and we'll hang it just there, shall we?' He pointed at the wall above the dining room fireplace where a watercolour of an English landscape had sat for as long as Frankie had lived.

'But what will Grandma say? She won't be happy about that.' Frankie bit her bottom lip, imagining the ruckus it could cause.

'I'll deal with Grandma. Besides, it's about time we made some changes around here.'

She helped her father to move the old painting then together they hung Jonas's photograph. On the dark papered wall, it looked right, as if it belonged there.

'I think this calls for a celebration, don't you?'

Hugo popped the cork on a bottle of champagne then poured it into the crystal flutes.

'You know what?' he asked as they clinked glasses.

'What?'

'I feel a bit… lost in here.'

'But we always eat in here. Except for when we have breakfast in the kitchen.' Something that had, admittedly, only happened since Grandma had been absent.

'I know but… I think we should kick back and relax. Let's take dinner into the drawing room and eat in front of the TV.'

'You mean have a carpet picnic?'

'Exactly!'

So they did. Hugo found an old festive movie on Netflix and they settled down to enjoy their Christmas dinner together.

When they'd finished the main course, they ate large portions of rich fruity Christmas pudding covered in sweet spicy brandy butter and Frankie felt as if she would burst.

'I really enjoyed that,' she said. 'Thanks, Dad.'

'It wasn't anything special. Not compared to the usual festive feasts.'

'But it was because we got to enjoy it together in such a relaxed way. I think it was the best Christmas dinner I've ever eaten.'

He smiled, peering out from under the gold paper crown that had slipped over his eyebrows as he ate.

'What do you think next year will bring, Dad?'

He frowned, causing the hat to slide even further down, so he pushed it back up, leaving it at a jaunty angle on his head. In the firelight, he looked relaxed and younger than he had done for as long as Frankie had known him, which was strange, considering the fact that she'd known him for almost thirty years, but it was as though a great weight had been lifted from his shoulders. This evening, he was wearing a Peruvian silk navy shirt, without a tie, so it was open at the neck, with a pair of fawn chinos. It was an outfit Frankie had bought him for Christmas and given him on Christmas Eve. It was also a less formal outfit than those her father usually wore; a strict upbringing meant that he rarely dressed so casually. He hadn't worn it to the hospital, opting for a suit as it was Christmas Day, but he was wearing it now and it really suited him. Frankie was moved by the fact that he'd changed into it and glad she'd gone for the smaller size because he'd also lost a few pounds over recent weeks, no doubt a benefit of drinking less, as if his need for single malt to help him sleep had faded.

'I have no idea, Frankie. It's been a strange year this one and things have happened that I could never have imagined. Good things that have made me happier than I've been in years. Obviously, I'm worried about Mother but I'm also delighted you've been reunited with Freya.'

'You were happy to see her too?'

'What do you think?' His smile lit up his face. 'However, I have to admit to missing her already.'

Frankie reached over and took his hand. 'I know, Dad. Me too.'

'Seeing her after all that time made me realize – not that I'd really ever forgotten – how precious she is, in here,' he placed his hand over his heart, 'and how precious time is. Mother being ill also confirmed that for me. Life's too short for living a half-life. We need to grab happiness while we can.'

'You're right. So, what're you waiting for?'

'Pardon?'

'You should go and tell Freya.'

'Tell her what?'

'That you love her.'

'Uh... I... uh...' His lips trembled and he blinked rapidly.

'Dad, it's obvious.'

'Frankie: I meant that I wanted to see more of her but going out there and declaring my love for her could be the last thing she wants.'

'It could but you won't know unless you try.'

'And what if she doesn't feel the same? I could mess up our friendship... I couldn't bear not to see her again. To lose her again.'

'Dad, I'm fairly certain that she loves you too. She's missed you as much as you've missed her. You two are meant to be together.'

'Where has my daughter the realist gone?' He sat up and peered around the room. 'Hello! Has someone replaced my sensible daughter with a romantic?'

Frankie laughed. 'Dad, stop! Just... go and see her. At least do that and see how it goes. Then... if it's right, you can tell her how you feel.'

'I can't just leave Mother.'

'We'll sort something out with the hospital. I don't think she's going to be rushing home, do you? I think that after the scare she had, she's glad to be there.'

He nodded. 'She told me today, when you'd gone out to get the car, that she's going to stay on for a few more weeks. She could come home with the right care package in place but said she likes it there and is happy to pay for an extended stay. I think it's a combination of her enjoying the attention and not wanting to burden us. She's been so poorly.'

'Well, there you are then.'

'Right… uh… do I pack now?'

She laughed. 'No, Dad! Now we are going to drink more champagne, eat our bodyweight in chocolates and watch Christmas TV. Tomorrow, we'll look at flight times and so on, and once we've arranged everything, we can head out to Oslo.'

'We?'

'Well, you don't think I'm going to stay home alone, do you, and miss seeing my mother again?'

'I'm so glad you said that.'

'Merry Christmas, Dad.'

'Merry Christmas to you.'

As they curled up on the sofa together, eating chocolates and drinking champagne, the snow fell outside. But Frankie's thoughts kept straying to Norway and her mother, wondering what she was doing and if she'd seen Jonas today. They'd sent texts early that morning then gone about their respective Christmases. Frankie had also sent Jonas a text, a polite message wishing him and his mother a good day, and he'd replied just as politely.

Yes, there was no way she was going to stay home when she had a chance of seeing her mother, and Jonas, again, even if it was just as a friend…

Chapter 31

'And this is the gallery.' Frankie and Hugo stopped in front of Freya's place.

Hugo gazed at the front of the building then straightened his jacket. He looked so smart today with his new jeans – he'd got Frankie to help him choose them in the Harrods sale – his light blue shirt and the waistcoat she'd made for him in a navy material with contrasting light-blue paisley trim around the collar and pockets. In spite of their desire to leave London as soon as possible and head to Oslo, they hadn't been able to leave until they'd ensured that Helen's care was sorted at the hospital and then they'd needed to book a flight. Which hadn't been easy over the holidays when everyone seemed to want to fly. Plus, there had been snow. More snow than they'd seen in years had fallen on Boxing Day and grounded all flights, much to their dismay.

They finally managed to book afternoon flights for the twenty-eighth of December, so with a slight delay too, it was late night when they arrived in Oslo. They went straight to the hotel where Frankie had stayed before and, after a light supper, headed to bed, keen to get to sleep so the next day would arrive.

'Do I look all right?' Hugo asked and a lump rose in Frankie's throat.

'Of course you do, Dad. You look lovely.'

'But do I look… old?'

'Old?'

'Well, yes. It's been worrying me, you see. I don't think your mother has changed much at all. Her hair is shorter but she's still slim and her skin is so good that she's barely aged but when I look in the mirror I see an old man.'

'Oh, Dad, you're so handsome, you just don't realize it.' She gently stroked his cheek. 'You're not old and you don't look old. You actually look younger of late and besides which, you've always reminded me of George Clooney.'

'Really?' He pushed a hand through his salt and pepper hair.

'Really. You're a very handsome man and the grey hair is distinguished.'

'When your mother and I got together, I had a head of thick dark brown hair. You don't think she looks at it now and finds it… ageing?'

'No, I don't. Look, George Clooney is fifty-six so you're only two years older than him. He's a heart-throb and has recently had twins with his younger wife. You're a successful businessman, you're funny and kind and… any woman would be lucky to have you.'

He coughed, clearly a bit embarrassed at the direction in which he'd led their conversation.

'Your mother still looks terribly good though, doesn't she?'

'She does. Right, shall we go in?'

Frankie was itching to see Freya again but understood that this was a big deal for her dad too. She pushed the door open and walked into the cool interior of the gallery. The bell tinkled and Freya looked up from where she was poring over books at the desk.

'Oh my darlings!' She jumped up and rushed over to them then hugged Frankie tight.

'Hi.'

Frankie breathed in her mother's now familiar perfume and swallowed her emotions, sneakily wiping away a tear before her mother released her.

When she did, Freya turned to Hugo.

'Hello, Hugo.'

'Freya.'

They stepped closer to each other then he lifted a hand and took one of hers. He raised it to his lips and held it there, closing his eyes briefly. Freya responded by reaching out to him with her other hand and pulling him close. They held each other for a while, lost in a world that was theirs, a combination of the past and the present, and Frankie had to choke back a sob. These two people, whom she loved so much, had been kept apart by her grandmother's harsh nature and rigid beliefs as well as by a whole load of misunderstandings and fears, and it had all been so unnecessary.

She stepped forwards and hugged them both. Her parents. Together. At last.

'I'm so glad to see you both.'

'We would have got here sooner but what with being unable to get a flight and needing to sort out care for Mother, it was difficult.'

'But you're staying for New Year, right?'

'Yes, of course. Try and stop us.' Hugo smiled boyishly and Frankie suspected she was seeing him as he had been all those years ago when he'd first fallen in love with her mother.

'Where's Jonas?' Frankie asked, realizing that he hadn't come through from the kitchen where she'd thought he might be.

'He had some friends come into town and he went to meet them. I'm not officially open today and have closed until the second week of January, but he came in early this morning to help me to go through some new stock and to sort out some orders that have to go out in the new year.'

Disappointment flooded through Frankie. Though she'd refused to admit it to herself, she'd been yearning to see him and had hoped he'd be as keen to see her too. Since he'd returned to Oslo, he had stayed in contact with her via text and they'd spoken twice on the phone but it had been quite formal and focused on her designs, which he'd informed her he'd left with his acquaintance that Thursday. He could have sent them to the boutique owner in an email but said he preferred to print them out as a proper portfolio, as his acquaintance was more likely to appreciate that personal touch. Frankie had longed to speak to him about them and about his feelings but inside she'd also cringed at her desire to do so. Jonas had made his feelings – or lack of them – clear so she had better accept that.

Besides, she was here to start her new venture, to pursue her new direction in life. It could all backfire and she'd end up starting from scratch in her old career, but she wanted to give it a shot. She also wanted to be closer to her mother if possible, because now she'd found her, she didn't want to let her go. And if the way her father was gazing at Freya was anything to go by, he didn't want to let her go either.

'Shall we go and get some lunch?' Freya asked.

'Don't you need to finish up here?' Frankie pointed at the desk.

'Give me ten minutes and I'll be ready.'

'Come and look around with me, Dad.' Frankie pointed at the displays.

'Love to,' he said, but he was following Freya with his eyes as she returned to the desk and sat down.

'Dad!' Frankie took hold of his arm then led him to the far end of the gallery. 'Aren't these beautiful?'

They stood in front of a range of photographs of the Norwegian wilderness. In one, a mother husky played with her pups, their fur thick and grey and their eyes bright blue.

'Wolves?' Hugo asked.

'Huskies, I think.'

In another, reindeer gathered in a field, their shaggy coats protecting them from a snow storm. The camera had captured the snow in the foreground and the detail of the photograph was incredible. The next was of a sled racing across the snow as a wild reindeer dragged it. The snow ahead of the sled was flawless, but behind it, the sled had left tracks that swerved from left to right, as if the beast had been writing a message on the landscape.

'I did that when I was here last time.'

'It looks rather marvellous.' Hugo nodded.

'We can see if Jonas can arrange a trip while we're here if you like.'

'That would be fabulous. As long as your mother comes too.'

He kept his eyes on the photos but his lips had curved upwards, as if he was smiling all to himself.

'I guess everything you do out here will involve my mother, right?'

A jangling of bracelets made her turn sharply. Freya was standing right behind them.

'I hope I will be involved, seeing as how I've missed you both so much.' Freya smiled.

'Wouldn't want to spend a minute more without you.' Hugo coughed then laughed and Frankie shook her head.

'I always thought you were shy and socially awkward, Dad, but it turns out you're actually quite the flirt.'

'It's your mother. She brings out the charmer in me.'

'Come on then, charmer, you can escort me to lunch.'

Freya tucked her arm into Hugo's and they walked to the door then she turned the lights off and Frankie followed them outside, a smile playing on her own lips. It was nice getting to see another side to her dad, even if she did wish Jonas was there too so she wouldn't feel like a complete gooseberry.

—

Freya took them to a bar that was warm and bright inside and where Frankie felt instantly relaxed. Light bounced off every surface and Michael Bublé played softly in the background, one of those catchy tunes that made her want to tap her feet.

'This is a great bar and they serve the best burgers.'

'Burgers?' Hugo asked, his eyebrows slightly raised.

'Yes, they're gourmet burgers. You can have lots of different types, including vegetarian ones with a wide variety of toppings. I've been here with Jonas in the past and brought a few customers here too.'

A waiter arrived and took their order then brought them some water. Hugo ordered a bottle of wine then Frankie excused herself to go to the bathroom.

She followed the waiter's directions and admired the bar as she passed it, with its mirrored walls and black and chrome decor. It certainly wasn't a cosy English pub but it was classy and stylish. Jen would love it there.

Laughter caught her attention just as she reached the short corridor that led to the toilets and she turned to see who was enjoying their afternoon.

She froze.

Did a double take.

In a corner booth, Jonas was sitting with a group of people, all of whom appeared to be physically perfect. Like him, they were tall and long-limbed. The women had flowing golden tresses and sparkly blue eyes and wore strappy silk tops with skinny jeans and fashionable boots. The men were scruffy-chic, with hair that was either long and blond or short and stylishly messy. They could easily have been the cast of a Viking movie being filmed locally. They were beautiful, strong, young and healthy and Frankie was suddenly aware of her own height, or lack of it, and her rather limp brown hair – she'd washed it last night when she'd showered the flight from her skin and hair, then gone to bed with it damp. Today, it was clean but flat. At least she did have on her good jeans and an Alexander McQueen floral shirt, but even so… she couldn't compare to those perfect women who were laughing and joking with Jonas and his friends.

'Excuse me.' She jumped as a man gently tapped her shoulder. 'I need to go through.'

'Oh… sorry.'

She stepped out of the way, realizing that she'd been caught staring. This would never do. She hurried into the ladies' toilet and locked herself in a cubicle. She really was an idiot. Jonas lived in Oslo; he had a whole life out here. What had she expected? That he never associated with beautiful women or enjoyed time out with friends? For all she knew, one of those women was his girlfriend or lover, perhaps more than one if he was anything like Rolo.

She shook her head. Time to get a grip. Jonas was a friend and she was behaving like some giddy school-girl who'd fallen for the first man who'd paid her some attention since she'd run away from her wedding. And he hadn't really paid her any attention that could have made her fall for him, anyway, had he? He'd been kind and respectful and even offered to help her out with her fashion-designing aspirations. If she had read anything into his behaviour and the things he'd said, then that was on her. Besides, he had rejected her outright at the airport, so why was she struggling to let him go?

He had never been hers in the first place, so she had no right to yearn for anything else and she certainly couldn't compete in the circles that he seemed to move in, could she?

She used the toilet then washed her hands and splashed some water onto her hot cheeks. She'd have some wine and a nice meal then go back to her hotel and take a nap. It was probably everything catching up with her, including the emotion of seeing her mother again.

When she walked out of the corridor though, a hand caught her arm.

'Frankie! I thought it was you.' The soft Norwegian inflections laced his words and her heart leapt as it recognized him.

'Jonas! You scared me.'

'I'm sorry. Sigfrid said a woman was staring at us but when I looked up you had disappeared into the toilets. Why didn't you come and say hello?'

'Oh… I stopped because I thought it was you but I wasn't sure and then a man asked me to move and I really needed to go… to use the loo.' Her cheeks burned as she tried to avoid eye contact. The blue of his eyes was so bright; his smile was so easy, that looking at him actually hurt her. She'd stupidly fallen for him in spite of all her vows to the contrary and now she didn't know what she was going to do. But she also felt awkward around him, as if he was a stranger and not the man she'd sat next to on a patchwork quilt as they'd eaten a picnic, or the one she'd posed in front of for photographs. It made her wonder if she'd really known him at all. If she'd turned him into the man she wanted him to be.

'Come and meet my friends.' He nodded at the corner booth and she looked over at the people who were currently staring at her, clearly interested in the strange woman who'd been sneakily observing them. They might even suspect her of being some crazed stalker, one of Jonas's admirers who'd mistaken him for Thor.

'Oh… no… better not. I'm with my parents.'

'That's OK. Freya knew I was coming here for lunch anyway and I told her that if she brought you here to come and say hi. You could join us, even.'

'Uh… I'm not sure. I mean… Dad just ordered some wine and they were chatting and—'

'That's decided then. We'll get a table moved next to ours and you can eat with us. We can order more wine… to share.' He smiled at her and her mind went completely blank. She couldn't think of an excuse to make to get out of having lunch with him and his gorgeous friends.

'OK. I'll go and get them.'

'Frankie?'

'Yes.'

'It's good to see you.'

Her mouth was dry and she struggled to swallow, but she managed to whisper, 'It's good to see you too.'

Then she walked away on legs as shaky as a baby giraffe's, and tried not to trip over her own feet. She'd imagined seeing Jonas again but in all of her fantasies, it hadn't been when he was in the company of such beautiful people. However, she'd have to put on her best smile and make small talk, because otherwise she was going to come across as a spoilt little rich girl from England, and she'd hate to seem that way.

Chapter 32

Frankie arrived back at their table to find her parents giggling.

'Oh, hello, love. We thought you'd got lost and Dad was about to send in a search party.' Freya chuckled and Hugo gazed adoringly at her.

'No… I bumped into Jonas, actually.'

'Yes, he said he'd probably be here. Is he with his gang?'

'Gang?'

'Friends. They're all photographers and bloggers and I've had work from quite a few of them in the gallery at different points. Like Sigfrid Nilson, for example. I take a lot of her work at the gallery and it sells like hot cakes.'

'Ah, right. Yes… I think that's probably who he's with.'

'Were they all strikingly attractive?'

Frankie nodded then took a big gulp of her wine. 'Extremely.'

'I swear it's the air in Norway. Some of these kids grow so tall.'

'He asked if we'd like to join them.' *Please say no…*

Freya placed a hand on Hugo's arm. 'Shall we?'

Frankie's dad smiled broadly. 'I'm easy. Whatever my two favourite women want to do is fine with me.'

'Come on then and you can meet some of Jonas's friends. They're all absolutely lovely.'

Frankie picked up her wine and her coat and led the way over to Jonas, even though her feet wanted to retrace their steps right out the front door.

Of course, Jonas's friends had to be lovely too, didn't they?

And they really were.

–

Two hours later, Frankie was holding her stomach as she'd laughed so much that it was aching, as was her face.

'No, he didn't!' she said to Hilda, the tallest of the blonde women, who had come to sit next to her.

'Oh he did, Frankie. He was such a rascal when we were younger and he was always up to mischief.'

It turned out that Jonas had known Hilda, Sigfrid and Astrid since kindergarten. They'd all shared stories of when they were very young, seemingly competing to see who could embarrass whom the most, and Frankie had laughed at each story as they got funnier and more outrageous.

The rest of Jonas's group included an Australian couple whom Astrid had met when travelling, Astrid's boyfriend, Fredrik, and two other men who were also long-term friends of Jonas.

As they ate, drank, talked and laughed, Frankie found it hard to believe that she'd been at all intimidated by the thought of joining these lovely people. She was so used to feeling that she didn't fit in with her peers back home that the warmth and easy way of Jonas's friends came as a surprise to her. There was no sense of pressure, no atmosphere of competition. Of course, not everyone she'd associated with in England was like that, but some of the acquaintances her grandmother had encouraged her to spend time with had been the epitome of highly competitive – in every area of their lives.

The evening came to an end all too soon and it was time to go. Frankie exchanged hugs and numbers with Hilda, Sigfrid and Astrid, and they agreed to meet up again when she was next in Oslo. Her parents had also seemed to enjoy their evening and they were arm in arm as they left the bar and went out into the icy air. Frankie couldn't believe how long they'd spent over dinner, and how the light had faded while they'd been inside, but then this late in December, daylight didn't last long.

Jonas walked outside with them and turned up his collar against the freezing air.

'Your friends are lovely,' Frankie said.

'They're a good bunch.' He smiled. 'And they really took to you, especially Astrid, Sigfrid and Hilda.'

'Astrid said she wants to see my designs.'

'She does, I know. I told her all about them... and about you.'

Frankie gazed at him, absorbing the lines of his face that were highlighted by the street lamps and the light from the restaurant. He had told his friends about her... but only because of her fashion designs and aspirations. And yet, Astrid had said something about Jonas telling her all about Frankie, how much he enjoyed her company and how he hadn't actually stopped talking about her since they'd met. Astrid had also said it wasn't like Jonas at all. Jonas had always been a free spirit, Astrid had said, but now, something about him was different. Frankie had put Astrid's comments down to the good wine and jovial atmosphere, as well as to the fact that they had got on so well but maybe it was something more...

'I hope you didn't tell them anything awful.' Frankie nudged him.

As he gazed at her, his pupils dilated, becoming deep dark pools, and she felt as if she could lose herself in his eyes.

'I'll walk you back to your hotel.'

'No, it's OK. We're going to walk Freya home then I'll walk back with Dad.'

'Don't your parents want some... time alone?'

Frankie looked at her parents who were standing in the middle of the street, gazing up, as Freya pointed out the star formations visible in the black Norwegian sky.

'Oh... I'm not sure. I'm not really sure how to act at the moment, to be honest. They're so sweet together but I don't want to make it obvious that I think they might be falling for each other all over again.' At least she hoped that was what was happening and that neither of them would end up getting hurt. It was as though their roles were reversed and she was the concerned parent, worrying that Freya and Hugo would fall too hard and too quickly and end up with more regrets. But then, they were adults, had lived a lot longer than she had, and they were entitled to their feelings. She just hoped it would work out the way they wanted it to.

'Well, if I insist on walking you back to the hotel, then they can have some time alone without having to ask for it.'

She nodded, her heart thundering as she contemplated what was happening here.

'Freya, Hugo, I'm going to walk back to the hotel with Frankie. I might even pop in for a drink at the bar.'

'OK, love.' Freya smiled then pulled her hat down over her ears. She whispered something to Hugo and he nodded. 'Hugo's coming back to mine for an hour.'

'If that's all right with Frankie?' her dad asked, looking slightly sheepish.

'Of course it is, Dad.' Frankie gave them both a hug and a kiss. 'Have fun.'

They walked away and Jonas offered her his arm.

'It's slippery this evening.'

'Of course. Thank you.'

She tucked her gloved hand into the crook of his arm, conscious of his strength and his size as they walked, knowing that should she slip, he'd save her easily. He had a way of making her feel safe without needing to say anything, just by being there.

When they reached the First Hotel Grims Grenka, they walked through the automatic doors and entered the warm, brightly lit lobby.

'Do you want a drink?' she asked.

'Sure. Why not?'

In the bar, they took seats at a corner table and a waiter took their drinks order. After all the wine they'd consumed earlier, they opted for coffee.

'So…' Frankie let the word hang in the air. 'What do you think about my parents?'

'I think they care about each other very much and that being reunited has made them both very happy.'

She nodded.

'I've known Freya for some time now and she has never shown a flicker of interest in another man. Not that she hasn't had offers – she's an attractive woman – but she always remained the consummate professional, never showed any interest in anyone other than in a business capacity. Not even the suave art collectors who came to the gallery and asked to take her out.'

'Dad was the same.'

'They were waiting for the right one, I suppose.'

'Isn't everyone?' The words flew from Frankie's mouth and she winced. 'I didn't mean that. I don't believe in all that romantic nonsense about everyone needing someone and there being a perfect match for everyone out there.'

'You don't?'

She shook her head. 'It's silly, isn't it?'

'So you don't think your parents are perfect for each other, then? Or that they've been unable to love anyone else because they knew they'd never find anyone to match up to the one they'd already found?'

'But they were apart for almost thirty years. How...' She paused. Whatever she said, she could see that her parents had feelings for each other, feelings that had evidently never died.

'You hear about it all the time,' Jonas said, smiling at the waiter as he delivered their coffees. 'People meet up with their first loves and get back together.'

'Jonas... you sound like a romantic now.'

His smile lit up his face. 'I don't think I've ever been called that before but I can take it.'

'You're right. My mother and father were forced apart and they're delighted to see each other. I do hope they can find a way to make this work though. They have lives in separate countries. Dad still has his job and wasn't planning on retiring any time soon... at least not until my mother came back into his life.'

Jonas blew on his coffee and steam billowed over the edge of the cup.

'I think that you need to stop worrying about them. They're old enough to know what they're doing and if they make each other happy, then they will find a way to be together.'

Frankie sipped her coffee; it was hot, strong and delicious and a shiver of delight ran down her spine.

'Good?'

'So good.'

'Like most Norwegian things.' He laughed. 'I'm meeting my contact from the boutique tomorrow, so I'll let you know how it goes. She's quite excited after seeing the portfolio of your designs.'

'That makes my stomach flip.'

'You're nervous?'

'Of course.'

'Don't be nervous, Frankie. You're one of the strongest people I've ever met.'

'Me?' She laughed. 'I'm not strong.'

'But you are. You coped your whole life without your mother. You got through school and university then set up in business. You dealt with a grandmother who could – it seems – bully a grown man into submission and yet you kept going and had the strength to walk away from a wedding you knew wasn't right. That takes so much courage, far more than walking down the aisle and going along with it. You're stronger than you realize. And then… you came searching for your mother and had enough love and compassion in your heart to forgive her, your father and your grandmother for what happened. You are strong.'

Frankie digested his words. She'd never thought of herself as a strong woman before; she just got by, got on with things, made a go of it. She often believed that she drifted along, allowing others like her grandmother and Rolo to control her direction. But Jonas believed that she was strong and that she'd done well throughout her life. She liked the way he saw her; no one had ever seen her like that before and it made her heart swell.

'Thank you.'

'What for?'

'For telling me that. I like how you see me. I'm not sure I deserve it but I'm grateful.'

'You should value yourself more. You're very special.'

He stretched his arms above his head.

'I think I need to get home. I'm quite tired after all that food and wine.'

Frankie smiled. 'I suspect I'm going to nod off as soon as my head hits the pillow.'

'Shall we call it a night then?'

They paid for their coffees then walked out of the bar and through to the lobby. Jonas put his coat back on then wound his scarf round his neck.

'I'll let you know how it goes tomorrow.'

'Please do.'

'Before I go... what are your plans for seeing in the new year?'

'I was just going to go along with what my parents wanted to do.'

'Why don't you come and watch the fireworks? We usually grab a few bottles of champagne then go down to the harbour. It's a great place to watch the display.'

'That sounds lovely.'

'You might have some good news to celebrate too.'

'I hope so.'

'I'll speak to Freya about the fireworks in the morning and speak to you later in the day.'

'OK, marvellous. See you tomorrow then.'

Jonas hesitated for a moment, leant forwards a bit, as if to kiss her cheek, then stepped backwards again.

'Goodnight, Jonas.'

'Goodnight, Frankie.'

She reached out and squeezed his hand then turned and walked to the lift before she was tempted to do more. She'd seen the easy way Jonas had with his female friends and with her mother, and it was evidently just his way. He had such a kind heart and he was showing her the same respect and friendship he showed everyone he met.

She was very lucky indeed to have him in her life.

Chapter 33

Late the next morning, Jonas hurried along the street to Freya's gallery. His smile was wide and he kept chuckling to himself. A few people who passed him looked at him curiously, as if suspecting him of early morning drinking. But it wasn't that. He had good, no, *great* news to share. He'd texted Frankie and told her to meet him at the gallery and he couldn't wait to see her face; he'd also sent Freya a text to ask her to get in a bottle of bubbly in for when he arrived.

He paused outside the door, took a deep breath and tried to force the smile from his lips. He was going to give it away as soon as she laid eyes on him if he didn't stop grinning. He tapped his boots on the wall outside to shake the snow from them then opened the door.

Inside, the lamp on the desk cast a golden glow in the corner but the rest of the gallery was in darkness. As they were closed until January, Freya didn't want anyone coming in when they saw the lights. Oslo was busy with tourists who'd arrived to see in the new year and they would be looking for things to do, and a walk around a gallery, in the warm, would likely bring them inside.

'Freya?' He peered through the gloom.

'She's in the kitchen making coffee.' Frankie stepped out of the shadows.

'Were you hiding?' he asked.

'No, I'd just… used the lavatory.' She gestured behind her.

'Ah! Sorry. Where's your father?'

'He said he had to go and get something.'

'Right.' Jonas nodded. Presumably, Hugo had gone out to get the champagne.

Freya emerged from behind a display board carrying a tray of mugs and a coffee pot. She placed the tray on the desk then poured coffee into three mugs. Jonas took one gratefully and wrapped his hands around the mug, savouring the heat as it warmed his frozen fingers.

The door to the gallery opened and Hugo entered, carrying a tote bag that Jonas was certain belonged to Freya.

'Did you get it?' Freya asked.

'Yes.' Hugo smiled as he walked over to the desk and put the bag down. He pulled out a large green bottle and Freya went to the desk drawer and brought out four small glasses.

'What's going on?' Frankie asked.

'I have good news…' Jonas drained his coffee then placed the cup on the tray on the desk.

Frankie stared at him, her face pale. 'Don't keep me in suspense, Jonas. I can't stand it.'

She worried her bottom lip and Jonas had to push his hands into his jeans pockets to prevent himself from picking her up and twirling her around.

Hugo popped the cork then filled the four glasses and Freya handed them out.

'OK… so, my contact with the boutique… absolutely loved your designs. She said she's never seen anything like them. They're beautiful, glamorous, classy and could be worn by just about anyone. She liked how they weren't designed just for skinny people and said that will appeal to her regular clientele.'

Frankie's mouth had opened and she was shaking her head.

'She also said that she wants to put in an order immediately after the new year and that she'll want to have a meeting with you to discuss future orders. But... get this... She wants every single garment you've made already so she can start selling them. She will speak to you about numbers and possible commission, et cetera, et cetera, but basically, she loved your work and also said she knew of other boutique owners who will do too.'

Frankie was still shaking her head.

'It's wonderful news, love.' Freya wrapped an arm around Frankie's shoulder. 'Aren't you happy?'

To Jonas's horror, Frankie crumpled in front of his eyes, almost folding over completely, and she started to cry. He looked at Hugo then at Freya but they both looked as confused as he was, so he went to Frankie and lifted her chin gently with his forefinger. 'Hey, Frankie. This is good news, no?'

She sniffed then nodded. He handed his champagne to Freya then smoothed his thumbs over Frankie's cheeks, wiping away her tears.

'I... am... happy...' Frankie squeaked.

'Are you sure?' Hugo said from behind them. 'You don't look very happy, darling.'

'She's emotional,' Freya said. 'It's a lot to take in.'

Jonas pulled Frankie into his arms and rubbed her back, trying to comfort and reassure her. Against his chest, she felt soft and female and that urge to protect her surged again. It was a primal instinct but it was combined with something even stronger, a deep desire for this woman, a longing to know her better, to be there for her when she was sad and to bring her joy.

When Frankie finally stepped back, her face and eyes were red and there was a large damp patch on his shirt front.

'Frankie? Are you OK?' Freya asked.

'Yes. Thank you so much, Jonas. I'm extremely happy. Delighted, in fact.'

'Well then, let's have a proper toast.' Hugo made sure they all had their glasses then he topped them up. 'To our gorgeous girl and her new venture. Frankie's fashion!'

They clinked glasses and Frankie finally smiled.

Jonas couldn't help himself then, he slid an arm around her shoulders and squeezed her tight as her parents chatted about how exciting this was, how successful she was going to be and all the wonderful possibilities that lay ahead for her. Just as parents should do, and he realized that he wanted this for her, probably just as much as they did.

At one point, Frankie looked up at him and the emotion in her green eyes almost knocked him sideways. In spite of all his reservations about Frankie and her life, her wealthy upbringing and how he could never offer her what she would want and need, he was falling for her hard and fast. He'd tried to rationalize it away in England, to deny it when he returned to Norway, but now that she was here again, he knew all hope of fighting it was lost.

–

'Where are we going?' Frankie asked as Freya opened a door at the back of the gallery and led her up a staircase.

'Wait and see.'

They'd left Jonas and Hugo in the gallery downstairs because Freya said she had an idea.

When they reached a short landing, Freya pulled some keys from her pocket then unlocked a door. It groaned as it opened, causing them both to shudder.

'Now, I know you have a whole life in London and that you probably want to go back there to carry on your design business, but just in case… there's room here for you to work, should you need it.'

Freya walked into a room that was the same size as the gallery downstairs but looked bigger because it was completely empty. The window was shuttered but daylight sneaked through the slats, creating enough light for them to see.

Frankie walked around the room then towards the back, where a doorway led into what appeared to be a kitchen area. Another door next to it, led to a small room containing a toilet and hand basin.

'Is this yours as well?' Frankie asked.

'I don't rent it but I have the keys as the owner asked me to keep a set in case anyone ever wanted to look around. There's a separate entrance from out the back, that's where the other door at the top of the stairs leads.'

Frankie crossed to the window and peered through the slats. Outside, people walked up and down the street and snowflakes drifted down, only to be swept up by gusts of wind and thrown against the windows and into the faces of passers-by. The flakes that made it to the ground settled on top of the snow that was already there, creating a picture-perfect Norwegian scene. It was beautiful, and even more so because Frankie was with Freya, her dad and Jonas, and there were possibilities here for the future too.

Freya joined her at the window.

'Frankie, I'm not putting any pressure on you. I know you have a life in London and that you need to get back because of your grandmother… but I also wanted to let you know that there are possibilities here. Should you want to consider them.'

Frankie turned to Freya and met her green eyes. Her heart soared as she pulled her into a hug.

'I'm not sure exactly what I'm going to do yet, and it's going to take some more thought, but I do know that this is a fabulous idea and I am so grateful.'

Freya nodded against her shoulder.

'Whatever you want is fine with me, Frankie. I just want to see you. A lot.'

'Me too.'

They hugged each other tightly and Frankie thought about what had happened in her life and about what could happen next. A fresh start, away from London and Rolo and the life she'd lived but never really felt comfortable in, could be exactly what she needed. Of course, there was Grandma, but she suspected that Helen Ashford would be fine whether Frankie was at her beck and call or not. Frankie and her dad had spent so long doing what Helen wanted them to do, being there for her when she called for them and living the life she'd chosen for them.

Now it was time to choose their own paths…

Chapter 34

'I've so many layers on, I can barely walk. I just hope I don't need the toilet.' Frankie shuffled along next to her father. 'And after that huge supper we just ate, everything's tighter than it should be anyway.'

'I know what you mean.' He chuckled. 'I'm not even sure if I'll be able to find a way out of the layers.'

They'd had a quiet supper at the hotel together, after an enjoyable day of sightseeing with Freya, while Jonas had spent the day with his mother. They'd eaten their fill of pork and ground beef meatballs and brown gravy served with herby carrots and boiled potatoes, then enjoyed *kanelbulle* for dessert; the sweet buttery cinnamon buns were fast becoming a favourite of Frankie's. They'd washed the food down with *gløgg* – the Norwegian mulled wine spiced with cloves and cinnamon and served with almonds and raisins. Norwegian food and drink was certainly satisfying and comforting, and something that Frankie could get used to.

Now, they were on their way to the harbour where they would meet Freya and Jonas. It was dark and very cold and the snowy ground was slippery underfoot, but Frankie was glowing. The good news she'd had about the boutique and the work space her mother had shown her above the gallery had all given her such a lift. She still hadn't come to any conclusions yet but at least she had options, for what felt like the first time in her life.

It was a bit scary, a bit daunting, a bit… exciting.

The streets of Oslo no longer seemed as strange. She was able to place familiar landmarks now and she enjoyed the sense of familiarity, as if she belonged there.

'It's a lovely city, isn't it?'

'Beautiful.' Her dad smiled at her and she noted, as they passed under a street light, and not for the first time recently, how much healthier he looked. For so many years, he'd seemed grey and serious, more serious than a man should ever be. But now… his skin glowed in the cold air, his eyes sparkled and he had a spring to his step that she couldn't recall ever seeing before.

'Dad, are you happy?'

He stopped suddenly and she had to turn back to face him.

'Happy?'

'Yes.'

'I…'

'I ask because when I was growing up, you never really seemed happy. You smiled occasionally and you never wallowed in despair – because you always kept so busy – but you never seemed happy.'

He met her gaze.

'Yes, Frankie, I am happy. It's a strange feeling, I'll give you that, but I'm getting used to it. I can't deny that I'm scared… having lost my… *happiness* once, I'm terrified of losing it again, but I am trying to be brave and to go with the flow.'

'I'm so glad. I love seeing you like this.'

'And I love seeing you like this!' He laughed then hugged her. 'Now come on or we'll miss the fireworks.'

They hurried along, breathing deeply of the icy air and trying not to slip. The snow had stopped late afternoon but was crisp and crunchy underfoot. Frankie suspected that her father was as undecided as she was about what to do next, but she also believed that that was OK. Sometimes, not knowing exactly what tomorrow had in store could be a good thing.

When they reached the harbour, she spotted Jonas through the mass of people; it was as if her eyes would seek him out in any crowd, anywhere. She waved to catch his attention, then led her dad towards him. It was New Year's Eve, she was in Oslo, her future looked exciting, and she had her mother back.

–

'Jonas!' Frankie waved at him again and he smiled as they reached him.

'At last. We wondered where you'd got to.'

Freya hugged Frankie then Hugo. 'We did. It's so busy here we were worried we wouldn't find you.'

'Let's try to find a quieter spot where we can stand together.' Jonas held out his hand and Frankie took it as if it was the most natural thing in the world. Behind her came her parents and they shuffled through the crowds until Jonas found them a space closer to the rail that overlooked the water.

'It's so cold.' Frankie was shaking in spite of her layers.

'It takes a bit of getting used to.' Jonas nodded. 'Come here. It's going to be a while and you'll just get colder.'

Frankie stepped closer and Jonas turned her around so she stood right in front of him then wrapped his arms around her. 'Body heat is the best thing for staying warm,' he whispered in her ear and his breath tickled her skin.

She nodded, unable to reply because words had deserted her.

Next to them, Frankie's parents stood arm in arm, both stamping to keep warm. A hush fell over the harbour as the onlookers waited in anticipation. The air seemed to crackle with excitement as one year was left behind and a new one was about to begin. And what a year it had been. Frankie's life had changed in many ways and all the changes were for the better.

Then the countdown to midnight began...

As the year turned, everyone cheered and shouts of 'Happy new year' in many different languages echoed around the harbour. Frankie turned in Jonas's arms and accepted his hug and kiss then she turned to do the same to her parents and froze.

Hugo and Freya were lost in each other, their arms wrapped around each other as they kissed. It was surreal and wonderful, strange yet right. They had found each other again and were kissing as if the world around them had ceased to exist.

'Look!' Jonas nudged her.

She followed his finger and there, in the rich inky ebony of the Norwegian sky, fireworks burst in hues of gold, green and red. People around them oohed and aahed, and Frankie tried to keep her eyes focused on the fireworks, but she couldn't help glancing back at her parents.

'You OK?' Jonas whispered.

'Yes.' She giggled. 'A bit surprised to see them kissing but also very happy about it.'

'It's a good way to start the year.' He wrapped his arms around her and squeezed her tight. He had said it was to keep her warm but Frankie hoped there was more to it than that. Much more.

Once the fireworks had finished, the air was hazy with smoke and heavy with the scents of sulphur and gunpowder with a hint of brine from the water underneath it all. Freya and Hugo seemed to emerge from their trance and they rejoined Frankie and Jonas.

'Happy new year!' Freya said before hugging them both.

'Yes, happy new year!' Hugo's eyes were bright and his cheeks flushed, in spite of the freezing conditions, and as he hugged Frankie, he whispered, 'Sorry about that.'

She leant back and met his eyes. 'Don't be sorry, Dad. It's wonderful.'

'I guess I couldn't wait any longer and lucky for me your mother seemed to feel the same.'

'What shall we do now?' Freya asked. 'Do you all want to come back to mine?'

'I promised Mum I'd head home to have a drink with her.' Jonas shrugged. 'Would you like to come with me, Frankie?'

'Oh!' She swallowed her surprise. 'Really?'

'She'd love to meet you.'

'She would?'

He nodded.

'I'll go back to your mother's then.' Hugo smiled bashfully. 'See you in the morning for breakfast?'

'Brunch more like, Dad.' Frankie smiled.

'Come on then.' Jonas took her hand and led her out of the crowds and away from the harbour. He was surefooted in the snow as only someone accustomed to these conditions could be. They walked briskly along dark streets and past revellers, the majority of whom, Jonas told her, would be heading home to spend time with family and friends as was Norwegian tradition.

When they stopped in front of a modest-looking apartment block, Jonas stopped and took her hands.

'Before we go inside… there's something I need to tell you.'

–

Jonas took a deep breath. He'd been nervous about asking Frankie to come back with him but he hadn't wanted the night to end at the harbour either. When Freya and Hugo had started kissing, he'd known they'd need time alone and the idea of sending Frankie back to her hotel alone on New Year's Eve was more than he could bear. So he'd swallowed his doubt and brought her back to his mum's apartment. Even though he knew now that Frankie had a good heart, he was also very aware of how different their backgrounds were.

'Frankie… my home isn't very… grand.'

'What?' She smiled, clearly thinking he was teasing her.

'I grew up here and it's quite simple. Homely but a lot smaller than yours.'

'It looks very nice.' She peered up at the building. 'With those lovely big windows, the rooms can't be that small.'

'The apartments are one- and two-bedroom and they are quite small. And simple. Not at all like your London home. You'll probably be surprised.'

'Jonas… do you think I care about that? You're taking me to meet your mum. I'm sure your home is lovely.'

'Don't say I didn't warn you.'

He pushed open the communal front door then led her towards the staircase. The lift didn't always work and it was often faster to take the stairs anyway.

By the time they reached the fourth floor, Frankie was red-faced and puffing.

'Sorry. I'm not unfit but it's all these clothes I'm wearing.'

'Of course!' He laughed. 'You can remove some layers once we get inside.'

They reached his mother's apartment and he pushed his key into the lock.

'Here you go.' He swung the door inwards and stood back. As Frankie entered, he knew that this would go one of two ways. Either she'd be horrified at how he lived and realize that she wanted the grandeur of her life back home, or... well, he'd have to wait and see.

'Mama?' Jonas called as they walked through the hallway and into the one room that served as lounge and kitchen.

'Coming,' his mother replied from her bedroom.

There was a scratching of claws on wood and Jonas paused, aware of what was coming.

Luna.

She bounded into the hallway and Jonas opened his arms then laughed as she jumped up at him, licking his face and neck as if he'd been gone for months and not just hours. When she was done welcoming him, she turned to Frankie.

'Luna, be gentle.'

The dog approached Frankie slowly and Jonas watched as Frankie's expression changed.

'It's OK, Frankie; she won't hurt you. She recognizes you.'

Frankie nodded then knelt down and held out her hand. Luna sniffed it, gave it a lick then moved closer and licked Frankie's face. Her big tail wagged furiously, and when she turned back to Jonas, her mouth was open as if in a wide smile.

'She likes you. You just had the Thorsen greeting.'

'Thank goodness for that. I'd imagine she can be quite intimidating if she doesn't take to someone.'

'Let me take your coat, hat, gloves and whatever else you need to remove, then we can go and sit down.'

Frankie handed him a pile of clothing and he took it to his small room to put on the bed. When he'd stripped off his own warm clothing, he went back through the door to find his mother kissing Frankie's cheeks.

'Happy new year, Frankie. It's good to meet you.'

'Same here, Mrs Thorsen.'

'Call me Aslaug, please.'

'You have a lovely home, Aslaug.'

'Thank you.'

Frankie sat on the two-seater sofa next to Jonas and accepted a mug of coffee from his mother. Aslaug Thorsen was a lot like her son: tall, blonde and blue-eyed. She had his calm manner and easy smile, and Frankie felt instantly comfortable with her. Luna lay on the floor in front of Jonas, her big paws under her chin, and though her eyes were closed, her tail wagged every so often, as if she was listening to the conversation.

They chatted about Aslaug's job as a receptionist for a law firm then about Frankie's change of career. Aslaug admitted that she'd seen some of Jonas's photographs of

Frankie's designs – he'd been keen to show her, apparently – and that she thought they were lovely. Frankie opened up about some of her new ideas and asked if Aslaug would be happy modelling some of them, which the older woman said she'd be delighted to do. It was a very different exchange to the ones she'd had with Rolo's mother, who she'd felt looked down on her and disapproved of her in many ways. Rolo's mother had never been openly rude or dismissive but Frankie had always sensed that her fiancé's mother wasn't her biggest fan.

After an hour of chatting, Aslaug yawned. 'I'd better go to bed. I'm all done in and I'm going to see a friend of mine out of town tomorrow.'

'Are you still taking Luna?' Jonas asked.

'I have to.' Aslaug smiled. 'She loves my friend and her children, so she'll have a fabulous time in their big garden.' She turned to Frankie. 'She's normally glued to Jonas's side but she does like to accompany me on day trips. Goodnight, Frankie. Goodnight, my boy.' Aslaug kissed Jonas's cheek then went to her room.

'Your mum is lovely.' Frankie smiled. She'd enjoyed meeting Aslaug and feeling as though she could be herself; she didn't feel any need to act on ceremony as she'd done with Rolo's mother and the rest of his family. Aslaug hadn't seemed to judge Frankie at all and it was refreshing.

'We Norwegians don't impose ourselves upon others and neither do we judge them. It's a good thing about living in Norway. Family is very important, as are friends, but no one will force their company on you or their opinions.'

'That sounds very different from my upbringing.'

He nodded. 'You would like it here.'

'Luna's very relaxed, isn't she? Considering that there have been fireworks tonight.'

'Things like that don't bother her. Give her ten minutes though and she'll be asking for her pre-bedtime walk. Obviously, it's a bit later tonight because I've been out. I took her before I left but she'll need to go again before bed.'

'How did you come to adopt her?'

'I was out on a shoot almost two years ago, taking photos for a tourist website. Luna was the runt of a litter born to a female from a dog-sledding team. She was so small and yet so determined to try to get to the food before the other puppies. Even so, she was being pushed out by the two bigger male pups at feeding time and the breeder didn't think she'd make it through the winter. I asked if I could have her.'

'He just gave her to you?'

'I took some photographs for his section of the website and he gave me Luna as payment.'

'She's a lucky girl… to be rescued by you.'

Jonas stroked Luna's head and she peered up at him, her bright blue eyes full of trust and loyalty. 'I'm the lucky one. She's a good companion.'

'It's clear that she loves you.'

'I'm loveable.' He winked. 'So my mum tells me.'

Frankie giggled. She couldn't disagree with Aslaug.

'I suppose I should get going.' She stood up. 'I don't want to make any noise and keep your mum awake.'

'I'll walk you back to the hotel.'

'There's no need.'

'I'm not letting you walk back at this time, and there will be stragglers wandering the streets looking for another party to go to. Besides which, I need to walk Luna.'

He went and got their coats, hats and other warm paraphernalia then they dressed quickly, until Frankie felt like an Egyptian mummy again.

–

They walked through the dark streets to Frankie's hotel in silence. They were clearly both tired so the silence was fine for Jonas. He was just happy to be with Frankie and to see how she'd reacted to his home, Luna and to his mum.

Of course, she could have been hiding her shock at the apartment's size and simplicity, but if so she had done it well and he was grateful for how well she'd got on with his mother. Aslaug was a quiet and serious woman who worked hard and lived a modest life, but she was also kind and caring and had done her best to give him a good upbringing.

Outside Frankie's hotel, they stopped and she smiled up at him.

'I had a great time tonight.'

'Me too. Thank you for...'

'For what?'

'For not judging.'

'Judging what?'

'My home.'

'What? Why would I judge your home, Jonas?' She frowned causing a tiny line to mar her pretty features.

'It's nothing like yours.'

She shook her head.

'Jonas, I don't care about that.'

'You don't?'

'Your home is warm, cosy and clean. Your mother is sweet, kind and funny and she clearly loves you deeply.

I'd have loved to grow up in a home like that, because that's what it is. Sometimes where I live didn't feel like a home at all… that's why I used to sleep in my cupboard, remember?'

'That image makes me so sad for you. But I was nervous about what you'd think. It's where I grew up and I am proud of it but you come from such wealth, your house is enormous and we're very different.' Luna leant against his legs, letting him know she was sensitive to his mood so he patted her head to reassure her that he was OK.

'We are, Jonas, but I think we're also very similar.'

'You do?'

She nodded, her green eyes wide as they roamed over his face.

'Jonas, I did grow up surrounded by money and privilege. I had whatever material things I could desire but you know what? All I ever wanted was to have my mother back and I'd have sacrificed everything else in a moment just to see her walk through the door. I'd have lived in a caravan or a shed if I could have grown up with her in my life.'

A tear trickled down her cheek and he automatically removed his glove and wiped it away.

'You really mean that?'

'Of course I do.'

He pulled off his other glove then cupped her face.

'Frankie, I could never give you everything that you've had throughout your life. I don't have much money and I still live with my mother.'

'I still live with my father and grandmother.'

He laughed. 'You have a bit more room than we do, but it suited me because I still wanted to travel and to be

315

free of the constraints of my own place and, of course, it meant that I could help Mum out with the rent. I watched her struggle while I was growing up and I couldn't bear to see her struggling again.'

'Of course not.'

'Since I've been selling more photographs at the gallery, though, I've been able to help make her more secure.'

'Glad to hear it. Jonas... I'm freezing.' She was trembling with the cold. 'I need to go inside.'

'Of course you do. Sorry... I'll let you go.'

'Would you come with me?'

'To the bar? I think it'll be closed now.'

'No, to my room.'

He gazed at her then pulled her closer and stroked the soft skin of her cheeks, ran his thumbs over her pretty lips then leant forwards and kissed them gently.

'Are you sure this is what you want?'

'I don't want you to go. I want to be with you tonight.'

'How can I say no to that? But I have Luna.' He looked down at the dog and she tilted her head to one side and let out a small whine.

'I'm sure I saw a sign saying that they allow dogs inside. If not, we can sneak her in.'

'I suppose it will be quiet now that it's so late... or rather early.'

'Come on, let's go find out.'

He kissed her again then she took his hand and they entered the hotel together.

Frankie hadn't judged him, his mother or his home. She was exactly as she seemed. Kind, sweet and friendly. Beautiful and desirable. And she wanted him too.

A new year had just begun and Jonas had a good feeling that it would be the best year yet...

Epilogue

'So, do you think we'll see them?' Hugo asked as they made themselves comfortable on the reindeer skin outside the *lavvu*.

'If we're lucky.' Freya smiled at him.

'I'm very lucky indeed.' He wrapped his arm around her. 'My luck changed when you came back into my life.'

Frankie shook her head. Over a year had passed since her parents had officially got back together on New Year's Eve, even renewing their wedding vows the following summer, and they were still in awe at being together again. They'd even both produced their original wedding rings and Frankie had thought it incredibly romantic how they'd kept the rings safe all that time. Seeing them reunited never failed to lift her heart, and although the sadness still lingered that they'd lost out on so much time, they kept reminding her that they had plenty of time ahead to enjoy as a family. Frankie and her father had moved out to Norway just before Christmas and were staying at Freya's home, and Jonas spent a lot of time there too, although he'd recently started hinting that he and Frankie should start looking for a place of their own. Frankie and her father also travelled back often to visit Helen, who had made a good recovery with the right balance of medication and had housekeeper Annie close by in case of emergencies. A nurse also visited her three times

317

a week as part of the private hospital's aftercare package. The softening that had come with Helen's illness and realization about her poor treatment of her family, especially her daughter-in-law, had also made Helen kinder to work for, and even though Annie was her housekeeper, she'd also become a close friend. Freya had gone back to the house with Frankie and Hugo a few times and Grandma had apologized to her for her behaviour in the past. It had been awkward and stilted, and the two women would never be close, but they'd managed to have their say and Freya had accepted Helen's apology. Frankie didn't think it was possible to get over a lifetime of hurt and loss, but her mother had been gracious and kind towards the woman who had pushed her away all those years ago, and it had made Frankie love her even more. Freya had a good heart and an enormous amount of compassion, and Grandma had been extremely penitent. The way that Freya accepted Grandma's apologies made life easier for Frankie and for her father, and they were both grateful for that.

'Here.' Jonas arrived at Frankie's side and handed out frothy hot chocolates and home-baked ginger-spiced biscuits.

'Thank you.'

'Are you warm enough?'

She shook her head. 'Apparently the best way to keep warm is body heat.'

'So they say.' He grinned then sat behind her and wrapped his arms and legs around her as Luna settled at his side, ever their watchful and loyal companion.

'Look!' Hugo shouted as he pointed up at the sky.

They all looked up and Frankie gasped.

'Do you want to get your camera out?'

'No, it's fine.'

'Are you sure?'

He squeezed her tighter. 'There'll be plenty of opportunity to take more photographs but right now I just want to hold you.'

Frankie leant back in his embrace and watched as above their heads, great swaying bands of green, blue and purple undulated and shimmered. Their movement was constant as they shifted and rolled, one moment seeming like ocean waves, the next like giant serpents, dancing to the tune of a snake charmer.

It was the most incredible thing she'd ever seen and her heart swelled with emotion.

'It's so beautiful,' she whispered.

'You're beautiful.' Jonas held her tight against his chest. 'I love you, Frankie Ashford. More than anything.'

She tore her eyes from the sky and turned in his embrace.

'I love you too.'

His blue eyes reflected the night sky and as she gazed into them, she knew she loved him more than anything too. But for Frankie, falling in love with Jonas had been a bonus in a long journey. By coming to Norway she'd found herself, had overcome her own doubts and fears about her mother, her career and her past. She had forgiven herself for running away from her wedding, for accepting Grandma's version of how her life should be for so long without question, for not following her heart. She had met her mother, and now she finally felt able to call her 'mum'. It had taken time and she hadn't known if she would ever be able to, then one day, on her thirtieth birthday, Freya had presented her with a silver bangle to match the one from her father and as she'd hugged her, the word had popped out. They'd both been shocked but also delighted. Frankie had also made peace with what her grandmother had done, with what Freya had done and with what her father had done, or rather failed to do. Life was not easy, it would never be neat and tidy, and there would, no doubt, be many more bumps in the road. Accepting that, as well as her past, had empowered Frankie. She'd thought she needed to find her mum to know herself, but in reality, she had needed to peel away the layers that the years had created around her and to look inside. With her new design business, regular commissions from Norwegian boutiques, including one for an outdoors range that Jonas had helped her with, and the workshop above her mum's gallery, Frankie felt fulfilled.

And then, of course, there was Jonas.

She wrapped her arms around him and kissed him, their connection deepening under the Norwegian sky, beneath the magical display she'd once only dreamt of seeing. And when he moved to his knees, took off her glove and then produced a beautiful white gold ring set with a sapphire that matched the colour of his eyes, they didn't even need words. This was what they both wanted, as equals, as lovers, as friends and as partners. He slid the ring onto her finger then sealed the deal with a kiss.

Her heart was full, her mind finally at peace, and she knew that she really had found love at the northern lights.

Acknowledgements

My thanks go to:

My husband and children, for your love, support and patience – even when I'm in my pyjamas all day because writing is more important than getting dressed. XXX

My three dogs for all the cuddles and for being my writing buddies, as well as listening to me read dialogue out loud to see if it works.

My warm and wonderful agent, Amanda Preston, at LBA. You're a star!

The fabulous team at Canelo. As always, your enthusiasm and hard work are deeply appreciated. In particular, thanks to Louise Cullen, Laura McCallen and Hannah Todd for your amazing editorial input, and to Liz Hatherall for adding polish in copyedits! To Iain Millar for helping to make my dream come true by signing me 2 years ago, and to Francesca Riccardi and Ellie Pilcher for patiently answering my questions and getting the books out there.

My very supportive author and blogger friends. I love you!

My readers who come back for more and who take the time to write reviews and share the book love. You guys rock!